*Wildflowers
of Louisiana
and Adjoining States*

CLAIR A. BROWN

**Louisiana State University Press**
BATON ROUGE

# Wildflowers of Louisiana
## and Adjoining States

*Published with the assistance
of the LSU Foundation*

ISBN 0–8071–0232–8 (cloth)
ISBN 0–8071–0780–8 (paper)
Library of Congress Catalog
Card Number 72–79327
Copyright © 1972 by Clair A. Brown
All rights reserved
Manufactured in the United States
of America
Printed by Moran Industries, Inc.
Baton Rouge, Louisiana
Designed by Dwight Agner
1980 printing

To my wife
CLARA DOUGLAS BROWN

# Contents

| | |
|---|---|
| **Preface** | ix |
| **Introduction** | xi |
| Nomenclature | xiv |
| Classification | xv |
| Flowers at Work | xvii |
| Flower Photography | xxii |
| Vanishing Wildflowers | xxiii |
| Vegetation of Louisiana | xxvii |
|    General ecology | xxvii |
|    Relationship to other floras | xxxi |
|    Vegetation regions | xxxii |
| Plant Identification Tips | xxxviii |
| **Part I: Monocotyledons** | 1 |
| **Part II: Dicotyledons** | 43 |
| **Glossary** | 227 |
| **Suggested References** | 233 |
| **Index** | 235 |

# Preface

This book comes as a climax to some forty-five years' study of plants. I began work on it in the spring of 1968, at the instigation of Chancellor Cecil G. Taylor, and took early retirement from LSU in 1970 to insure completion of the project.

The majority of the photographs were made expressly for the book, and in the course of taking them I traveled more than 20,000 miles. But photography was only part of the work: while securing the illustrations I collected voucher specimens in triplicate. One specimen was deposited in the Louisiana State University Herbarium. Duplicate specimens were deposited in the U.S. National Herbarium at the Smithsonian Institution in Washington, D.C., and in the New York Botanical Garden. These voucher specimens were used to determine the correctness of the identification. Some of the more difficult specimens were taken to the U.S. National Herbarium for comparison with authentically determined material. The actual knowledge of where and what to look for represents a synthesis of many years of study, and travel of more than 100,000 miles.

I would like to express grateful appreciation and thanks to the LSU Foundation for its substantial financial assistance toward publication and to Chancellor Taylor for his interest and encouragement in making a dream a reality.

I am deeply indebted to my many colleagues, and to people in the state, too numerous to mention individually, for help in locating plants as well as for allowing me to trespass on their properties.

I wish to give special mention to the late Dr. Caroline Dormon for her interest and suggestions; to Mr. and Mrs. Frank Gladney for allowing me to take material from their garden in Baton Rouge as well as from the preserve they established at Gloster, Mississippi; to Mrs. A. Louise Radau, Saucier, Mississippi, for keeping me informed about the plants in her area; to Dr. Arnold Lewis, who accompanied me on many field trips in Mississippi and who kindly furnished the color slide of witch hazel which is far better than mine; to C. Heiser for identifications in the genus *Helianthus;* and to Dr. Harold W. Rickett for suggestions and encouragement.

CLAIR A. BROWN

# Introduction

Louisiana has a rich and varied native flora which has been augmented with many introduced plants. Many of these have escaped from cultivation and a few have become pests. Unfortunately no complete inventory of the flora exists. However, nearly 3,000 species have been recorded for the state. It is probable that the number exceeds 4,000 and it may go close to 4,500. There are some 800 to 1,000 species which are worthy of illustration because of their mass effects, abundance, color, appreciation by the general public, and peculiarities of flower structure, or oddities of distribution and ecological relationships cherished by the professional botanists. Unfortunately the cost of publication, in particular color illustration, makes it necessary to select a smaller number. These selections are chiefly the author's judgment of what may make an interesting, colorful, and educational book. It was considered advisable to illustrate certain segments of the plant population which have not been included in some of the other wildflower books. A number of the illustrations were chosen to depict features which would help in the identification of a plant. For example, some plants are so tall that the flower cluster is all that can be included in the photograph, and the diagnostic leaves at the base of the plant cannot be seen. The author believes the inclusion of these parts with the flower cluster is a necessity. However, there is a philosophy to make the flowers large and describe the leaves, and this has been done here in some instances.

*Scope*

Although the term *wildflower* seems self-explanatory, there are different interpretations. Fundamentally it refers to any native plant growing without cultivation. Yet there are those who restrict the term to plants with pretty flowers. One of the more recent publications excludes trees and shrubs, partly because many of these have such inconspicuous flowers. Should introduced plants which escape from cultivation be included? Many of these introductions are so widespread and abundant that they are considered as naturalized by botanists. The general public, not realizing they are introductions, considers these as native. They form a conspicuous part of the flora. There are some plants like the daffodil and certain gladiolus species which have persisted long after the home where they grew has disappeared, and which are escaping to a limited extent. A few of these have been included because of their historical significance.

There are both native and naturalized plants with mini-flowers which are abundant, aggressive, and often difficult to control. These are designated as weeds. The aggregation of these mini-flowered plants gives character and color to the roadside vegetation. Therefore the author has included trees, shrubs, and herbaceous plants, both native and naturalized, which produce spectacular bloom crops, as well as some of the mini-flowered types. The latter, because of their size, are often difficult to photograph and have little appeal to the average wildflower enthusiast.

*Why Study Plants?*

It is well known, but little appreciated, that plants play an important role in our daily lives. Food, fuel, clothing, and shelter are all too brief designation of their impact.

Plants not only furnish the staff of life but also manufacture the life-sustaining oxygen of the air without which we cannot live.

They furnish us with many luxuries such as fruits, drugs, and spices. They stimulate our appreciation of the aesthetic appearance of structure and beauty. The present interest in environment stresses their role in the purification of the atmosphere, trapping of dusts, amelioration of some of the climatic factors, and reduction of noise pollution. Their restful green soothes our weary eyes.

Man has found he can improve the beauty of flowers and crop yields in both quality and quantity by hybridization of plants which have desirable potentialities. He has introduced disease resistance in some plants by the use of a parent which has been considered inferior in other ways.

Cotton, jute, ramie, linen, hemp, sisal, and abaca are some of the important fiber plants which can be made into fabrics. Tea, coffee, and cacao, the source of chocolate, are universally used by man. Paper is produced from a variety of plants.

Many of the early studies on plants were related to their supposed or actual medicinal properties. The production of cortisone from *Rawolfia* is one of the more recent medicinal discoveries. Fungi have contributed penicillin and many of the newer antibiotics.

Nature has placed toxic compounds in some common plants which give trouble to man and beast: snow-on-the-mountain, wisteria, Jerusalem cherry, oleander, cherry-laurel, poison ivy, and sumac are some examples. Other plants such as marijuana, coca, and poppy are sources of more potent drugs.

There are still greater quantities of wild plants which are food plants for birds, mammals, and man. Elderberry, mulberry, black cherry, pokeweed, goatweed, and wild rice are a few of the conspicuous ones. Among our wildlife, ducks, geese, quail, deer, muskrat, and nutria eat a variety of plants which are passed by as unattractive. Many of these grow in water and wet areas. Deer browse on many more kinds of plants than most people realize. The research on wildlife food resources is extensive and emphasizes the need for a knowledge of plants; food value, methods of reproduction, general biology, and ecology are under investigation.

Some plants fall into the category of weeds. Inasmuch as some weeds materially hinder crop production, the prevailing attitude is to kill weeds in general. However, they have an important role in healing man-made scars on the landscape. They take over barren areas too poor for agricultural purposes, retard erosion, and eventually improve the soil to the point it can be cropped.

There are numerous ways in which knowledge of plants and the ecological conditions under which they grow are important. Several species of *Astragalus* are selenium accumulators; thus their presence in an area is a good indication that selenium exists in the soil. These plants are toxic to livestock. Other minerals such as iron, copper, and gold have been located on the basis of the presence of indicator plants. The red cedars and junipers across part of Texas have been correlated with the presence of limestone deposits.

Many early surveys in Louisiana were very sketchy when the land was worth fifty cents an acre. The discovery of oil in an area has resulted in more precise surveys which have been coupled with the use of the vegetation for determination of ownership of the land. Louisiana law designates the mean high-water level as the boundary of lakes and the mean low-water level for the state's ownership of the beds of navigable streams. Here the vegetation has been used to determine these levels in the absence of stream gauges.

The breeding of varieties resistant to given diseases and the increase in yields from certain hybridization have been important contributions to Louisiana agriculture.

All of the above-mentioned features are related to plant identification or recognition, which is the major theme of this book.

## Nomenclature

The naming of a plant, although related to its classification, is a separate and distinct feature. Carolus Linnaeus, the Swedish naturalist, is credited with the establishment of a binomial system of nomenclature in which every plant has a generic and specific name. International Botanical Congresses adopted a rule that the first validly published name, starting with Linnaeus (1753), should be the name to use, and set up rules governing the technical details of nomenclature which have been modified from time to time at the various Botanical Congresses. The purpose of these rules is to establish a uniformity of names. However, if you look through a series of technical plant identification manuals published in the last fifty years, you will find as many as eight different names for the same plant. In part this results from the use of the American Code of Nomenclature as well as the International Code. In part it results from differences of opinion and interpretation of the one- or two-line descriptions of the earlier taxonomists. Because there are some differences in the currently available manuals, the writer has chosen to use the names in the magnificent *Wild Flowers of the Southeastern United States* by Dr. Harold W. Rickett of the New York Botanical Garden. Some scientific names used in other books are listed for correlation purposes.

Scientific names are composed of three parts. The first or generic name is equivalent to our family name, the second or specific name is equivalent to our given name, and the third part gives the authorities responsible for the name. Our bald cypress was first described by Linnaeus, who gave it the specific name *disticha* and placed it in the genus *Cupressus;* thus we write *Cupressus disticha* L. Later L. C. Richard transferred the specific name to the genus *Taxodium;* thus *Taxodium distichum* (L.) Rich. A scientific name is not complete without the authorities, although there are numerous situations in which the authority names are omitted.

## Classification

Plants are grouped into categories based upon similarity of flower and fruit characteristics. Members within a group are separated by differences in the distinguishing features. The International Botanical Congress recognizes the following categories in descending sequence: Division, Class, Order, Family, Genus, Species, Subspecies, Variety, and Forma. Some botanists use the term *Phylum* as a category, although it is not recognized by the International Botanical Congress. The family is defined as a group of related genera (plural), and the genus (singular) is defined as a group of related species. The species is a unit of botanical classification and is difficult to define or interpret. One of the frequently used concepts is that a species is a population with individuals so alike they could have been derived from the same parents. Another, but perhaps more vague, definition is that the species is the considered opinion of a competent taxonomist. At one time the ability of plants to come true to type from seed was fundamental to the species concept. It is now recognized that some species are very variable, and there are explanations for most of these variations. Inasmuch as the species is composed of individuals, there are bound to be some minor differences among the individuals of a population. Part of these may be caused by different environmental conditions and part by their inheritance or genetic makeup. The species may be divided into subunits such as subspecies, varieties, forms, clones, and cultivars. Here again botanists are not unanimous in their subdivision of the species. The term *variety*, widely used, has two meanings. The varieties in botanical usage are variations, often quite constant, which are not of sufficient magnitude to be called a species. They are plants which show minor differences from the typical representative of the species. The term *variety* has been used in other ways. Some use it as a popular designation for species. It is widely used in the case of cultivated plants—thus in roses, camellias, daylilies, and many other plants there are horticultural or agronomic varieties which are recognizable, named, and often more distinct than botanical varieties or species. The botanical variety can be subdivided into forms for which the Latin name is preceded by the term *forma* or the abbreviation *f*. The term *clone* is applied to a unit perpetuated vegetatively. The term *cultivar*, abbreviated *cv*, is used to designate man-made hybrids and selections.

Inasmuch as the botanists do not agree as to what constitutes a species it is no wonder the layman is confused and has difficulty understanding the different appearing plants he finds. The inconsistencies that arise from the valid use of one set of characters in one genus and not in another cause confusion—for example, flower color. Also, what appears to be an easily distinguished feature that separates two specimens may be so variable when applied to a number of plants that it has no value.

Thus the species is usually the synthesis of the features of many individual specimens. However, many of our species have been described from a single specimen. There is no agreement as to the number of specimens one must have to describe a new species.

There are instances where a botanist finds essentially the same type of plant but finds features which were not given in the brief Linnaean description and uses these features to describe another species.

## Flowers at Work

Those who have seen strawberry blossoms know the flowers are promises of strawberries to come. The work of flowers is to make fruit and seeds. If you will look at several kinds of flowers, you will notice that they are different in many details but alike in others. Let us examine a flower so we can see the different parts and learn about the work they do. Most of the flowers have structures that are used to make fruits or are covering parts. Look at the strawberry blossom (Fig. 1). The fruit-forming parts are *stamens* and *pistils*. Each of these has its own duties. The top part of the stamen is enlarged to form the *anther*, a part which contains the dustlike grains called *pollen*. The pistil is usually swollen at the base *(ovary)* and contains *ovules* which will develop into seeds. At the top of the pistils are *stigmas*, which are usually sticky and trap pollen grains. The pollen germinates to produce a tube which grows down into ovules where it discharges sperm nuclei that unite with the ovule nucleus. This process—fertilization—is necessary for the flower to produce fruits and seeds.

 The bright showy parts around the stamens and pistils are called petals, collectively the *corolla*. They vary in shape, size, color, and number, yet are the same for each kind of flower. Sometimes the petals may be absent; at other times they are grown together so that they fall in one piece *(united corolla)* (Fig. 2b). The petals have work to do. Their color, shape, and odor attract bees and other insects which carry the pollen from the stamens to the pistils *(pollination)*. Many flowers reward bees with a sweet substance, *nectar*, which the bees make into honey. The petals also protect the stamens and pistils in the unopened bud. There are usually some green parts outside of the petals. These are called *sepals*, collectively *calyx* (Fig. 1). They cover the flower bud before it opens. The collective term *perianth* is used when the sepals and petals are so alike that it is difficult to distinguish which is which.

Botanists make use of the flower parts to classify plants into such categories as species, genera, and families. Thus the knowledge of the flower parts is helpful in the identification of plants. When you look at a flower, see if you can find all of these parts. People who are engaged in hybridization or development of new types must be able to recognize them.

Thus a typical flower is composed of pistil(s), stamens, petals, and sepals, all inserted on a *receptacle*. There are many modifications too numerous to include here. A *polypetalous flower* has all petals separate and distinct from each other, such as in the strawberry (Fig. 1). Usually there are as many petals as there are sepals except in double flowers. Petals fuse with each other to produce a *united corolla*, such as in *Lamium* (Fig. 2b). The corolla may be radially symmetrical or regular (Fig. 2a) in contrast to an irregular corolla in which there are differences in shape, size, number of parts, and texture. The *Lamium* is an example of an irregular (bilabiate) type of corolla.

The Legume family is divided into three subfamilies on the basis of flower structure. Subfamily I, *Mimosoideae* has very small, regular flowers crowded into a head. Stamens, usually twenty, which extend beyond the corolla lobes, are like pins on a pincushion (see *Mimosa, Schrankia,* and *Neptunia*). The corolla in subfamily II, *Caesalpinioideae*, is sometimes irregular, sometime fused, and sometimes partly open. It has ten distinct stamens as in *Cassia*. Sometimes the flower is pea-shaped as in redbud. The largest subfamily, *Papilionoideae*, has pea-shaped blossoms (Fig. 3) consisting of a *standard* or *banner*, two wing petals more or less fused to the *keel*. This is composed of two petals fused along one margin. The *calyx* consists of five *sepals* more or less fused. The *stamens*, typically ten, are mostly arranged in groups of $9 + 1$, or $5 + 5$. Here the filaments form a sheath around the *superior ovary* with nine united and one free. The fruit is a *legume*—that is, usually a dehiscent pod produced by a one-celled superior ovary.

The Sunflower or Aster family has a highly modified form of flower structure. Here the individual flower is subordinate to the flower head (Fig. 4). This head consists of a *receptacle* which has a variety of shapes—flat, concave, convex, surrounded by layers of green bracts called *involucral bracts* or *phyllaries*. The individual flowers may be *ligulate* or *discoid*, and the heads may have all ligulate or all discoid flowers, or as in the majority of species, a combination of both.

The family has been divided into two subfamilies, the *Tubuliflorae* and the *Liguliflorae*, on the basis of the kinds of flowers present. The flower head of the Tubuliflorae consists of a marginal row of ligulate flowers and the center with disk flowers. A few members have only disk flowers. The individual disk flower usually has a tubular corolla with five lobes, and the stamens are inserted on the corolla. The anthers are united to form a ring around the style. These are *perfect flowers*, that is, they have both stamens and pistil. One of the methods of self-pollination is for the stigma to contact the pollen as it elongates up through the pollen tube. The individual ligulate or ray flowers have a flat, strap-shaped corolla and vary from sterile to staminate to perfect.

The second subfamily, the *Liguliflorae*, has all ligulate flowers (see false dandelion). Both flower types have an inferior ovary which is united with the modified calyx called a *pappus*. The pappus consists of filiform bristles, plumose bristles, scales, and spinelike short teeth. The fruit is called an *achene*.

The Milkweed family has a highly specialized flower structure. There are in addition to the calyx and corolla, structures designated as *hoods* and *horns*. The pollen comes out in paired masses called *pollinia*, suggestive of saddlebags. The Spurge family has only a single stamen or a single pistil for a flower, and these are usually borne in a *cyathium*—a cuplike involucre bearing the flowers from within the base.

Some flowers have accessory parts—for example, the fringe on the maypop and the crown in the spider lily. Some plants have naked flowers, no calyx or corolla, like the willow. Plants which have the stamens and pistils in separate flowers but in different locations on the plant are *monoecious*—the cat-tails, for example. Plants which have the pistils or female flowers on one plant and the staminate or male flowers on another are *dioecious*. Most hollies and maples are dioecious, although some irregularities are known.

xx

◀ *Fig. 1.* Strawberry blossom with two petals removed to show all parts. This flower has many stamens and pistils. The "berry" develops from the fleshy receptacle. The "seeds" are actually fruits. Enlarged.

*Fig. 3.* White clover blossom. This is an example of an irregular flower with a united corolla. The large petal in the back is the standard. The keel, composed of two petals, is in the center and has a wing petal on each side. One lobe of the united calyx is against the keel. Enlarged.

◀ *Fig. 2 a.* A polypetalous flower showing five white, separate, two-lobed petals, stamens, pistil, and sepals. This flower is regular or radially symmetrical in shape. Enlarged.

*Fig. 2 b.* A polypetalous flower with clawed petals. The stamens are adjacent to the style which has a globose stigma. There are two horizontal bracts near the base of the flower. Enlarged.

*Fig. 2 c. Lamium* flower. The flower has a united corolla (gamopetalous). It is also irregular or bilabiate. The calyx is at the bottom. Enlarged.

*Fig 4.* A compositae head of *Helianthus*. This consists of 13 ray or ligulate flowers around the margin and numerous disk flowers in the dark center. Reduced.

## Flower Photography

Flower photography can be an interesting and instructive hobby. One of the early books illustrated with color photography was *Wild Flowers of New York* by Homer D. House. Every picture was made as an 8 x 10-inch autochrome plate. Exposures were long, and special equipment was used to keep off the breezes. Modern equipment and films have simplified this procedure.

The writer has used a variety of equipment in color photography: a 4 x 5 cut-film camera, which is heavy, a 2 ¼ twin-lens reflex, and several 35mm single-lens reflex units. The bulk of the pictures reproduced in this book were made with the 35mm cameras. Extension tubes or bellows were used to secure close-up photos along with a variable magnification supplementary lens. Later a 40mm macrokilar lens was used to secure magnifications up to two times natural size. Exposures were determined with a separate photo-electric meter as well as with a behind-the-lens meter, by reading light reflected from green foliage or from a gray meter card. All color photography is a system of compromises. If the greens are reasonable, the other colors usually are in good balance. When plants are posed against a black velvet background, the meter reading should be from a gray card or green foliage. The lack of reflection from the velvet causes the meter to indicate more time than is actually required.

Flower photography can be divided into three main groups, namely, habitat photos, flower portraits, and arrangements. Good habitat pictures are not luck but represent skillful selection of the plants in good light and proper position to show their identification characteristics attractively. The art of visualization is what makes a good habitat illustration. One should not have detracting, out-of-focus images of additional vegetation. Some plants grow in habitats too shady for normal photography and thus electronic flash may be used. Some habitats are so cluttered that good photos *in situ* are not possible.

Flower portraits are generally close-up illustrations to show most of the taxonomic details needed for identification. The writer believes that artificial backgrounds, such as black velvet, are not only permissible but are often necessary to show the flower to the best advantage. The artificial background eliminates the hodgepodge of detracting out-of-focus details which can confuse the viewer. At times plants are so situated that you can use the sky as a background. Electronic flash lights the scene and is reflected to the camera. One photographer so arranges the plant in relation to its background that there is nothing to reflect light and thus achieves a dark background. To do this requires time and patience. Light-colored flowers show best against a dark background. Another photographer poses his plants so the blossoms are contrasted against deep shadows and thus accomplishes a dark background. The writer has pinned specimens to the black velvet, he has used a needle holder, and more recently a laboratory stand with a test-tube clamp. The specimen is placed in a split rubber cork and clamped. This gives a more natural posing of the plant than where the specimens are pinned. Blue colors are sometimes difficult to capture in open sun, and light shade will give better color rendition.

Some plants have a short bloom season of a week or ten days, whereas others may bloom over a period of three months, and the photographer must take these differences into account. During the course of preparation of this book, weather conditions unfavorable for photography resulted in some plants passing through the flowering cycle. Then again, unfavorable climatic conditions resulted in a speedup or delay of flowering based upon blooming dates taken from herbarium specimens. There is also a time lag from south to north Louisiana of ten days or more and this was helpful in getting certain species. For example, redbud and dogwood may be in good flower, or even out of flower in south Louisiana before these species flower along the northern tier of parishes. Some plants do not flower every year and thus were not found in known localities. Sometimes man or nature has altered the environment. In such cases, additional field work was necessary to locate them.

## Vanishing Wildflowers

People normally associate the term *vanishing* with wildlife such as birds and mammals. It is difficult to think of plants as vanishing. Yet the plight of many kinds has been recognized by plant lovers as well as professional botanists. It is well known that as the human population builds up in an area, the attractive plants disappear. This concern about the disappearance of plants has led to the formation of conservation organizations, in particular to the Wild Flower Preservation Society, whose slogan is "Enjoy, do not destroy." They have published lists of plants which should not be picked because they are in danger of extermination. These organizations have had their impact upon many state legislatures who have passed laws designed to protect the more endangered species. Most of these efforts fall into the category of making it unlawful for the individual to pick designated plants. The Louisiana legislature, recognizing that it could not legislate relative to private lands, passed a law to prohibit picking on the highway right-of-way. It has long been illegal to pick flowers in the national parks and in many state parks. Very often such regulations are forgotten and not enforced.

The Louisiana Garden Club Federation endorsed the conservation concept and extended it by preparation of a comprehensive list of wild plants which should not be used in flower arrangements unless grown in the garden of the exhibitor. The Federation has also campaigned against the custom of cutting wild holly trees for Christmas decorations.

The purpose of this discussion is to direct attention to man-made changes in the environment which destroy thousands of plants quickly and more effectively than uncontrolled picking. It is well known that farmers in the cultivation of the fields and the conversion of wooded areas to farmland, as has happened in Louisiana in the past decade, have destroyed thousands of acres. More than a million acres of bottomland hardwoods have been bulldozed and burnt to plant soy beans. Even some organizations interested in perpetual timber sources are clearing natural second growth in order to establish extensive even-aged stands for future use. These activities have destroyed many kinds of rare and interesting plants. Unfortunately this is their prerogative.

The development of modern weed-killers whose use has increased crop yields of three to six tons of sugarcane per acre and as much as ten barrels of rice per acre in very weedy sites has produced profound changes in the vegetation. These increased yields, along with lower costs of crop production, resulted in the adoption of the use of herbicides as a standard agricultural practice. The difficulties in getting ground equipment through flooded rice fields led to the aerial application of herbicides, insecticides, and fertilizers. Some of the scientists in weed control research did not know that dusts and sprays would drift five to twenty-five miles from point of application and produce injuries to sensitive plants at these distances. The aerial application of herbicides not only controlled weeds in the cultivated fields but also drifted into non-agricultural areas with toxic effects to some wildflowers.

The migration of people from the cities to rural areas following World War II has had an adverse effect upon native vegetation. Hundreds of miles of vacant rural roadside have developed into someone's front yard. Areas that once were good collecting areas for a botanist are now lawns and cultivated fields.

Demands for highway beautification have led highway departments to construct the roadside so that it can be mowed readily or sprayed with weed-killers. These nicely manicured shoulders of mowed right-of-way improve the looks as well as the safety of the highway. A certain percentage of the cost of federal aid to highways in the 1920's was spent for planting trees and shrubs along the roadside. Today many of the planted trees have been removed because so many people were killed when their cars hit them. More attention is given now to construction that will make maintenance easier.

Mowing is a form of weed control. It has been demonstrated that mowing a pasture two to four times a year for three or four years in succession has eliminated many of plants. Thus mowing, now a standard practice, has eliminated some of the native plants. The brown dead vegetation resulting from the application of herbicides is not only a dreary sight as compared to the restful green of the natural vegetation, but also a potential fire hazard.

Our wetlands have been drained or dammed and as a result many kinds of plants have died. The summer-blooming wild azalea, *Rhododendron serrulatum*, was once abundant along the meandering sloughs in the pine flatwoods between Hammond and Slidell. Today it is difficult to find a living plant of the species in this area. All the gravel roads have been blacktopped or paved with concrete. The sloughs that formerly passed under these roads have been deepened and straightened to get water away from the roadbed. This lowered the water table and changed the boggy marginal habitat of the sloughs to dry land which is not suitable for this azalea. Many other kinds of plants have also disappeared. This change of the environment made it possible for less desirable plants to invade the habitat.

Road builders have run roughshod over acres of interesting and rare plants and passed through parks and preserves. There are many instances where a slight shift in the highway location could have saved endangered species. Our new superhighways and interstates have taken an unbelievable toll, not only on wild land but also on rich farmland as well and have displaced human occupants. These highways require a right-of-way 300 feet or more wide. A strip eight feet wide by a mile long is an acre in extent. Thus the 300-foot right-of-way takes out some 40 acres per mile. Some highway departments have made an attempt to plant these highly disturbed road shoulders with attractive flowering herbs. The Texas Highway Commission, for example, has planted bluebonnet seed successfully. Crimson clover has been planted along miles of Louisiana's new highways, and produced a spectacular sight the first year. However, aggressive and/or better adapted plants have crowded out the crimson clover.

Botanists on university campuses have picked such plants as *Trillium* and *Podophyllum* for class use without seriously depleting these plants. After the semiwild habitats became lawns with weekly mowing, these plants disappeared. It has been observed that the placement of plants on the wildflower preservation or the "thou shall not" lists is a kiss of death because so many thoughtless people have taken the attitude "this is something I must have for my garden." Many would not recognize the plant except when in bloom, and the digging of wild plants at this time usually results in their death. Plants are transplanted without due consideration of the problem of matching the environment in which they grow. The acid-soil-loving wild azaleas have been transplanted to the alluvial floodplain soils of the Mississippi River, which are generally alkaline in nature, and as a result these plants died. Many other examples could be cited. Sometimes it is soil acidity differences, sometimes the soil texture, and sometimes the moisture requirements are not compatible. The purple and the yellow foxgloves are root parasites on certain grasses and trees. These plants will not grow if the host plant is not present. The hairy lupine of Louisiana's Florida Parishes and southern Mississippi can be raised from seed. The digging of this plant usually breaks the fine taproot and the plant dies.

Most of our wild plants can be propagated vegetatively by hardwood or softwood cutting and by division of the rhizomes or stolons, as well as from seed. People should learn to grow more of the wild plants from seed. Some seeds remain dormant for two or more years. Some dry out quickly and die. These should be planted immediately. Iris seed, for example, have a corky waterproof covering. If one waits for the seed pod to open normally, the corky covering will be brown in color, and these seeds usually take two years to germinate. However, if planted when the corky covering is white to slightly pink, the seeds will germinate sooner. If the corky covering is removed at this stage, the seeds will germinate in ten days' to two weeks' time. There are a number of ways to break dormancy in seeds. Pour boiling hot water on redbud seed and let them soak until the water is cold. This will not only speed germination but will greatly increase the percentage that germinate.

It should be the objective of garden clubs to learn the conditions necessary to get our attractive wildings to grow from seeds or cuttings. The vanishing natural habitat of many of our wildflowers points the need for establishment of preserves where the natural habitats will be maintained. This has been done to a limited extent. If the habitat destruction is as bad in the next ten years as it has been in the past, the only knowledge that certain plants grew in Louisiana will be from specimens preserved in the Louisiana herbaria. It will not be possible a decade from now to easily find all of the plants illustrated herein.

## Vegetation of Louisiana

### General ecology
The vegetation of the state can be divided into several regions based upon the presence of certain diagnostic species. The map

(p. xxxiv) shows the general distribution of these regions in a simplified grouping of the vegetation based largely upon the original arborescent flora. Each of the regions can be subdivided into a number of communities based upon minor differences of the environment and the flora. Specific plants are found in one part of the state and not in others. Many factors are responsible for these conditions. Some of the more important are the individual requirements of the species, their relative tolerance or adaptability, and the variation of the environmental conditions. This diversity of the vegetation can best be understood through a knowledge of the various factors which affect plants. These are usually grouped into three major categories: Climatic factors, such as temperature and rainfall; *Edaphic* factors, those operating from the geology and soils and finally, *Biotic* factors, the relationships of plants to plants, plants to insects, birds, mammals, and to man.

*1. Climatic factors.* The blooming seasons of southern plants are quite different from their northern counterparts. Oranges can be raised commercially below New Orleans and peaches in north Louisiana, whereas Baton Rouge, is too far north to grow oranges and too far south to grow peaches commercially. Peaches require a certain number of hours around zero degrees Fahrenheit to break bud dormancy. Poinsettias are usually killed in Baton Rouge by the cold spells prior to Christmas, whereas in New Orleans they usually thrive all winter. If there is a killing freeze the last of November or the first of December, American elm will bloom the first week of January and winged elm about the middle of January, followed by red maple the first of February in the Baton Rouge area. It takes this freeze to break the dormancy of American elm. However, some winters are so mild that a freeze of this kind does not occur. Then the flowering of the elms may be delayed into February. Cypress normally starts shedding its pollen in mid-December and continues into February. Slash pine, one of the earliest of pines, starts pollen liberation in January. Mild winters result in a variety of plants blooming in December, such as butter weed, clovers, sow thistle, daisy fleabane, violets and dandelions. Cold fronts frequently pass over Louisiana in late January and February and thus delay the spring bloom. The extreme cold of 1962 killed large citrus trees in the Baton Rouge area which had been bearing for more than ten years, as well as in the citrus area below New Orleans. Thus the extreme temperatures, not the means, are a set of limiting factors for the growth of tropical plants in the semitropical environment.

The quantity and distribution of the rainfall gives us the equivalent of three floras. There is a spring dry spell which starts about mid-April and extends until the June rains (if they come). Our spring blooming plants start to mature and dry up. Thus the spring plants which reached their peak of bloom in March and April will be gone by June. There is a summer flora which is enhanced in volume when stimulated by the midsummer rains. This gives way to a more xeric fall flora of the usual September-October dry spell which may extend into November.

There is a bloom lag from south to north within the state of about ten days between Baton Rouge and Alexandria and another five to ten days to Ruston and Shreveport.

Tropical storms have upset the physiology in plants which lost the bulk of their leaves in a September or October storm. They will put out a new crop of leaves and flowers a month to six weeks later. The fall of 1970 saw an abundance of the out-of-normal-season blooming for the false garlic and the yellow jessamine. Normally spring blooming plants, they were in blossom in several locations in October and November of 1971. Coral honeysuckle was in blossom every month in 1971.

2. *Edaphic factors.* The relationship of plants to the geology and soils is quite easy to see, but more difficult to understand are all the factors which may operate independently but probably are more effective collectively. Soil acidity, moisture, texture, salinity and other mineral content, drainage, aeration, and leachability are some of the more important factors.

Free floating, submerged and emergent aquatics or plants which tolerate a nearly saturated soil will form definite zonations around ponds and lakes as well as along streams. Six inches of difference in elevation are more significant in changing the plant communities in Louisiana than 100 feet in the mountains. One can observe that the vegetation on the natural levees in the marsh is different from the marsh proper. The weed flora on the contour levees in a rice field is quite different from the weeds of the rice field. This slight difference in elevation is related to drainage, moisture content, and aeriation.

The floodplains of the Red and Mississippi rivers are generally alkaline and plants from the acid-soil pineland will usually die when transplanted to alkaline soils. Thus the absence from the floodplain of plants which are on adjacent uplands is conspicuous and significant. For example, sugar maple, post oak, white oak, tulip-tree, black cherry, and magnolia are generally absent from the alluvial soils.

The shape of the bole of the cypress tree is related to the frequency and duration of flooding. High-conical, bottle-based trees occur in areas of considerable water-level and aeriation changes, whereas those with columnar or low-conical boles grow in areas with very slight or no water-level changes. There are marked differences in vegetation on sandy versus loam versus clayey soils.

3. *Biotic factors*. As indicated, biotic factors cover the relationships between or among organisms. The yucca moth is needed for seed set in the yucca. Many members of the Figwort family, such as species of Agalinis, Aureolaria, and Seymeria, are root parasites on grasses or trees. The Indian pipe and beech drops are saprophytes on the roots of beech.

The aggressiveness of some plants is related to their ability to thrive not only in the open but in intense competition. This aggressiveness in Japanese honeysuckle leads us to consider it a bad weed. At one time tolerant versus intolerant in trees was correlated to shade. Then came the trenched plot, where the seedling and sapling survived, whereas the same species died on the nontrenched plots. Then root competition became a favorite explanation. There are studies now which show that mustards, Johnson grass, and willows, to name a few, give off toxic compounds which either inhibit seed germination or greatly retard the development of other plants. This antibiotic reaction is widespread.

Alfalfa seed had to be inoculated with a root nodule organism for alfalfa to make satisfactory growth in some midwestern soils. It has been shown that mycorrhizal forming organisms on the roots of certain forest trees are necessary for the trees to develop properly in certain soils.

Thus biotic relationships between organisms may be the reason for the presence of a wildflower in one area and not in another.

*Relationship to other floras*

If you look at the distribution range cited in various plant identification manuals, you will notice that many of the plants found in Louisiana are also found in Mississippi, Arkansas, Tennessee, Kentucky, Illinois, and Indiana, as well as in Missouri and Iowa. Plants are no respecters of political boundaries. Many of these come down the Mississippi Valley. They are found in the highlands on each side of the Mississippi floodplain as well as on the floodplain proper. Then there is a smaller, more relict northern element which may be found in certain restricted localities, such as the Tunica Hills (West Feliciana Parish) and the hills near Coshandra and other places in north Louisiana. The Mississippi River carries many seeds.

There is a Texas element which gets into western Louisiana from Caddo Parish south to Cameron Parish. In fact, there may be two distinct Texas elements, the first exemplified by the vegetation of the sand hill "prairie" near Goldonna, Louisiana, where one can find *Penstemon murrayanus, Streptanthus, hyacinthoides, Eriogonium longifolium,* and *Opuntia drummondii.* Along the coast we find *Opuntia lindheimeri,* which is very abundant on the sandy cheniers from Pecan Island to the Sabine River. Along with this is the narrow-leaf gromwell. Many of our coastal plants extend from Texas to Florida and up the Atlantic seaboard to Virginia. Then there is a distinct floridiana element which gets into eastern Louisiana. Mobile Bay and the Pearl River are barriers for the westward movement of some of these plants. A few, like *Sarracenia purpurea* and *S. leucophylla,* work their way into southern Mississippi but do not cross the Pearl River Valley into Louisiana although there are suitable habitats.

One of the big phytogeographic puzzles is the distribution of longleaf pine. It is common in most of the Florida Parishes, with just a trace in East Baton Rouge Parish. Then comes the big jump across the Mississippi floodplain and the prairie west of Opelousas, almost to Kinder. Here this pine follows a sand ridge south to Iowa, Louisiana. It in turn extends northward over the Pleistocene terrace formations onto the Miocene and Eocene formations. Again its range is divided by the Red River. It has been observed that certain plants which grow with longleaf pine in one location will be found wherever longleaf pine occurs. Thus it is possible to generalize distribution statements.

There is a tropical element from the Caribbean or South America via Florida, or via Mexico and Texas. Some of this is natural, but much is related to man's introduction of these plants, and a few have become serious weeds—for instance, the water hyacinth. Many of the European and Asiatic plants growing without cultivation are related to man's activities. The Persian clover was first found in the United States in Georgia in 1921. It became widespread in Louisiana immediately following the 1927 flood. Today it is a serious pest for people who wish to grow white Dutch clover seed. It was just a few years ago that three introduced grasses were found in our fields. New plants are constantly being introduced, consciously or unknowingly and they may become serious pests.

*Vegetation regions*
The following vegetation regions are based upon records about the original vegetation. Today's vegetation is quite different. A Forest Service map made several years ago shows that longleaf pine had a less restricted range then than it has now. Also the abundance of loblolly pine is so different that the Forest Service has made different vegetation regions.

*1. Marsh region.* There are some 4.2 million acres of marshland in Louisiana which are unique in origin and biota. These marshes fringe the Gulf of Mexico from border to border and extend inland for varying distances. The marshes are of considerable economic importance as the native habitat of fur-bearing animals and the winter feeding grounds of ducks and geese as well as the nursery for shrimp, oysters, blue crabs, and crawfish. There are extensive oil fields under the marshes and the recreation value of this region is likewise important.

The marshes can be divided into fresh and saline with a transition zone designated as brackish based upon the salt content of the soil and water. There are numerous local habitats within each of these types which have outstanding vegetation differences. There are mounds of different heights, stream bank natural levees, cheniers, ponds, and small sand dunes, as well as soil differences from sand to organic materials. There are thousand of acres of marshland in which the water level is about equal to that of the root zone of the marsh plants except in dry periods. The saline marshes are usually more firm than the brackish or fresh marshes. Here the principal plants are the oyster grass, salt meadow grass, black rush, couch grass, with minor quantities of black mangrove, sea-oxeye, glassworts, and saltwort. A slight elevation may have silverling, rattlebox, and marsh elder.

The brackish marshes are composed of plants characteristic of both the saline and fresh marshes—that is, saline plants which will tolerate some degree of freshness and fresh-water plants which will tolerate some salinity. There are no species which grow in brackish marshes exclusively. However, some species, like couch grass, may be very abundant.

The fresh-water marshes have the largest number of species. It is interesting to watch the vegetation changes on the natural levees of some of the major streams in going downstream from a mixture of hardwoods to forests of live oak-palmetto to willows to a shrub cover of silvering and marsh elder to the marsh grasses.

Associated with the above vegetation units are numerous herbs which also change. Slight elevations of about six inches to a foot will be reflected by a difference in the plant cover. The fresh-water ponds, lakes, and streams have a rich variety of aquatic plants: parrots feather, alligator weed, water-hyacinth, water-lettuce, water-lilies (white, yellow, and blue), along with the large lotus, arrowheads and Louisiana irises. The well known roseau is helping hold soils against the gradual subsidence of the habitat in many areas. Alligator weed, despised in cultivated fields and on some stream margins, is valuable for holding the soil in the lower reaches of the Mississippi River.

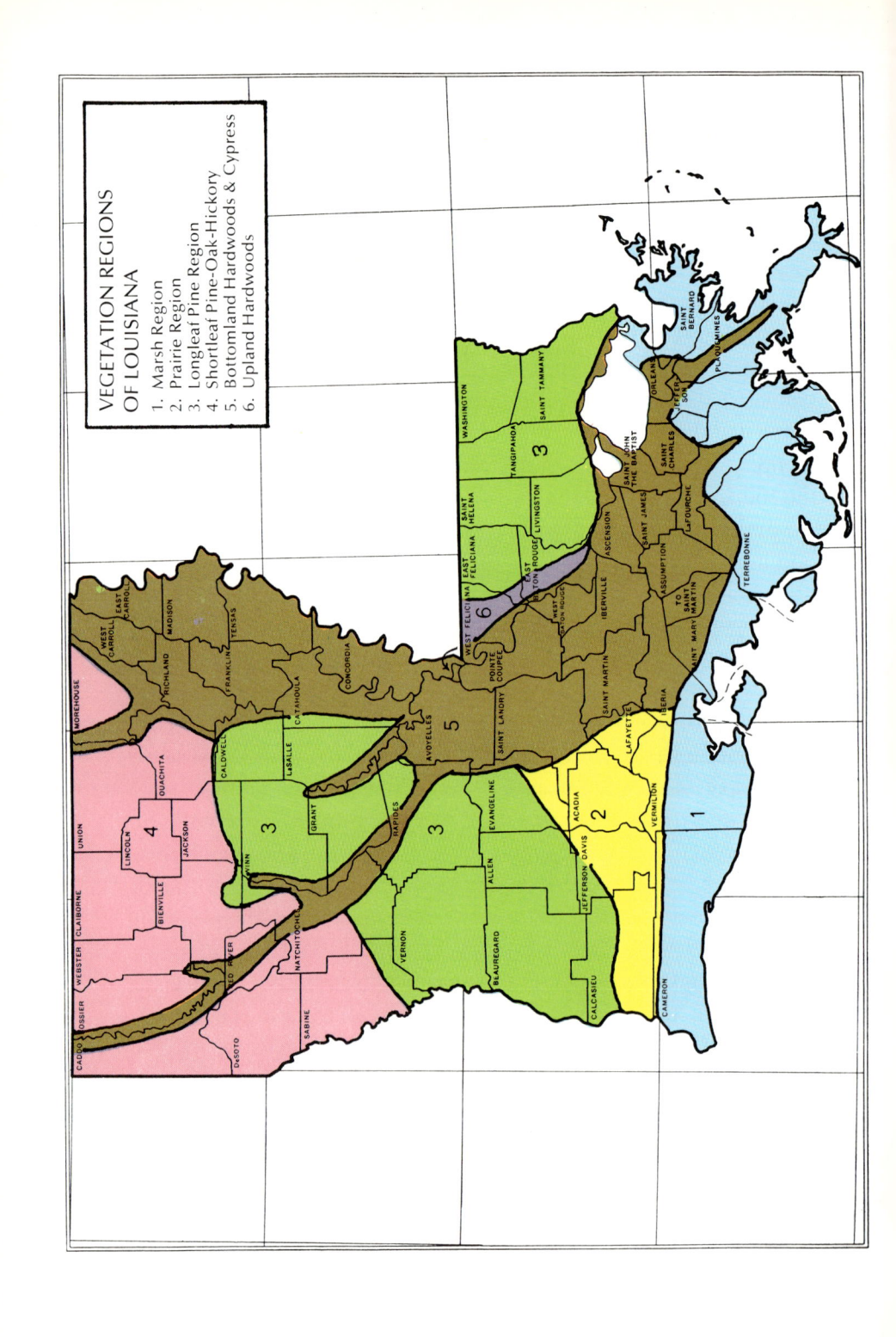

VEGETATION REGIONS
OF LOUISIANA
1. Marsh Region
2. Prairie Region
3. Longleaf Pine Region
4. Shortleaf Pine-Oak-Hickory
5. Bottomland Hardwoods & Cypress
6. Upland Hardwoods

*2. Prairie region.* The term *prairie* was coined to designate natural treeless areas, and these usually have less than 20 inches of annual rainfall, a climatic feature. The Louisiana prairies in the southwestern portion of the state have from 50 to 60 inches or more of rain. Thus something other than climate is responsible for the treeless condition. There is an edaphic feature, consisting of an impervious clay pan 6 to 18 inches below the surface, occasionally deeper, which prevents not only the downward percolation of water but also the upward movement of capillary water. This clay pan is the feature that holds water on the land for rice culture. Prairie soils are water-saturated in February and by the dry period in May they are so dry that the soil runs off the soil auger like sugar off a tin scoop. If you get below the clay pan, which is about 6 inches thick, the soil has plenty of moisture. Tree planting will be successful in the prairie if you dig the hole below the clay pan. The tree vegetation in towns between Lafayette and Lake Charles is astonishing. The spoil banks for irrigation and drainage canals soon develop a woody vegetation. Most of the prairie area has been under intensive cultivation or grazing so that it is doubtful that any virgin prairie sod exists. However, along the railroad between Lafayette and Lake Charles there are small patches which were not scooped out to form the railroad birn. Here we find many of the attractive prairie species. The same condition exists between Opelousas and Kinder.

If you fly over this prairie, you will notice a southward converging drainage pattern with trees along the streams forming a band of woods only a few hundred feet wide. There are marais ponds with such trees as the American elm, swamp red maple, green ash, and other hardwoods if the ponds dry out in May. The marais ponds with cypress and swamp tupelo usually do not dry out until October. There is a more or less sandy ridge, a few feet higher than the prairie proper, which extends from Kinder to Iowa, Louisiana, and which was covered originally with longleaf pine. No matter where you stand in the prairie, you can see a rim of trees in the distant background. Thus our southwestern prairie area is not one big prairie but is divided into many by a network of streams. Many of these have received distinctive names. In the final analysis, trees are found on better drained and poorer drained sites than the prairie proper.

The presence of indigo, sundew, butterwort, blazing-star, and many others is the same as in the pine flatwoods. This similarity of vegetation suggests that the prairie would have been pine flatwoods, as in eastern Louisiana, had not the development of the clay pan effectively prevented the establishment of the pine. The remnant of prairie vegetation, aside from the grasses, sedges, and rushes, has quantities of milkweed, blue-star, compass-plant, clover, vetch, spiderwort, obedient plant, sneezeweed, blazing-star, and indigo.

3. *Longleaf pine region.* The abundance of this species gave rise to the terms *longleaf pine belt*, and the *Southeastern Evergreen Formation*. Longleaf pine occurred in both hill areas as well as level areas known as flatwoods. It occurred in both relatively pure open stands of magnificent trees as contrasted to dense second growth stands. Associated with it in eastern Louisiana were slash, shortleaf, and spruce pines, and in the wetter flatwoods a form of cypress. Meandering sloughs through the flatwoods had a variety of hardwoods, such as swamp black gum, sweet bay, water oak, black-jack oak, gallberry, silverling, and ericaceous shrubs. The flatwoods had an extensive array of wildflowers, ground orchids, pitcher-plants, sundews, gentians, rose-gentians, and indigos. The pinehill areas consist of small rolling hills with more or less impeded drainage courses and branch bottoms, which produced a variety of habitats, in particular boggy sites often with sphagnum. Southern Mississippi has many real sphagnum bogs, with pitcher plants in abundance.

4. *Shortleaf pine-oak-hickory region.* The northwestern corner of the state has less rainfall than the rest of the state, about 45 inches as compared to 60 or more inches. This is a rolling hill country in which the hills are sandy and the bottomlands vary from sandy to heavy clays. The original vegetation was composed of shortleaf pine, a variety of oaks, such as post oak, black-jack oak, and southern red oak, and numerous hickories, among them sand hickory, white hickory, Louisiana hickory, and nutmeg hickory. Loblolly pine, now one of the predominant species in much of the

area, was of secondary importance. It was most abundant along the eroding slopes of the smaller streams. The ability of loblolly pine to reseed on denuded soils and its rapidity of growth account for its present abundance in the state. In some places it is called old-field pine, which emphasizes its ability to take over idle acres. Large pure stands of shortleaf pine occurred in some places, and in others the forest was a mixture of pine and hardwoods in varying proportions. Along the smaller streams such hardwoods as red gum, hawthorn, dogwood, redbud, oaks, basswood, and hackberry were common trees. A few of the wetter sites like Caddo Lake, Bodcau Bayou, and others had cypress, willow oak, overcup oak, swamp privet, and water elm. There are many sweet bay boggy habitats. The herbaceous vegetation in these areas is not too well known, but such plants as goldenrods, asters, blazing-stars, wind-flower, drummond rain-lily, trout-lily, yellow violet, and bloodroot are frequent.

5. *Bottom land hardwoods and cypress.* The alluvial or floodplain soils of the major streams such as the Red, Sabine, Pearl, Atchafalaya, and Mississippi rivers had a hardwood vegetation on the better drained soils and cypress and its associates in the swampy areas. These floodplains have lakes, old stream channels, backwater swamps, rim swamps, rim streams, natural levees, and levee slopes whose soils vary from sand to silt to heavy gumbo clays. This gives a variety of habitats and thus a variety of plants. Prior to levee construction the front lands received new sands and silts from each major flood and had a growth of cottonwood, sycamore, red gum, black willow, hackberry, swamp-privet, honey locust, water locust, and green ash. This type of habitat is rich in goldenrods, asters, ironweed, sennas, bitterweed, and dogfennel. Small streams and wet depressions had spider-lily and irises.

These front lands were better drained and were soon brought into cultivation and are now sugarcane fields in the southern portion of the state and cotton fields in the northern section.

The cypress swamp, a unique vegetation type, had tupelo gum, swamp red maple, green ash, American elm, palmetto, water-elm, swamp-privet, and pumpkin ash. Some of these cypress swamps had a relatively low water-level fluctuation and others had as much as

25 feet normally and as much as 40 feet in extreme floods. The fragrant ladies' tresses orchid, swamp-lily, pickerel-weed, irises, and white water-lilies are a few of the herbaceous plants found in the swamps.

6. *Upland hardwood region.* Only a small area east of the Mississippi River has been shown on the map as Upland Hardwoods. Narrow strips of this vegetation type too small to be shown, occurred on the margin of the prairie in Lafayette Parish, on bluffs at Chico State Park, near Grand Ecore in Natchitoches Parish, along the escarpment of the Ouachita River from Monroe to Columbia to Duty, and small areas in Webster and Lincoln parishes. The characteristic trees are white oak, sugar maple, beech, black cherry, tulip-tree, shagbark hickory, cherrybark oak, dogwood, and redbud. Wooded areas containing some or all of these plants have abundant moisture and a good soil. The herbaceous flora is rich and varied. Different plants will be found in different areas of the state. Lady's slipper, crane-fly orchid, Indian pipe, mandrake, claytonia, and trilliums are a few of the surprises one might find.

## Plant Identification Tips

There are two ways to identify plants with this book. One is to thumb through page by page to match the plants with an illustration. This is time consuming. The other way is to use the following tips to locate possible groups or families for a quicker match. The flowering plants are divided into two major groups, namely, monocotyledonous and dicotyledonous plants, commonly abbreviated as monocots and dicots.

Monocots have parts of the flower in twos or threes or multiples, leaves usually parallel-veined (except *Trillium, Smilax,* and Palms), no cambium, scattered vascular bundles.

Dicots have parts of the flowers in fours and fives or multiples, leaves usually net-veined, vascular bundles in a ring or united into a woody cylinder, cambium present.

The following are a few of the more important or abundant groups or families:

*Monocot Groups*
Individual flowers inconspicuous, small, covered with bracts or embedded in a spadix—Arum, Sedge, Bur-reed, Cat-tail, or Pipewort families. Flowers regular, three sepals, three petals, six stamens, ovary superior—Lily family. Flowers similar but with inferior ovary—Amaryllis family. Perianth very irregular, with odd shapes, fringes, spurs—Orchid family. Flowers with three stamens, perianth regular to irregular, ovary inferior—Iris family.

*Dicot Groups*
Plants with three to five petals, many stamens, many free pistils—Crowfoot family. Plants with pistils more or less united, many stamens, and five petals—Rose family. Corolla composed of keel, wings, and standard, more or less united, ten stamens, and fruit a pod or legume—Legume family. Plants mainly woody, united corolla, regular to irregular in shape, ovary inferior—Heath family. Plants with united anther, ray and disk flower, or only all ray or all disk, usually with a pappus, inferior ovary—Sunflower family. Flowers irregular, two-lipped, superior ovaries—Mint and Figwort families.

Plants with milky juice can be found in the Spurge, Dogbane, Milkweed, and Lobelia families, as well as in the Water-plantain family of the monocots. Plants with tendrils are in the Legume, Maypop, Gourd, and Grape families.

Plants lacking chlorophyll can be found in the Orchid, Heath, and Morning-glory families. Aquatic plants can be found in the Arum, Frog's-bit, Water-plantain, Bur-reed, Pickerel-weed, Water-lily, and Water-shield families.

The Mallow family has the stamens on a tube in the center of the flower. Flowers in umbels are in the Parsley family and also in the Milkweed family.

At times critical identification may be needed. Botanists in charge of plant identification are usually willing to make identifications if adequate material is sent. A specimen suitable to place in the herbarium will compensate for the time it takes to make the identification and write a letter.

Take all of a plant under three feet tall, including roots, bend into twelve-inch lengths, in the form of a *V* or *N*. In the case of woody material, send branches twelve to fourteen inches long. Be sure the specimen has flowers or fruit. Pack flat between two pieces of cardboard. Number if more than one specimen is sent at a time. Any data such as tree or shrub, color of flowers, and conditions under which it grows will be helpful. Do not pack in plastic bags; such material usually rots in transit, especialy if it lies over a weekend. Do not send too many plants at one time. Mail to the botany department at most universities. Someone will see that it gets to the proper person.

xl

# Part I
# Monocotyledons

## Cat-tails
*Typha latifolia* L. (Right)
*Typha domingensis* Pers. (Left)
Cat-tail family

*T. latifolia* L. has stems up to 6 feet tall with numerous flat leaves which overtop the flower clusters. Pistillate and staminate spikes contiguous. Pistillate spikes 5 to 7 inches long, about 1 inch in diameter, dark brown to black. Pollen in tetrads. Widely distributed in wet sites. Also Texas, Arkansas, and Mississippi. Spring to summer.

The flower spikes of *T. domingensis* Pers. overtop the leaves with a space between the pistillate and staminate portions. Pistillate spikes cinnamon brown, longer, and more slender than those of *T. latifolia* L. Pollen grains single. Abundant in fresh-water marshes along the Gulf Coast. Also Texas and Mississippi. Spring to summer.

## Bur-reed
*Sparganium americanum* Nutt.
Bur-reed family

Perennial. Leaves linear, 14 to 24 inches long by ½ inch wide, submerged flaccid, emergent more or less erect. Flower stalk bracted, 24 to 30 inches tall. Inflorescence monoecious. Pistillate heads 2 to 5, sessile, 1 to 1¼ inches in diameter, composed of radially aligned flowers. Individual fruits not constricted. Staminate heads several, apical. Locally common in southeastern Louisiana, along streams, margins of marshes, and cypress swamps. Also Texas, Arkansas, and Mississippi. April to June.

**4** *Sagittaria lancifolia* L.
Water-plantain family

Plants perennial, stout, on rhizomes 1 to 2 inches in diameter with persistent leaf bases. Leaves paddle-shaped, up to 3 feet tall. Blades 8 to 24 inches long, broadly lanceolate, elliptical to ovate, base cuneate to rounded. Flower scape taller than leaves. Flowers in whorls, white, 3 conspicuous petals, 1½ inches in diameter. A conspicuous member of the fresh-water marshes. Also Texas and Mississippi. Spring bloom, late March into May, and occasionally to frost.

*Sagittaria graminea* Michx.
Water-plantain family

Plants perennial, slender, from small diameter rhizomes with persistent leaf bases. Leaves 18 to 24 inches tall, glabrous, blades linear to lanceolate, 8 to 10 inches long by ½ inch wide, petioles strongly sheathing, juice milky. Flower scape often taller than leaves. Flowers in whorls, upper staminate, lower pistillate. Flowers white, about ½ inch in diameter. Petals 3, white, stamens and pistils numerous in respective flowers. Abundant in roadside ditches, widespread. Also Texas and Mississippi. March to August. Sporadic later part of year.

**Arrowhead**
*Sagittaria latifolia* Willd.
Water-plantain family

A robust perennial with long stolons about ¼ inch in diameter with plantlets at the nodes and apex. Leaves up to 4 feet tall, variable, narrow to broad basal lobes, arrowhead-shaped, 6 to 14 inches long. Flower scape usually shorter than the leaves, whorls of white flowers. Peduncles often branched. Flowers 1 to 1¼ inches in diameter. Widely distributed in fresh marshes, ponds, streams, and ditches. Also Texas, Arkansas, and Mississippi. April into November.

**Ottelia**
*Ottelia alismoides* (L.) Pers.
Frog's-bit family

A submerged aquatic whose blossoms appear above the water. Leaves usually totally submerged, blade about 10 inches long, broadly ovate to cordate, very thin, conspicuous veins. Flower stalk angular, 12 to 18 inches long, holding flower about 2 inches above the water. Flower 1 to 1½ inches wide, slightly fragrant, white. Petals broadly obovate. Calyx with several longitudinal, irregular wings. A South Pacific plant first found in Louisiana by Miss Olive Hester of Lafayette. "Big burn" and McCain's pond in Cameron Parish. Its presence in this artificial pond remains unexplainable. Flowers May to June.

## 6    Leafy Three Square
*Scirpus robustus* Pursh
Sedge family

A gregarious perennial up to 5 feet tall. Culm triangular. Leaves dark green about 2 feet long by ½ inch wide, three ranked. Inflorescence consisting of 1 to several ovoid to cylinderical spikelets 1 to 1½ inches long. Spikelets reddish brown, composed of spirally arranged scales covering inconspicuous flowers. A very important food plant for muskrats and ducks. Very abundant in fresh to brackish marshes of southern Louisiana. Also Mississippi. May to July.

THREE SQUARE, *S. olneyi* Gray, a companion species is quite similar. The cluster of spikelets is smaller, and they are on one side of a triangular culm. Very abundant and important as a food plant.

## White-topped Sedge
*Dichromena colorata* (L.) Hitchc.
Sedge family

What many people driving through the pinelands believe to be a white lily is not a lily but a sedge which belongs to the family *Cyperaceae*. These have modified leaves or bracts which become white except for the tips. Numerous inconspicuous flowers are hidden in clusters of small spikelets at the base of the bracts. It is most abundant in the moist pinelands, but also occurs in the prairies of southwestern Louisiana and in some of the coastal marshes where the salinity ranges from brackish to distinctly salty. Also Texas and Mississippi. April to August.

## Palmetto
*Sabal minor* (Jacq.) Pers.
Palm family

A shrub with two growth phases, acaulescent on dry hills in north Louisiana, or with short stems up to 10 feet tall in areas of water level changes. Leaves consist of a stout unarmed petiole and a fan-shaped blade 1 to 3 feet in diameter, divided into numerous segments. Flower cluster, elongate, up to 6 feet long, branched. Individual flowers tiny, whitish. Fruit is black, dry, hard, less than ½ inch in diameter. Abundant and widely distributed from the dry hills of north Louisiana to the cypress swamps of the alluvial floodplains, where it develops a trunk. This form has been named *S. louisiana*, (Darby) Bomhard

SAW PALMETTO, *Serenoa repens* (Bartr.) Small, has small spines on the petiole. Rare in Louisiana. Along Bayou Lacomb, St. Tammany Parish. Also Mississippi. April.

## Indian-turnip, Jack-in-the-pulpit
*Arisaema triphyllum* (L.) Schott
Arum family

Plants with two leaves, each with three leaflets. Flowers are inserted on a straight spadix enclosed in a tubular spathe with a flap on top. Spathe striped with red and brown lines. Fruit is a cluster of bright red berries. The corm should not be eaten because it contains stinging crystals. Widely distributed in Louisiana uplands, absent from the Red and Mississippi floodplains. Also Texas, Arkansas, and Mississippi. March to May. Some plants have 5 leaflets on each leaf or 5 on one and 3 on the other. The all-green spathe projects above the level of the leaves. This is listed as *A. quinatum* (Nutt.) Schott.

*A. dracontium* (L.) Schott, the GREEN DRAGON, consists of a single leaf with several leaflets and a light green spathe with a slender spadix which protrudes from the spathe.

## Elephant's-ear
*Colocasia antiquorum* (L.) Schott
Arum family

A fleshy, frost-sensitive herb about 3 to 4 feet high under Louisiana conditions. Leaf blades drooping from stout petioles, 2½ to 3 feet long, oblong-ovate to cordate, with shallow sinus, not reaching petiole. Flower scape shorter than petioles, spathe portion cylindrical to tapering, yellow with slight opening at margins. Does not produce tubers, but ropelike stolons several feet long. A widespread introduction which has become a pest in gardens and along streams in the fresh-water marshes. From the Pearl River to the Sabine River. Summer to fall. Foliage contains irritating raphides.

**Golden-club, Golden-torch**
*Orontium aquaticum* L.
Arum family

Emergent aquatic growing in clumps from a stout rhizome. Leaves long, petioled, elliptic to broadly ovate. Blades entire, up to 18 inches long, acute at apex, a distinctive bluish green. Flowers tiny, sunken in a golden yellow apical portion of the spadix, the lower part is whitish. Scape erect in flower and decumbent in fruit. Widely distributed in bogs and streams in acid soil areas, most abundant in the Florida Parishes. Sensitive to frost but recovers quickly. Also Texas and Mississippi. March into November.

**White-arum**
*Peltandra sagittaefolia* (Michx.) Morong.
Arum family

A fleshy plant 2 to 3 feet tall. Leaves 6 to 12 inches long, hastate to ovate-hastate with conspicuous spreading basal lobes on a long petiole. Flower stalk erect, about 18 inches long. Spathe white, tubular at base and flaring open at the top exposing the spadix. Rare. Confined to pineland bogs. Also Mississippi. June to August.

## 10 Arrow-arum
*Peltandra virginica* (L.) Kunth
Arum family

A fleshy perennial, 12 to 20 inches tall. Leaves broadly triangular with sharp divergent basal lobes. Scape shorter than leaves, erect in flower, reflexed in fruit. Spathe green, tubular, tapering to a sharp point. Margin opening slightly over the flowers, crisped, light yellow. Pistillate flowers basal on spadix, staminate near the apex. Common in fresh marshes and cypress swamps. Texas and Mississippi. April to June.

## Water-lettuce
*Pistia stratiotes* L.
Arum family

Plants free-floating or rooting in soft muck when water levels drop. Plants consist of a rosette of many overlapping leaves. Blades up to 10 inches long, obovate, strongly ribbed. Flower spathe small, nearly ½ inch long, inconspicuous. Very abundant, often a pest as it clogs streams and lakes in lower Louisiana. Usually covered with aphids. Also Texas and Mississippi. April.

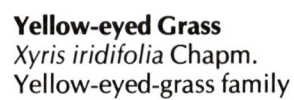

**Yellow-eyed Grass**
*Xyris iridifolia* Chapm.
Yellow-eyed-grass family

An herbaceous perennial growing in small clumps with irislike leaves. Leaves flat, linear, 16 to 24 inches long by ½ inch wide. Flower scape taller than the leaves, terminated with a solitary ovoid spike. Bracts of the spike reddish brown, indurated, each bract subtending a solitary flower. Calyx green, corolla of 3 yellow petals, flower about ½ inch wide. Very common in fresh marshes, wet pine flatwoods, edges of streams, and cypress swamps. Also Texas and Mississippi. June to September. Several other species occur in Louisiana.

**Hard-heads, Pipewort**
*Eriocaulon decangulare* L.
Pipewort family

Plant has a basal rosette of thin, linear-lanceolate leaves about 4 to 6 inches long, with one to several naked flower stalks about 2 feet tall, crowned with a whitish compact, dense head, consisting of tiny flowers and bracts. Widely distributed in wet sites in the acid pinelands, bogs, and pond margins. Also Texas and Mississippi. Spring. Several other species are known to occur in the state.

**Spanish-moss, Barb-d'Espanole**
*Tillandsia usneoides* L.
Pineapple family

The plant body is composed of a woody core surrounded by a thin layer of soft greenish tissue, coated with thin grayish scales. These trap dust and absorb water for the plant. Flowers about ¼ inch in diameter, emerald green with 3 petals. The flower structure shows its relationship to the pineapple. It is an epiphyte, that is, a plant which is supported by other plants but does not receive nourishment from them. It is not a parasite. The only time it may damage a tree is when the weight of the wet moss causes branches to break during a tropical storm. It does not shade out a tree, but rather lives in the shade. It also grows on insulated wire. Widely distributed. Also Texas, Arkansas, and Mississippi. May.

**Day-flower**
*Commelina erecta* L.
Dayflower family

Perennial herb. Stems ascending to erect, branched. Leaves linear to lanceolate, 3 to 6 inches long. Sheath ciliate. Flower cluster borne inside spathes. Spathe margin united near base. Flower ½ to ⅜ inch wide, 2 back petals blue, larger than the white front petal which is often obscure. Widespread in moist sites and gardens. A weed. Also Texas, Arkansas and Mississippi. April to frost.

### Spiderwort
*Tradescantia virginiana* L.
Dayflower family

Perennial herb about 16 to 20 inches tall, erect. Leaves linear, about 16 inches long by ¾ inch wide. Flower cluster terminal, pedicels and sepals densely pilose. Petals blue, occasionally pure pink, about ¾ inch wide. Widely distributed in dry pinelands, not on Mississippi or Red river floodplains. Also Texas, Arkansas, and Mississippi. April.

*T. ohioensis* Raf. is glabrous and glaucous, usually 24 to 30 inches tall, with inflated sheaths. Flowers typically blue, occasionally pink, 1 inch in diameter. Confined to alluvial and terrace soils. Common in wet habitats. At times a bad weed in gardens. *T. hirsutiflora* Bush is densely pubescent all over. Flowers blue, pink, and white. Chiefly in pinelands.

### Water-hyacinth, "Lilie"
*Eichhornia crassipes* (Mart.) Solms.
(=*Piaropus crassipes* (Mart.) Brit.)
Pickerel-weed family

The date this plant was imported into the United States is uncertain. It is an aquatic herb, free-floating or occasionally rooting in the mud, and is quite variable in size. The petioles of the smaller plants are inflated ("bulbs") and are more conspicuous than the reniform blades. The spicate flower cluster, often 6 to 16 inches long has many funnel-form, irregular flowers, bluish-purple to lavender with a conspicuous yellow eye spot in the top petal. Widely distributed in lakes, bayous, swamps, and fresh-water marshes. Vegetative division is so rapid that streams are clogged. Seeds will germinate after several years' storage. A beautiful pest very sensitive to 2,4-D. Now illegal to transport in Louisiana. Also Texas and Mississippi. April until frost.

14 **Pickerel-weed**
*Pontederia cordata* L.
Pickerel-weed family

A perennial herb with creeping rhizomes. Plants 2 to 3 feet tall. Leaves erect, long-petioled, blades about 6 to 8 inches long, deltoid-ovate with a deeply cordate base. Flower stalk 6 to 8 inches long with a single subtending leaf. Flowers irregular, deep blue, closely inserted on spike, blooming in succession that keeps the flower stalk in blossom for several days. Common in wet sites, fresh-water marshes, streams, and lakes. Also Texas, Arkansas, and Mississippi. April into November. Frost sensitive.

**Colic-root**
*Aletris aurea* Walt.
Lily family

A perennial herb with short, thick rhizomes and a conspicuous basal rosette of leaves. Leaves thin, lanceolate, about 4 to 8 inches long. Flower stalk with several yellow flowers. Flowers campanulate to semiglobose, about ¼ inch in diameter when perianth lobes are inflexed, wrinkled, roughened. Pinelands and prairie soils. Absent from alluvial soils. Also Texas and Mississippi. July.

**Colic-root**
*Aletris lutea* Small
Lily family

Very similar to *A. aurea*. Flower more cylindrical, slightly constricted below the apex to the spreading tiny perianth lobes, ⅜ inch long. Blooms from the bottom upward. Rickett suggests this may be a hybrid between *A. aurea* and *A. farinosa*. Common in pine bogs and wet sites in the pinelands. Also Mississippi. July.

WHITE COLIC ROOT, *A. farinosa* L., is the white counterpart of this species. Usually a taller plant 24 to 30 inches tall. Moist pinelands, absent from alluvial soils, more abundant in western Louisiana. Also Texas and Mississippi.

**Wild Onion**
*Allium canadense* L.
Lily family

A perennial bulbous plant with a typical onion odor. Bulbs with a distinct net-fibrous coat. Leaves shiny, dark green, flat, about 12 inches long. Scape round, longer than the leaves, terminated with a spathe and a mixture of bulblets and flowers, or at times all bulblets or all flowers. Flowers perfect, white with pink tints, about ¼ inch long. Fruit a capsule. Widely distributed, most abundant on alluvial and terrace soils, at times a bad weed. Also Texas, Arkansas, and Mississippi. March to May.

### Wild Onion
*Allium arenicola* Small
Lily family

This can be recognized by the compact cluster of tiny white to pinkish flowers at the summit of the scape. These plants grow in clusters from small offshoot bulbs with a fibrous, matted outer coat. The plants are about 12 inches tall. The leaves are cylindrical and have the typical onion odor. The perianth is about ¼ inch long with the outer segments (sepals) a little wider than the inner segments or petals. It is common in the pinelands of eastern and western Louisiana. Also Texas, Arkansas, and Mississippi. March to June.

### Featherbells
*Stenanthium gramineum* (Ker) Morong
Lily family

Perennial herb up to 5 feet tall. Leaves both basal and cauline up to 2 feet long by ¾ inch wide, reduced upward. Flower cluster a panicle of racemes. Flowers white, perfect, and unisexual in same cluster, about ¼ wide. Pedicels shorter than the individual flowers. Margins of bogs in Florida Parishes, pinelands. Also Mississippi. June to September.

FLY POISON, *Amianthium muscaetoxicum* (Walt.) Gray, is quite similar, but has only 1 raceme with the pedicels longer than the respective flowers. North Louisiana.

**Wild-hyacinth**
*Camassia scilloides* (Raf.) Cory
Lily family

Perennial bulbous herb up to 2 feet tall. Leaves several, basal, linear, 12 to 18 inches long by ¼ to ½ inch wide. Flower cluster a bracted raceme up to 12 inches long. Bracts as long as, to a little longer than, the pedicels. Flowers perfect, symmetrical, light blue, about 1 inch long. Mixed woods in north Louisiana. Also Texas, Arkansas, and Mississippi. April to May.

**Catesby Lily, Leopard Lily, Pine Lily**
*Lilium catesbaei* Walt.
Lily family

A bog-inhabiting plant usually with one terminal erect flower. Scaly bulb about 1 inch in diameter. Stem leaves lanceolate, about 2 to 5 inches long by ¼ inch wide, mostly appressed to the stem. Open flower about 5 inches in diameter. The perianth lobes are stalked, lanceolate, with the apical portion marked with red, whereas the basal portion is marked with yellow and dark spots. Stigma about 3 inches long, exceeds the conspicuous stamens. This plant has such exacting requirements that it should not be transplanted into gardens. Pineland bogs in Louisiana and Mississippi. August to September.

## 18  Carolina Lily
*Lilium michauxii* Poir.
(=*L. carolinianum* Michx.)
   *linianum*)
Lily family

A rare plant in Louisiana. Stem comes from a small scaly bulb and varies from 1 to 4 feet tall. Lower stem leaves in whorls of 3 to 7 with the upper leaves greatly reduced either opposite or alternate. Leaves fleshy, about 3 inches long, oblanceolate to obovate, broadest near the tip. Flower 1, occasionally 2, nodding, 3 to 5 inches in diameter. Perianth segments strongly reflexed, orange-red to yellowish in the throat, purple-spotted. Well-drained, sandy, pine-hardwood areas. Kisatchie Forest and southeastern Louisiana. Also Texas and Mississippi. July to August. Specimen courtesy of Charles Allen, St. Helena Parish.

## False Garlic
*Nothoscordum bivalve* (L.) Brit.
Lily family

This plant has no onion or garlic odor. Bulb with scaly coat and offset bulblets. Leaves round to flat to slightly channeled on inner face, about ⅛ inch wide. Flower cluster a few long-stalked white flowers about ½ inch in diameter with a green to brown strip on 3 petaloid-sepals. Widely distributed and a pest in gardens and lawns. It is closely related to the onion, and some botanists place it in the genus *Allium*. Also Texas, Arkansas, and Mississippi. It usually blooms from late February into April, and some years from September into October.

*N. fragrans* (Vent.) Kunth is a bigger plant with leaves ¼ to ⅜ inch wide, no onion odor. Blooms from April into June. Widespread, a bad weed.

## Greenbriar
*Smilax laurifolia* L.
Lily family

Perennial, stout, high-climbing vine, usually very spiny, upper branches may be smooth. Leaves oblong-lanceolate, leathery, evergreen, usually with enrolled margin, 3 to 5 inches long, 3-nerved, tendrils present. Flowers in umbels in axils of leaves, small, inconspicuous. Fruit a 1-seeded berry, greenish the first year, turning a blue-black the second year when ripe. Widespread and abundant, margins of swamps and wet woods, especially abundant in margins of bog in pinelands. Also Texas, Arkansas, and Mississippi. April.

## Greenbriar, Sawbriar
*Smilax bona-nox* L.
Lily family

A woody vine from thickened, knotty rhizomes. Lower stems with stout spines. Leaves variable, pandurate to broadly cordate, with or without marginal cilia, reticulate, petioles about 1 inch long. Flowers small, inconspicuous, axillary peduncles about 2 inches long. Fruit globose, about ¼ inch in diameter, black. Abundant and widely distributed in Louisiana, absent from the marshlands. Also Texas, Arkansas, and Mississippi. Flowers in April. Fruit ripe September to October.

**20**  **Greenbriar**
*Smilax walteri* Pursh
Lily family

Perennial, slender, high-climbing vine, very thorny below, branchlets smooth. Leaves firm, deciduous, ovate to broadly ovate, 3 to 6 inches long, reticulate. Flowers in axil of leaves, yellowish, inconspicuous. Fruit red, globose, about ¼ inch in diameter, persistent after leaves are shed. Widely distributed along streams and in cypress swamps. Flowers April. Ripe fruit November to January.

**False Asphodel**
*Tofieldia racemosa* (Walt.) BSP.
Lily family

Perennial herb, basal leaves erect, 8 to 12 inches long by ¼ inch wide. Scape leaf single, bractlike, below middle. Scape rough. Flower cluster apical, creamy white, opens from apex downward. Flowers about ¼ inch in diameter, 2 to 3 at each node near the base of the flower cluster. Confined to wet sites in the pinelands. Also Texas, Arkansas, and Mississippi. June to September.

**Red Trillium, Wake Robin**
*Trillium sessile* L.
Lily family

The perennial corm sends up a scape with three leaflike bracts at the apex plus a sessile flower which has an unpleasant odor. Bracts 3 to 6 inches long, oval to suborbicular, and usually definitely mottled. Flowers 1 to 2½ inches long. Sepals green, widespreading but not reflexed, lanceolate. Petals linear-lanceolate without a clawlike base. The petals elongate slightly as the flower ages and turn from the deep maroon to a yellowish green. There are plants with clear yellow petals. Widely distributed in Louisiana and generally absent from the Mississippi floodplain. Also Texas, Arkansas, and Mississippi.

*T. ludovicianum* Harbinson has a clawlike base to the petals. *T. recurvatum* Beck has clawed petals, reflexed sepals, and stalks to the leaflike blades.

**Bellwort**
*Uvularia perfoliata* L.
Lily family

A perennial herb. Stem simple or once-branched, 6 to 12 inches tall. Leaves perfoliate, elliptic lanceolate, 3 to 5 inches long. Flower nodding, yellow, about 1 inch long. Perianth papillose on inside. Rare. Tunica Hills in West Feleciana, scattered moist rich woods, in north Louisiana. Also Texas, Arkansas, and Mississippi. Late March, April to May.

*U. sessilifolia* Sm. is very similar, but smaller and can be distinguished by the absence of the papillose condition.

## Camass
*Zigadenus glaberrimus* Michx.
Lily family

Slender, 3 to 5 feet tall, from a perennial horizontal, scaly rootstalk. The basal leaves 12 to 16 inches long, strongly keeled, and reduced in size up the stem. Flower cluster paniculate, with ascending branches bearing 6 to 10 flowers. The individual flowers are whitish to yellow tinged with reddish color, 1 inch in diameter. The sepals are slightly smaller than the three petals. The petals have 2 well-developed greenish glands marked with purple spots. The petals are about ½ inch long with a distinctly clawed base. It is related to the POISON CAMASS and is suspected of being toxic. Pineland bogs. Also Texas and Mississippi. August to September.

## Camass
*Zigadenus leimanthoides* Gray
Lily family

Perennial herb with erect stems to 5 feet tall. Leaves chiefly basal, linear, about 20 inches long by ½ inch wide. Flower cluster a pyramidal panicle about 20 inches long. Branchlets ascending, densely flowered near the apex. Flowers greenish white, about ½ inch wide, lower fertile, upper sterile or staminate. Perianth with one gland per segment. Rare. Found in boggy sites in wet pine flatwoods. Also Texas and Mississippi. June to September.

## Yucca, Bear-grass
*Yucca louisianensis* Trel.
Lily family

Perennial 6 to 8 feet tall. Leaves mainly basal, scalelike on flower scape, linear-lanceolate, 2 feet long by ½ to ¾ inch wide, few marginal fibers, apices sharp-pointed. Inflorescence a panicle of bracted racemes, 2 to 3 feet high. Panicle branches pubescent. Flowers white, bell-shaped, about 1 to 1¼ inches long, waxy, generally not fruiting due to the absence of the yucca moth. Widely distributed in the dry, sandy, or upland soils. Also Texas and Mississippi. April to June. Reported in the past as *Y. filamentosa*.

*Y. treculeana*, *Y. aloifolia*, and *Y. smallii* have been reported for the state.

## Golden Canna
*Canna flaccida* Salisb.
Canna family

A large perennial up to 6 feet tall. Leaf blades 10 to 20 inches long, marked with parallel veins. Flowers in apical clusters, irregular in shape, yellow. Confined to the fresh-water marshes. Also Texas and Mississippi. Blooms in fall.

There are several acres of a white flowered species. *C. glauca* L. just off Highway 82 near the Intercoastal canal. *C. indica*, L. with reddish flowers, is known to have been an escape for more than 100 years. A cultivated hybrid, *C. X generalis* Bailey, with large red and yellow spotted flowers, is getting established in the fresh-water marshes near Pilottown.

## 24 Agave, American Aloe
*Agave virginica* L.
Amaryllis family

A perennial herb with thick fleshy roots and a rosette of succulent leaves. Basal leaves 10 to 15 inches long, lanceolate to oblong, spatulate with acute to acuminate apices, frequently spotted with purple, greatly reduced in size up the stem. Stem 3 to 5 feet tall. Flower cluster a spike of many fragrant, greenish flowers about 1 inch long. Stamens exerted, filaments and anther conspicuous in freshly opened flower; anthers detach easily. Fruit a globose capsule about ¾ inch in diameter with many flat black seeds. Also Texas, Arkansas, and Mississippi. April to May.

## Copper-lily
*Habranthus texanus* (Herb.) Steud.
Amaryllis family

Bulbs small, about 1 inch in diameter. Leaves basal developing after the flower, short, narrowly linear. Scape slender, about 6 to 8 inches tall. Flower orange-yellow, opening early in morning, closing in afternoon, funnel-shaped, declinate, about 1 inch in diameter. Stamens in fascicles, 4 different lengths. Very abundant on lawns of several residences in Natchitoches. Escape on banks of Cane River and in small spots on Northwestern University campus. April.

**Drummond Rain-lily**
*Cooperia drummondii* Herb.
Amaryllis family

A native rain-lily which is easy to grow from seed. The black-coated bulb produces 2 to 5 linear leaves which elongate after blooming. The flower stalk is about 8 inches tall and bears a single flower, white inside and pinkish outside. The flower is more or less expanded, about ½ to 1 inch wide. The spathe under the flower is about 2 inches long. A rare plant, most abundant in the black soils around Caddo Lake and on the prairie soils at Lake Charles. Also Texas. October.

**Swamp-lily**
*Crinum americanum* L.
Amaryllis family

Large, long-necked stoloniferous bulb. Strap-shaped leaves 3 to 4 feet long by 2 to 3 inches wide. Flower stalk about 1 inch in diameter by 2 to 3½ feet tall, with usually 4 flowers at apex. Flower white with pinkish markings. Perianth lobes 3 to 4 inches long by ½ inch wide, bending backward to form a ball-shaped blossom. Stamen filaments colored. Common in fresh-water marshes and cypress swamps of lower Louisiana. Will thrive in cultivation. Also Texas and Mississippi. May into November.

### Spider-lily
*Hymenocallis occidentalis* (LeConte) Kunth
Amaryllis family

Bulbs 4 to 5 inches in diameter, covered with black scales. Leaves numerous, linear, about 2 feet long by 1½ to 2 inches wide. Scape solid, 2-edged, ½ to ¾ inch in diameter, varies from shorter to longer than the leaves. Spathe membranaceous. Flowers 2 to 6 per scape, white, fragrant, inferior ovary, perianth tube 3 to 4 inches long, opening into 6 long white lobes about 4 to 6 inches long by ¼ inch wide. Crown thin, membranaceous, about 1½ inches in diameter. Stamen filaments adnate to crown. Fruit a capsule with large, green, fleshy seeds. Widely distributed in wet sites. Also Texas, Arkansas, and Mississippi. March to May. Some authors use the name *H. liriosme* (Raf.) Shinners.

*H. eulae* Shinners is a summer blooming species which lacks leaves at blooming time.

### Yellow Star-grass
*Hypoxis hirsuta* (L.) Cov.
Amaryllis family

Plant from a corm. Leaves few, linear, 6 to 14 inches long, ⅛ to ¼ inch wide, densely pilose. Flower scape shorter than leaves, 1 to several flowered, usually only one open at a time. Flowers yellow, about ½ inch in diameter, with 6 lanceolate perianth segments. Fruit a capsule with shiny black seeds. Widely distributed in Louisiana, pastures, pinelands and prairie. Absent from the Mississippi floodplain. Also Texas, Arkansas, and Mississippi. Late February into April.

**Atamasco-lily**
*Zephyranthes atamasco* (L.) Herb.
Amaryllis family

Bulb produces a flowering scape and leaves. Leaves 8 to 12 inches long by less than ½ inch wide. Scape naked, terminated by a sheath and a solitary flower. Perianth tubular, white, more or less united. Stigmas 3, exceeding the stamens in length. Sandy pineland. Rare. Mississippi. March to April. Cultivated in Louisiana.

**White Rain-lily**
*Zephyranthes candida* (Lindl.)
Herb.
Amaryllis family

Bulbs small, less than ½ inch in diameter, in dense clumps. Leaves 8 to 12 inches long, about ¼ inch wide. Scape to 12 inches tall, terminated by a solitary flower. Perianth usually white, saucer-shaped, about 1½ inches in diameter, stigma as long as stamens. Cultivated. Escape from cultivation, persisting for long intervals. Also Texas and Mississippi. April to May.

PINK RAIN-LILY, *Z. grandiflora* Lindl., with flowers from pink to rose is widely cultivated in Louisiana.

## 28 Gold-crest
*Lophiola americana* (Pursh) Wood
Bloodwort family

Perennial herb 2 to 3 feet tall with elongate rootstalks, glabrous below, pubescent near the top. Leaves erect, 12 inches long by about ¼ wide. Flower cluster dense, flat to rounded. Perianth bright yellow, about ¼ inch wide, strongly pubescent on inner face. Stamens 6. Pedicel and peduncles copiously woolly. The genus is sometimes placed in the lily family. Bogs and wet pinelands, St. Tammany and Washington parishes. Also Mississippi. June to September.

## Redroot
*Lachnanthes caroliana* (Lam.) Dandy
Bloodwort family

A perennial herb 2 to 3 feet tall with red roots and rhizomes, pubescent near the top. Leaves erect about 12 inches long. Flower cluster dense, flat to rounded, pubescent. Flower yellow, small, less than ½ inch long. Petals narrow, strap-shaped. Stamens 3. Bogs and moist pinelands. St. Tammany and Washington parishes. Also Mississippi. June to September.

Similar to *Lophiola* but distinguished by number of stamens and the more open flower cluster.

**Hebertia**
*Alophia drummondii* (Grah.) Foster
(=*Herbertia caerulea* Herb.)
Iris family

A perennial, bulb about 1 inch in diameter, coated with brown scales. Leaves narrowly linear, about 10 to 12 inches long, sheathing the bulb. Scape about 10 to 12 inches tall, bearing a spathe with 1 or 2 erect flowers. Perianth about 2 inches wide, 3 outer segments, cuneate-obovate, spreading, pale to dark violet, whitish near the base with violet spots. Inner segments much smaller. Style branches 3, with bifid stigmas. Capsule erect. Prairie and grassy areas in longleaf pineland. Rare in Louisiana. Also Texas. April to May.

**Pinewoods-lily**
*Eustylis purpurea* (Herb.) Engelm. & Gray (= *Nemastylis purpurea* Herb.)
Iris family

A perennial bulb with black scales. Leaves linear-lanceolate, about 18 to 24 inches long by 1 inch wide, plaited, veins distinct. Scape about 30 inches tall, slender, simple to branched, bearing a single apical spathe which contains several flowers. Perianth cup-shaped to flat, of 3 outer segments, spreading, about 1½ inches wide, light to deep purple. Inner perianth segments 3, dwarfed, cupped, or crimped. Flower opens in the morning and closes in the afternoon, with a succession of new ones each day. Abundant in longleaf pinewoods. Vernon Parish northward into Winn Parish. Also Texas. May to June.

**Zig-zag-stemmed Iris**
*Iris brevicaulis* Raf.
(=*I. foliosa* Mack. & Bush)

Perennial, rhizome slender about 1 inch in diameter. Stem zig-zag about 2 feet tall. Leaves lax, linear, about 2 feet long by 1½ inches wide. Flowers along the scape, bracted, below the level of the leaves, deep blue. Falls 4 to 5 inches long, claw portion tight, blade portion widespreading, oval with yellow signal patch. Standard shorter than the falls. Crest on stigma arch entire to toothed. Capsule 6-angled. Widely distributed in wet sites, fresh marshes, streams, and ponds. Also Texas and Mississippi. March to April.

**Copper-colored Iris, Red Iris**
*Iris fulva* Ker
Iris family

This iris was first collected near New Orleans in 1811. It is a perennial plant with a stout rhizome. Leaves basal, linear, about 3 feet long. Flower stalk up to 5 feet, with leaflike bracts subtending the flowers. Flowers red or copper-red, orange-red, and occasionally yellow, 1½ to 2½ inches long. The arched spreading sepals (falls) are larger than the drooping petals (standards). The stigma arch lacks a distinct appendage. Stamens under the stigma arch. Capsule 6-angled. One of the parents of the numerous Louisiana hybrids. Common and widely distributed in fresh marshes, stream banks, and wet depressions in the alluvial floodplain. Also Texas and Mississippi. Late March to May.

**Giant-blue Iris**
*Iris giganticaerulea* Small
Iris family

Plants 5 to 6 feet tall in the fresh-water marshes. The flower parts in iris have different names. The falls (sepals) are 3 inches long by 1¼ inches wide. The falls are marked with a distinct whitish signal patch with a prominent yellow center. The standards (erect petals) are 3 inches long and ½ to ¾ inch wide. The stigma arch, which lies over the fall, has a distinct crest about ½ inch long. The stamens are under the three stigma arches. The flowers vary from pale blue to deep indigo. Capsule 6-angled. Most abundant in the fresh-water habitats in lower Louisiana. Also Texas and Mississippi. March to April. One of the parents of many hybrids.

**German Iris, Flags**
*Iris germanica* L.
Iris family

The specific name is applied to many color forms which have resulted from extensive hybridization. A perennial herb with stout rootstalks. Basal leaves sword-shaped, 1 to 1½ feet tall by 1 to 1½ inches wide. Flower scape terminal with 2 white flowers with green bracts. Falls 1½ inches in diameter with yellow beard. Standards slightly larger than falls, converging at apex. Persistent for many years at old house sites and gradually escaping from cultivation. This strain is better adapted to Louisiana conditions than the newer hybrids. March to April.

**Yellow Flag**
*Iris pseudacorus* L.
Iris family

Another Old World iris which has escaped from cultivation. Plants to 5 feet tall in large clumps, very vigorous. Leaves erect, linear, about 1 inch wide and 3 to 4 feet tall. Two flowers at apex and often in axil of upper leaf, yellow falls suborbicular to ovate 1½ inches broad, marked with a series of dots arranged in a *v*, no beard or crest. Standards erect, linear, with obtuse apex. Capsule 3-angled, erect, cylindrical, 2 to 4 inches long. Extensively naturalized. Atchafalaya floodway, especially from Lake Verret to Morgan City, also along Highway 82 from Pecan Island to Cameron. April to May.

**Southern-blue Flag**
*Iris virginica* L.
Iris family

Perennial, rhizome stout. Flower scape up to 3 feet tall. Leaves about 2 feet long, lax. Flowers about 3 inches long, apical on bracted scape, taller than the leaves. Color varied, typically blue, also white with lavender or blue lines in falls. Falls with distinct yellow signal patch. Standards erect, obovate to spatulate, shorter than the falls. Capsule 3-angled. Wet sites in marshes, pinelands, and alluvial soils. Also Texas, Arkansas, and Mississippi. March to April.

**Celestial-lily**
*Nemastylis geminiflora* Nutt.
Iris family

This plant buries its bulbs by producing a new bulb below the old bulb with frequently as many as 6 bulbs in a row. The new scape and leaves push up through the old bulb. The leaves are strongly veined, somewhat folded, and vary from 12 to 20 inches long. The light blue flowers open flat, 2 to 2½ inches in diameter. The sepals and petals are similar in appearance. Usually 2 flowers from the apical spathe. These short-lived flowers open in the morning. A rare plant in the pinelands of north Louisiana. Also Texas. April to May.

**Blue-eyed-grass**
*Sisyrinchium capillare* Bicknell
Iris family

Plants in tufts with old leaf bases as capillary fibers. Leaves 8 to 12 inches long, by less than $1/16$ inch wide, needle-like, slightly 2-edged when fresh. Flower stalks slightly longer than leaves, slightly flattened, terminated by two spathes which enclose several blue flowers. Flowers about ½ inch wide. Widely distributed in Louisiana. Also Arkansas and Mississippi. March into May.

**Blue-eyed-grass**
*Sisyrinchium atlanticum* Bicknell
Iris family

Plants in tufts, without last year's capillary fibers, 8 to 12 inches tall. Leaves flat, 6 inches long by 1/16 wide, flower stalk varying from shorter to longer than the leaves, usually with one bract about midway on the scape from which emerge 2 to 4 pedunculate spathes. Purple spot at base of the spathe. Flowers blue, about ½ inch in diameter. Widely distributed, high ground in the marsh, prairie soils, and into the pine-oak-hickory uplands. Also Texas, Arkansas, and Mississippi. March into May.

*S. exile* Bicknell has small yellow flowers with a purple or brown vein in the perianth parts. Hybridizes with other species.

**Grass-pink Orchid**
*Calopogon pulchellus* (Salisb.) R.Br.
Orchid family

Plant erect, slender, 18 to 24 inches tall. Leaves linear, basal, 10 to 12 inches long, by 2 inches wide, distinctly veined. Flower stalk simple or branched, bearing 3 to 10 flowers which open from the bottom upward. Flowers rose-pink to whitish, about 2 inches in diameter, sepals and petals distinct, spreading. Lower lip uppermost, with narrow base and obtuse apex, bearded with yellow and pink hairs. Rare in Louisiana. Most abundant in pineland bogs, occasional in wet pine flatwoods. Also Texas and Mississippi. April to June.

PALE GRASS-PINK, *C. pallidus* Chapm. is distinguished from the above by slender leaves less than ¼ inch wide, smaller and paler flowers.

**Spreading-pogonia**
*Cleistes divaricata* (L.) Ames
Orchid family

An erect, slender herb, 24 to 30 inches tall. Leaf solitary, attached above the middle of the scape, oblong-lanceolate, 3 to 5 inches long. Flower 1, occasionally more, terminal. Sepals erect, spreading, dark, 1½ to 2 inches long by ⅛ inch wide. Petals pink to white, nearly 1½ inches long, lower lip conspicuously crested, about as long as the petals. Most abundant in moist pineland bogs, occasional on drier sandy sites. Also Texas, Arkansas, and Mississippi. May to July.

**Yellow Lady's-slipper**
*Cypripedium calceolus* L.
Orchid family

Perennial herb, 20 to 24 inches tall. It has several strongly veined leaves about 6 inches long by 3 to 4 inches wide with 1, occasionally 2, flowers at stem apex. The yellowish sepals are speckled with reddish brown spots. The lateral petals are twisted to crisped, and the outstanding feature is the yellow inflated lip about 2½ inches long. It has been collected in Natchitoches and Caldwell parishes. Mr. John Lynch, Lafayette, has developed techniques of growing this plant in his green house, pollinating the flowers, and raising seedlings. Also Texas, Arkansas, and Mississippi. April.

**Tree Orchid, Green-fly Orchid**
*Epidendrum conopseum* R. Br.
Orchid family

This is the only native, epiphytic orchid thus far found in Louisiana. Its mass of cordlike greenish roots cling tightly to the bark of trees, some entering fissures and under layers of bark. Stems ascending to erect, short. Leaves leathery, dark green, oblong to linear-lanceolate, 2 to 4 inches long. Flower cluster short, few-flowered. Flowers greenish yellow when fresh, about ½ inch wide. Fruit a many-seeded drooping capsule. Found on magnolia, tupelo gum, and some oaks, usually in the crown or on trunks in shady areas. Extensively killed by the severe freeze of 1962. Widely distributed in lower Louisiana. Also Mississippi. June to August.

**White Fringed Orchid**
*Habenaria blephariglottis* (Willd.) Hook.
Orchid family

This is a replica of *H. ciliaris* in white. Flower cluster compact up to 6 inches long. The individual flowers have a slender spur 1½ inches long. Lower lip is entire with a distinct fringe. Pineland bogs along the Gulf Coast into Mississippi. It apparently has not yet been found in Louisiana. July to August.

*H. leucophea* (Nutt.) Gray can be distinguished by the 3-parted lower lip which is then fringed. Reported for Louisiana by Caroline Dormon.

**Yellow Fringed Orchid**
*Habenaria ciliaris* (L.) R. Br.
Orchid family

This is a spectacular plant with its orange inflorescence, projecting just above the surrounding plants in boggy habitats. The slightly fleshy lower leaves are lanceolate, about 10 inches long by 1¼ inches wide. The conspicuous flower cluster is 3 to 5 inches long. The individual flowers are about 1½ inches long with a conspicuous spur and a well-developed fringe on the lower lip. It occurs in moist boggy sites in the pinelands. Texas, Arkansas, and Mississippi. July into September.

Distinguished from *H. cristata* (Michx.) R. Br. by the larger flower cluster, flower, spur, and fringe.

## 38 Yellow Crested Orchid
*Habenaria cristata* (Michx.) R. Br.
Orchid family

This orchid is a smaller edition of *H. ciliaris* and usually grows with it. The spur is less than ½ inch long. The fringe on the lower lip is smaller, more delicate, and less conspicuous than in *H. ciliaris* (L.) R. Br. Widely distributed in moist, boggy pineland sites. Also Texas, Arkansas, and Mississippi. July to September.

## Snowy Orchid
*Habenaria nivea* (Nutt.) Spreng.
Orchid family

A terresterial orchid from small tubers. Plants slender, erect, 8 to 24 inches tall. Leaves basal, 2 or 3, linear, 4 to 12 inches long. Flower cluster terminal, compact, with many flowers. Flowers white, about ⅜ inch in diameter, lip uppermost. Spur conspicuous, more or less horizontal, about ¾ inch long. Widely distributed in moist pinelands and bogs. Especially abundant in the depressions between the pimple mounds in the longleaf pine near Kinder. Also Texas and Mississippi. June to August.

**Water-spider Orchid**
*Habenaria repens* Nutt.
Orchid family

A perennial aquatic herb rooted in masses of floating water hyacinths or soft muck. Stems 24 to 30 inches tall, leafy. Leaves oblong to linear-lanceolate, strongly ribbed, about 10 inches long by 1 inch wide. Flower cluster a raceme of bracted light greenish flowers. Perianth divided into narrow lobes, somewhat reflexed, about ½ inch wide. Resembles a spider. Very abundant in southern Louisiana in canals and water bodies which are infested with water hyacinth. Also Texas and Mississippi. April to October.

**Crested-coral-root**
*Hexalectris spicata* (Walt.) Barnh.
Orchid family

A nongreen orchid about 30 inches tall. The flesh-colored stem has several purplish sheathing bracts, and the flower cluster is from 8 to 12 inches long. The individual flower is more than 1 inch long. The narrowly oval sepals are larger than the petals. Widely distributed, local in moist mixed pine hardwoods. Also Texas, Arkansas, and Mississippi. June to August.

## 40 Southern Twayblade
*Listera australis* Lindl.
Orchid family

This is a delicate, inconspicuous orchid. The slender plant is about 6 inches tall with two opposite, sessile, ovate to elliptic leaves which are about ½ inch long. The flower stalk and flowers are a dull reddish brown. One of the outstanding features is the lower lip is divided into two divergent segments about ¼ inch long. It is widely distributed in moist pine and hardwood sites, but absent from the Mississippi floodplain. Also Texas, Arkansas, and Mississippi. March to April.

## Green Adders-mouth Orchid
*Malaxis unifolia* Michx.
Orchid family

A plant with tiny flowers. Plants are up to 10 inches tall, with a single green leaf midway on the scape. The ovate to oval leaf is 3 to 4 inches long by 1 to 2 inches wide. The flower cluster has many greenish white, tiny flowers nearly ⅛ inch in diameter on slender pedicels. Rare. Found in boggy sites in pine-hardwood areas. Also Texas, Arkansas, and Mississippi. May to June.

**Beard Flower, Rose Pogonia**
*Pogonia ophioglossoides* (L.) Ker
Orchid family

Plants with slender stems about 2 feet tall. Leaves solitary, attached about midway on stem, narrowly oval, 2 to 3 inches long. Flowers 1, occasionally 2, pink to white about 1 inch long. Lower lip has 3 lines of elongated papillae. Frequent in wet pineland and bogs. Also Texas, Arkansas, and Mississippi. March to May.

**Crane-fly Orchid**
*Tipularia discolor* Nutt.
Orchid family

This species can be identified part of the year on the basis of a single, strongly veined, ovate leaf about 3 inches long which is purplish below. It rots away prior to sending up the bloom stalk which is about two feet tall. This naked stalk has many scattered flowers about ½ inch in diameter. The flower parts are all slender, with the calyx and spur longer than the petals. The flower parts are yellowish to purplish. Widely distributed, more abundant in beech-magnolia woods, absent from the Mississippi River floodplain. Also Texas, Arkansas, and Mississippi. March to April.

### Fragrant Ladies' Tresses
*Spiranthes odorata* (Nutt.) Lindl.
Orchid family

A perennial herb 22 to 36 inches tall with stolons. Leaves mainly basal or on lower part of flower stalk, linear to linear-lanceolate, 8 to 10 inches long by about ½ inch wide. Flower cluster 8 to 10 inches long, terminal, pubescent, densely flowered, spirally arranged, very fragrant. Flowers white, about ½ inch long, lower lip broadly ovate. Abundant in standing water, cypress swamps, common in fresh marshes. Also Texas and Mississippi. August to frost.

### Ladies' Tresses, Cork-screw Orchids
Orchid family

These require the services of an expert for identification. *Spiranthes grayi* Ames has the smallest flowers—about ⅛ inch long. *S. gracilis* (Bigel.) Beck usually has a broad green stripe on the lower lip. *S. praecox* (Walt.) Wats. 4 short green lines on the lower lip. *S. ovalis* Lindl. is a very slender plant with lip less than ¼ inch long. *S. vernalis* Engelm. & Gray has a rusty pubescent spike with crowded flowers. *S. longilabris* Lindl. has the flower more secund than spiral; the lower lip is broad at the base and tapers to the apex. These orchids grow in a variety of habitats, bloom in spring and fall. Widely distributed in Louisiana. Also Texas, Arkansas, and Mississippi.

# Part II
# Dicotyledons

**Lizard's-tail**
*Saururus cernuus* L.
Lizard's-tail family

A perennial, colony-forming herb about 3 feet tall with extensive rhizomes. Leaves cauline, alternate, petioled. Blades about 6 inches long, cordate to broadly ovate, distinct converging veins. Flower cluster slender, nodding or trailing at tip, blooming from base upward. Flowers white, crowded, no perianth. Very common and abundant in wet sites, cypress swamps, usually in standing water. Also Texas, Arkansas, and Mississippi. April to July.

**American Mistletoe**
*Phoradendron tomentosum* (DC.) Gray
(=*P. flavescens* (Pursh) Nutt.)
Mistletoe family

This plant has a long Christmas tradition inherited from ancient folklore. The plant absorbs mainly water and minerals from its host, a semiparasite. Stems fragile, smooth green. Leaves opposite, obovate to orbicular, thick, about 1 inch long. Plants dioecious. Flowers minute, in short yellowish racemes, pollen sheds from late January into February. Fruit white berries about 1/8 inch in diameter with a sticky substance which is toxic to humans. Keep away from children. Birds spread this pest by eating the fruits and rubbing their beaks on branches. Widely distributed on hardwood trees. Also, Texas, Arkansas, and Mississippi. Fruit December into February.

### Wild-ginger, Jug-plant
*Hexastylis arifolia* (Michx.) Small
Birthwort family

An evergreen perennial herb spreading by means of underground rhizomes and seeds. Leaves leathery, triangular-hastate, 6 to 8 inches long, about as wide, dark green and somewhat mottled above, basal lobes rounded. Flowers lack petals. Calyx jug-shaped, about 1 inch long, with three erect to slightly spreading calyx lobes, yellowish green, somewhat leathery, fragile, borne on slender pedicels, just peeping out of the leaf duff. Widely distributed in mixed acid woods. Also Arkansas and Mississippi. April.

### Smartweed
*Polygonum punctatum* Ell. (Left)
Knotweed family

Annual, sometimes perennial, with ascending green stems about 3 feet tall. Leaves lanceolate, 4 to 6 inches long, punctate. Ocrea longer than wide, ciliate. Flower clusters of numerous slender erect racemes. Sepals greenish white, punctuate with yellowish glands. No corolla. Achenes black, triangular. The only species with punctate glands. Widespread in wet areas, a weed in gardens. Also Texas, Arkansas, and Mississippi. May to frost.

### *P. hydropiperoides* Michx. (Right)

Very similar but with larger leaves and a fuller raceme, with pink petallike sepals. Coexistent with the above species.

PRINCE'S FEATHER, *P. orientale* L., is a more robust plant up to 8 feet tall with drooping racemes. Escape from cultivation. Other species exist in Louisiana.

## Sea-purslane
*Sesuvium portulacastrum* L.
Carpetweed family

A perennial herb with creeping stems that root at the nodes. Leaves opposite, succulent, spatulate, about 2 inches long. Flower short-stalked, solitary in the leaf axils. Sepals 5 opening star-shaped, about ½ inch wide. No petals. Common along the Gulf Coast in saline, sandy soils and on the mudlumps at the mouth of the Mississippi River. Also Texas and Mississippi. March until frost.

*S. maritimum* (Walt.) BSP. is an annual with erect stems and essentially sessile flowers.

## Fire Pink
*Silene virginica* L.
Pink family

An herbaceous perennial 12 to 16 inches tall. Basal leaves 4 to 5 inches long, oblanceolate, generally glabrous. Stem about ⅛ inch in diameter has one to two pairs of greatly reduced leaves, glandular, sticky. Flowers two per node, terminal, on axillary branches, crimson, 1¾ inches long, about the same in diameter. Calyx tubular, about 1 inch long, petals 5, notched at apex. Rare in north Louisiana. Also Arkansas and Mississippi. April.

**48** **Spatterdock, Yellow Cow-lily**
*Nuphar advena* (Ait.) Ait. f.
Water-lily family

A perennial aquatic herb from large rhizomes. Leaves ovate to suborbicular, 4 to 16 inches long, apex rounded, sinus more or less open, erect to floating in deep water. Flower 1 to 2 inches in diameter, elevated above the water on stout pedicel. Flower consists of two rows of sepals, green to yellow outside, yellow inside, many reduced petals, many stamens, and a thickened disk on top of the ovary. Widely distributed in bayous, lakes, and roadside ditches. Also Texas, Arkansas, and Mississippi. March to October.

**White Water-lily**
*Nymphaea odorata* Ait.
Water-lily family

Plants from stout rhizomes rooted in mud. Leaves floating to emergent, chiefly orbicular, 3 to 10 inches wide with open sinus. Flower white, floating to emergent, fragrant. Petals many, stamens numerous, grading into petaloid stamens. Opens in morning and closes in afternoon. Fresh marshes, cypress swamps, ponds, and ditches. Also Texas, Arkansas, and Mississippi. April to July. Summer blossoms smaller than spring blossoms. *N. tuberosa* Paine differs by the presence of tuber offshoots from the rhizome, and lack of odor to the flowers. Most Louisiana water-lilies lack the odor. Among botanists there is a trend to consider this as not distinct from the above.

### Yellow Water-lily, Banana-lily
*Nymphaea mexicana* Zucc.
Water-lily family

Rootstalk erect, stoloniferous at apex. Leaves floating to emergent when crowded, oval to suborbicular, 4 to 8 inches wide. Flowers emergent, yellow, 3 to 5 inches wide. Petals numerous, stamens numerous. Fruit about 1 inch in diameter, many-seeded. Ponds and lakes. Not common, cultivated. Also Texas and Mississippi. April to July.

The native BLUE WATER-LILY, *N. elegans* Hook., has emergent flowers about 2 inches in diameter, on slender pedicels. Petals few. Marshes in southwest Louisiana, in particular Cameron and Calcasieu parishes. Also Texas. April to July.

### American Lotus, Water-Chinquapin
*Nelumbo lutea* (Willd.) Pers.
Water-lily family

An aquatic with large circular leaves 1½ to 2 feet across. The petiole is attached on the under side of the blade at the center. Thus the leaves form small umbrellas. The flowers are 4 to 6 inches wide, creamy yellow with many petals and stamens. The pistil is about an inch in diameter and develops into a large funnel-shaped fruit about 4 inches in diameter. The apex of the fruit contains several cavities, each has a single seed which shakes out of the fruit when ripe. The seeds have a very hard coat and can remain dormant for many years. The rhizome is attached to the bottom of ponds, lakes, and streams, and the leaves may emerge through 3 to 5 feet of water. It is widely distributed in the state and is sometimes planted as an ornamental, but it is so vigorous that it can become a weed in a few years. Also Texas, Arkansas, and Mississippi. April to July.

### 50 Water-shield
*Brasenia schreberi* Gmel.
Water-lily family

An attached perennial aquatic with floating leaves. Leaves long-petioled. Blade peltately attached on flexible petioles, broadly oval, 3 to 4 inches long, upper surface smooth, lower surface and petiole coated with a sticky gelatinous jell. Flowers purple, emergent, small, about 1 inch long. Widely distributed in borrow pits, lakes, and sluggish branch bottoms. Also Texas, Arkansas, and Mississippi. April to May.

### Wind-flower
*Anemone caroliniana* Walt.
Crowfoot family

Perennial from a tuber. Basal leaves long-petioled, about 4 inches long. Blade 1 inch long, 2 to 3 times divided, segments lanceolate to flabelliforme. Scape 12 to 14 inches tall with 1 sessile divided leaf about midway. Flower, solitary, terminal, sepals linear, about ½ inch long, no petals. Individual pistils many, forming a spiral conelike structure 1½ to 2 inches long which separates into many very hairy flat achenes. Abundant along Highway 2 west of Plain Dealing, Louisiana. Also Texas, Arkansas, and Mississippi. February to April.

## Leather-flower, Clematis
*Clematis crispa* L.
Crowfoot family

A perennial plant with annual climbing stems. Leaves compound, 2 to 5 pairs of leaflets. Leaflets variable in shape, entire to slightly lobed. Flower solitary on a naked stalk, nodding, color varies bluish to pinkish to violet, composed of petallike sepals, no petals, many stamens, and many pistils. Sepals 1 to 2 inches long, thick on the part exposed in bud, spreading near the apex into a thin, undulate and crisped margin. Fruit a long-beaked achene, densely short, pubescent. Widely distributed on alluvial soils and along streams in the pinelands, climbing on herbs and shrubs. Also Texas, Arkansas, and Mississippi. Late March to June and scattered blossoms into October.

## Japanese Virgin's-bower
*Clematis dioscoreifolia* Levl. & Van.
Crowfoot family

A tall, woody climber with trailing stems 10 feet or more long. The leaves are 3 to 5, foliate with entire leaflets about 2 inches long that are spear-shaped. The flower cluster is flat-topped with opposite branching of the peduncles. Flowers white, about 1 inch in diameter, with many stamens, and 4 white petaloid sepals which are pubescent on the back. An escape from cultivation. Native of Japan. Widely distributed in Texas, Louisiana, and Mississippi. July to September.

The native VIRGIN'S-BOWER, *C. virginiana* L., has toothed leaflets and smaller flower clusters.

**Early Buttercup**
*Ranunculus fascicularis* Muhl.
Crowfoot family

A perennial herb with a cluster of cylindrical tubers. Leaves mainly basal and variously divided. Flowers yellow, about ½ inch in diameter, with 3 to 5 petals, reflexed sepals, many stamens, and many pistils. It is widely distributed in prairie soils but not confined to them. Also Texas, Arkansas, and Mississippi. March to April.

**Spiny Buttercup**
*Ranunculus muricatus* L.
Crowfoot family

A winter annual that starts growth in November, frequently in clumps. Stem stout, ascending to erect, freely branched. Leaves forming a basal rosette, also on stems. Blades 3- to 5-lobed, cleft, glabrous, and fleshy. Flower yellow, about ¾ inch in diameter. Petals distinct, about ¼ inch long. Pistils separate, many which develop into achenes with distinct short spines on the sides. Naturalized in Louisiana. Very abundant, widespread, lawns, gardens, roadside ditches, often in standing water. Also Texas, Arkansas, and Mississippi. March to May.

**Blue Larkspur**
*Delphinium carolinianum* Walt.
Crowfoot family

Perennial herb with thickened roots. Stem 2 to 3 feet tall. Leaves about 3 inches wide, deeply divided into narrow, linear segments. Racemes elongate with blue flowers about 1 inch in diameter, irregular with a spur about ¾ inch long. Widely distributed in dry soils. Most abundant in the western and northern parts of the state. Absent from the alluvial floodplain. Also Texas, Arkansas, and Mississippi. April to June.

**May-apple, Mandrake**
*Podophyllum peltatum* L.
Barberry family

A perennial, gregarious herb, 18 to 20 inches tall. Leaves 1 or 2, peltately attached, lobed, 12 or more inches in diameter, light green, thin. Flowers white, about 2 inches in diameter, solitary, at junction of two petioles, nodding. Bracts and calyx shed with the opening of the flower. Corolla of 6 to 9 waxy white petals. Many stamens. Fruit a yellow berry about 3 inches long, edible in small amounts. Widely distributed on the Prairie Terrace and older areas. Also Texas, Arkansas, and Mississippi. April to May.

## 54 Carolina Moonseed
*Cocculus carolinus* (L.) DC.
Moonseed family

A high climbing semiwoody, twining vine. Leaves alternate, broadly ovate to deltoid, 1 to 4 inches long, margin entire, palmately veined. Flowers, tiny, greenish yellow in short axillary racemes, dioecious with 6 petals. Fruit bright red, succulent with one flat coiled seed less than ¼ inch in diameter. Widely distributed along streams. Also Texas, Arkansas, and Mississippi. Flowers May to June. Fruit September to November.

CUPSEED, *Calycocarpum lyoni*, (Pursh) Gray, a closely related vine, has 3 to 5 lobed leaves, a fleshy fruit with a cup-shaped, hard seed, frequently grows with the moonseed.

## Tulip-tree, Yellow-poplar
*Liriodendron tulipifera* L.
Magnolia family

A large tree with outstanding leaf shape and flower. Leaf blades 4 to 8 inches long, 4-lobed, apex truncate to distinctly notched. Petioles 4 to 8 inches long. Flower tulip-shaped, about 2 inches long, greenish yellow usually with orange markings. Fruit 2 to 3 inches long, conical, gradually shattering into 1-seeded winged fruits. Widely distributed in lower Louisiana, along streams in pinehill areas, absent from the Red and Mississippi river floodplains. Also Texas (an introduction?), Arkansas, and Mississippi. March to April.

**Star-bush, Star-anise**
*Illicium floridanum* Ellis
Magnolia family

An evergreen shrub. Leaves elliptic 4 to 12 inches long, clustered at branch apices. Frequently blooms with unfolding of new leaves. Flowers several in apex of branchlets, dark red with many strap-shaped petals. Foliage and flowers ill-scented. Fruit fleshy at first, flat radiating carples about 1¼ inches in diameter. A stream-bottom plant in the Florida Parishes. Also Mississippi. March to May.

**Cucumbertree**
*Magnolia acuminata* L.
Magnolia family

A medium-sized tree. Leaves 5 to 7 inches long, deciduous, oval to slightly obovate. Flowers greenish yellow, 4 to 5 inches wide. Fruit 2½ to 3 inches long, cylindrical to irregular, fancifully resembling a cucumber. Occasional, wide distribution on upland soils, absent from the floodplain. Also Arkansas and Mississippi. April.

### Southern Magnolia, Evergreen Magnolia
*Magnolia grandiflora* L.
Magnolia family

A large, slow-growing tree with smooth to appressed scaly gray bark. Leaves evergreen, leathery, 5 to 10 inches long, dark shiny green above, usually rusty below. Flowers white, polypetalous, 7 to 10 inches wide, fetid-fragrant, discolor easily when bruised. First opens about 9 A.M., closes at night, opens next day with all stamens shed, and remains open. Fruit ovoid conelike 3 to 4 inches long with bright red seeds on threads. Most abundant in south Louisiana along small streams above the floodstage. Absent from the floodplains of the Red and Mississippi rivers, or rare on high ridges. Also Texas, Arkansas, and Mississippi. Main bloom April to June with occasional blossoms into November.

### Bigleaf Magnolia, "Cowcumber"
*Magnolia macrophylla* Michx.
Magnolia family

A small tree with smooth, light gray bark. Leaves alternate, deciduous, 1 to 3 feet long by 8 to 12 inches wide, cordate base, light green above, silvery green below. Flowers white, 10 to 15 inches wide with purple blotches on the three inner petals. Fruit ovoid to subglobose, light purple at first, soon turning black. Usually along small streams in the Florida Parishes, Winn and Grant of central Louisiana, and less common to Sabine and Vernon parishes. Also Mississippi. May to June.

## Southern Sweet Bay, Swamp Bay
*Magnolia virginiana* L.
Magnolia family

A large, slow-growing tree which holds its leaves over winter and sheds them just before the new leaves start. Leaves 5 to 8 inches long, elliptic to obovate, dark green above, white silky below. Flower 2 to 3 inches wide, fragrant. Flower opens about 3 P.M. and closes 10 P.M, reopens next day and stays open. Common along branch bottoms and in poorly drained sites in the pinelands. Absent from the Mississippi and Red river floodplains. Also Texas, Arkansas, and Mississippi. April into July.

## Pawpaw
*Asimina triloba* (L.) Dunal
Custard-apple family

A small tree. Flowers appear before and during the development of new leaves. Mature leaves ovate to oblong or obovate, 6 to 12 inches long. The flowers are borne on rusty pubescent pedicels about ½ inch long. Flowers green at first becoming a dull purple-brown, distinct veins in the separate petals. Fruit 3 to 6 inches long, green to brown rind with an edible pulp and several large flattened brown seeds. Widely distributed in Louisiana, usually absent from the Mississippi floodplain. Also Texas, Arkansas, and Mississippi. March to April.

DWARF PAWPAW, *A. parviflora* (Michx.) Dunal, is a shrub seldom over 3 feet tall, with flowers less than ½ inch broad.

### 58 White Prickly-poppy
*Argemone albiflora* Hornem.
Poppy family

Erect herb 3 to 4 feet tall, occasionally branched. Leaves lanceolate to obovate, 3 to 6 inches long, irregularly divided, very glaucous, at times mottled, margins spiny. Flowers white, 4 to 6 inches in diameter, cup-shaped to nearly flat with conspicuous staminal center about equal in length to the pistil. Latex white, drying yellow. Fruit a capsule with spines, many blackish seed. A sporadic weed along roadsides. More abundant in Cameron Parish. Common in Texas, also Arkansas and Mississippi. April to June.

MEXICAN POPPY, *A. mexicana* L., can be recognized by its bright yellow flower. Occasional.

### Golden-corydalis
*Corydalis micrantha* (Engelm.) Gray
(= *C. halei* Small)
Fumitory family

A glaucous green winter annual with the leaves forming a basal rosette. Leaves pinnatifid and incised again. Stems decumbent to erect about 1 foot tall. Flowers yellow, irregular, about ¾ inch long, composed of 4 petals and a microscopic calyx. One of the outer petals is prolonged into a small blunt spur. The short slender pod produces shiny black seeds. Widely distributed, cultivated fields, roadsides, on alluvial and hill soils. Also Texas, Arkansas, and Mississippi. March to April.

**Spiderflower**
*Cleome houtteana* Raf.
Caper family

Robust, much-branched annual herb to 8 feet tall with spines on stem at petiole bases. Leaves palmately compound, on long petioles. Leaflets 5 to 9, oblanceolate to elliptic, about 6 inches long, margin serrulate, pubescent, and glandular. Upper stem leaves abundant, reduced to simple bracts about 1½ inches long. Flower cluster dense. Flowers irregular, petals 4, pink to purple, stalked, 1½ inches long, stamens 6, longer than petals, pistil long-stalked. Fruit a linear capsule about 5 inches long. Widely dispersed but only locally common. Cultivated strains (Pink Queen) have larger, more showy flower clusters. Often escapes from cultivation. Also Texas and Mississippi. April to October.

*Streptanthus hyacinthoides* Hook.
Mustard family

A rare plant in Louisiana. Perennial about 3 feet tall. Inflorescence a raceme about 1 foot long, sometimes branched. Leaves linear, 2 to 3 inches long by ⅛ inch wide. Flowers about ½ inch long, indigo blue. Bud erect, turning at right angles to the stem and drooping conspicuously as they open. The flower consists of 4 blue sepals, 6 stamens, 4 reflexed petals which are purplish in the reflexed area, white above and below. Deep sand on western edge of Winn Parish near Goldonna. Also Texas. May to June.

**Water Cress**
*Nasturtium officinale* R. Br.
Mustard family

A succulent perennial rooting extensively from the stem in water or wet sites, producing dense mats. Plants 6 to 12 inches tall in the spring, taller later in the year. Leaves alternate, pinnately divided, 4 to 6 inches long, with 5 to 9 segments, shape of segments variable, flowers white, small, about ¼ inch in diameter, dense short racemes which elongate in fruit. Petals clawed. Capsule spreading-ascending. Naturalized from Europe, locally common in spring runs, small brooks, and ponds. Also Arkansas. April.

## Yellow Pitcher-plant, Fly Catcher, Frog Belly
*Sarracenia alata* Wood
(=*S. sledgei* Macfarlane)
Pitcher-plant family

This is one of our interesting insectivorous plants. Early in the spring, it blooms in part before the leaves are fully developed, whereas later the hollow tubular leaves can be found with the open flowers. These hollow leaves are about 2 feet tall and have a zone of hairs so arranged that insects which get inside are unable to crawl out. These leaves have a certain amount of liquid inside them, and the insects drown. There is some evidence these plants utilize the nitrogenous matter from the insects. However, living rotifers, paramecia, insect larvae, and other tiny worms live in the matrix at the base of the leaves. Most abundant in the moist pine flatwoods. Also Texas and Mississippi. March to April.

## Purple Trumpet Pitcher-plant
*Sarracenia drummondii* Croom
(= *S. leucophylla* Raf.)
Pitcher-plant family

Leaves erect, trumpet-shaped, about 3 feet tall, upper part of trumpet white, marked with purple veination. Scape erect, nodding at apex, about as long or longer than the leaves. Flower nodding 2½ to 3 inches in diameter, petals fiddle-shaped, purple. Bogs and pine-cypress flatwoods on U.S. 90 east of Moss Point, Mississippi. April.

*S. purpurea* L. grows with the above species, and there is one Louisiana collection. The leaves are about 8 inches long, inflated, with an erect hood. Flower scape taller than the leaves, flowers 2½ inches wide.

### Parrots Pitcher-plant
*Sarracenia psittacina* Michx.
Pitcher-plant family

Perennial herb. Leaves forming a basal rosette which may be flat on the ground, or semierect, 4 to 6 inches long, basal part of leaf flat, winged, apex inflated, beaklike, orfice on side. Scape 12 to 24 inches tall, solitary flower apical, nodding, 1½ to 2½ inches long. Petals red, drooping. Umbrellalike structure in center of flower is a prolongation from the style. Stigma on inner surface. Frequent in the wet pine flatwoods of St. Tammany, Tangipahoa, and Washington parishes. Also Mississippi. May to June.

### Sundew
*Drosera brevifolia* Pursh
Sundew family

A small plant with a basal rosette of leaves about 1 inch in diameter, flat on the ground. Leaves about ¾ inch long, spatulate, on short pubescent petioles. Blade covered with glandular hairs. Flower scape glandular pubescent with several apical flower buds, opening one at a time. Flowers pink or white. Very small insects get trapped in the sticky substance of the glandular leaf hairs, and the blade rolls over them. They are digested by enzyme activity. If you unroll a rolled leaf you will find the exoskeleton of the insect. Widely distributed in the southwestern prairies, dry longleaf pinelands, as well as in boggy sites. Also Texas, Arkansas, and Mississippi. April to June. Difficult to distinguish from the more northern *D. rotundifolia* L.

**Narrow-leaved Sundew**
*Drosera intermedia* Hayne
Sundew family

Plants with both basal rosettes and leaves on the flower scape. Leaves 2 to 3 inches long. Blade nearly ½ inch long, usually spatulate, covered with gland-tipped hairs. Petiole 2 inches long, slender, and glabrous. Scape nodding at apex. Flower white, nearly ½ inch wide. Roadside borrow pits, ponds, and bogs in the pinelands. Also Texas and Mississippi. June to September.

**Thread-leaf Sundew**
*Drosera filiformis* Raf.
Sundew family

Leaves clustered, erect, filamentous, up to 14 inches tall by less than ⅛ inch in diameter, often curled at apex. Glandular hairs, very abundant. Flower scape longer than the leaves, nodding at apex. Flowers bloom from the bottom up with no more than 2 open at one time, petals deep pink, about ½ inch long. Pineland bogs in southern Mississippi. June to September.

**64** **Climbing Hydrangea, Wood-vamp**
*Decumaria barbara* L.
Saxifrage family

A high-climbing woody vine with aerial rootlets. Leaves opposite, ovate to broadly oval, or elliptic, 3 to 5 inches long, dark green above. Flower cluster flat, compound. Flowers numerous, small, white, fragrant. Fruit a small capsule with longitudinal ribs. Widely distributed in mixed woods, usually climbing into trees along small streams. Also Mississippi. April to June.

**Oak-leaved Hydrangea**
*Hydrangea quercifolia* Bartram
Saxifrage family

A straggly woody shrub up to 12 feet tall. Leaves opposite, coarsely lobed, green above and white, short, hairy below. Similar to some oaks, hence the common name. Flower cluster 6 to 10 inches long, compact. Two types of flowers, sterile flowers (or ray flowers), with petallike modifications of the calyx mixed with the inconspicuous perfect flowers. The rays turn reddish and finally brown. This shrub makes an unusual garden plant. Abundant in the bluff and hill pinelands and is absent from the Mississippi floodplain. Also Arkansas and Mississippi. April to June.

*H. arborescens* L. a small shrub with ovate, serrate leaves and a flat flower cluster with a marginal row of sterile flowers has been found in West Feliciana Parish.

**Virginia-willow**
*Itea virginica* L.
Saxifrage family

A small shrub, usually under 6 feet tall. Leaves alternate, deciduous, 2 to 3 inches long, elliptic to obovate with a minutely serrate margin. Flower cluster compact, about 4 inches long, more or less drooping. Flowers white, tiny, less than ¼ inch long. Widely distributed in wooded swamps, and along streams in pinelands. Also Texas, Arkansas, and Mississippi. April into June.

**Witch-hazel**
*Hamamelis virginiana* L.
Witch-hazel family

A large shrub. Leaves deciduous, oval, obovate to nearly orbicular, 2 to 4½ inches long, margin undulate to crenately lobed, slightly rough, pubescent above, more pubescent below. Flowers after leaves are shed, yellow with 4 strap-shaped petals about 1 inch long. Fruit a woody capsule about ½ inch long which ejects 2 shiny black seeds on opening. Widespread along well-drained streams in the pinelands. Late November into January.

65

## 66 Service-berry, June-berry, Shad-bush
*Amelanchier arborea* (Michx. f.) Fernald
Rose family

A small tree. Leaves alternate, deciduous, 1¾ to 3 inches long, ovate to oblong, base rounded to cordate, margins finely serrate, slightly soft, hairy, above, densely white, tomentose below when unfolding, losing this pubescence about the time the fruit is ripe. Flowers white, in compact clusters, petals 5, erect. Fruit purplish, about ¼ inch in diameter. Occasional, but widely distributed in Louisiana. Also Texas, Arkansas, and Mississippi. Late March to April.

## Mayhaw, Riverflat Hawthorn
*Crataegus opaca* Hook. & Arn.
Rose family

A small tree. Branches thorny. Leaves alternate, deciduous, 2 to 3 inches long, elliptic to oblong, sometimes spatulate, dark green above, rusty pubescent below along the veins. Flowers white, 1 inch in diameter, unfolding before and with the leaves. Fruits depressed globose ½ to ¾ inch in diameter, shiny, somewhat translucent, green to reddish. Widely distributed in low, wet woods and in "mayhaw slashes." Also Texas, Arkansas, and Mississippi. February to March. Fruit May to June. The fruit makes a fine jelly. Plants in standing water have a delayed bloom period. Many other species are known to occur in Louisiana.

## Wild Strawberry
*Fragaria virginiana* Duchesne

Now relatively rare, the plant is found in St. Helena, Washington, and St. Tammany parishes. There are historical records of its abundance at the Muster Grounds during the Civil War in Washington Parish. Strawberry Ridge is cited in the boundary survey between Washington and St. Tammany parishes. It was one of the parents of the hybrid named "Marion Bell." This species can be recognized by the 3-foliolate leaves, white flowers about ¾ inch in diameter, and a small, delicious fruit less than ½ inch in diameter. Also Texas, Arkansas, and Mississippi. March to April.

The abundant YELLOW-FLOWERED STRAWBERRY, *Duchesnea indica* (Andrz.) Focke, was originally described as native to the West Indies and is incorrectly cited as a native of India. The attractive fruit is flat and tasteless.

## Chickasaw Plum
*Prunus angustifolia* Marsh.
Rose family

A shrub forming dense thickets. Leaves elliptic to oblanceolate, 1¼ to 2½ inches long, margin crenate, glandular, shiny above, glabrous or slightly hairy below. Flowers small, numerous, white. Fruit a drupe, nearly globose, red or yellow, edible. Widely distributed in hill sections, absent from the Mississippi floodplain. Also Texas, Arkansas, and Mississippi. Flowers February to March. Fruit ripe May to June.

## 68 Laurel-cherry, Cherry-laurel, Mock-orange
*Prunus caroliniana* (Mill.) Ait.
Rose family

A small tree frequently used as an ornamental. Leaves evergreen, elliptic to elliptic-lanceolate, 1½ to 3 inches long, margin usually entire, occasionally remotely spinulose. Flower clusters axillary, short copious racemes. Flowers white, about ¼ inch in diameter. Fruit a black drupe with a leathery skin. Fruit intoxicates birds. Wilted leaves are toxic to cattle. Widely distributed in Louisiana, especially along small streams and thickets. Also Texas, Arkansas, and Mississippi. Flowers February to March. Fruit ripens in fall and persists to spring.

## Black Cherry
*Prunus serotina* Ehrh.
Rose family

A large tree noted for its lumber. In Louisiana its fruit is used to make cherry bounce. Leaves at blooming are small and enlarge after flowering. Leaves dark green, shiny above, oblong to ovate, 2 to 5 inches long, with a crenate-serrate margin and acute tip. Flowers in slender racemes 2 to 3 inches long. Individual flowers, less than ½ inch wide, on a slender pedicel. Ripe fruit purple-black about ¼ inch in diameter. Widely distributed in Louisiana, generally absent from the Mississippi floodplain. Also Texas, Arkansas, and Mississippi. February to April.

**Southern Crab Apple, Wild Crab Apple**
*Pyrus angustifolia* Ait.
(= *Malus angustifolia* (Ait.) Michx.)
Rose family

A small much-branched tree. Leaves alternate, deciduous, 1 to 2½ inches long by ½ to ¾ inch wide, elliptic to oblong ovate, apex rounded to acute, base cuneate, margin crenate-serrate. Flowers about 1 inch in diameter, 3 to 5 in cluster. Buds deep pink, open petals pink to white, definitely clawed. Fruit a minature apple, depressed at the ends, yellow-green, about 1 inch in diameter. Widely distributed in the state along small stream bottoms, moist woods, absent from the Mississippi floodplain. Also Texas, Arkansas, and Mississippi. Flowers March to April. Fruit September.

**Red Chokeberry**
*Pyrus arbutifolia* (L.) L. f.
(= *Aronia arbutifolia* (L.) Ell.)
Rose family

A shrub usually in clumps, up to 6 feet tall. Leaves alternate, deciduous, very tomentose when young, more or less persisting, 1 to 1¾ inches long, elliptic to oval, or obovate. Flower clusters both terminal and axillary, many-flowered. Buds red. Flowers small about ½ inch in diameter, white. Fruit red, about ⅛ inch in diameter, bitter, calyx and pedicels tomentose. Boggy branch bottoms, in pinelands. Also Texas, Arkansas, and Mississippi. Flowers March to April. Fruit ripe in October.

### Chickasaw Rose, Macartney Rose
*Rosa bracteata* Wendl.
Rose family

This is another Asiatic rose which has escaped from cultivation and become a pest. Individual plants form dense hemisphaerical clumps 6 feet or more high. Branches pubescent, densely set with curved prickles. Leaves evergreen, compound, 3 to 5 inches long, with 5 to 9 minutely toothed leaflets. Flowers white, single, opening cup-shaped to flat, are about 2 inches wide. Bracts under the fruits, conspicuous, dissected, pubescent. Widely distributed in Louisiana. Also Texas, Arkansas, and Mississippi. April into May with scattered flowers until frost. Its long bloom season and its 5 to 10 leaflets distinguish it from the CHEROKEE ROSE which has only 3 leaflets. Cattle eat the fruit, and seedlings come up from their droppings.

### Cherokee Rose
*Rosa laevigata* Michx.
Rose family

A high-climbing shrub with glabrous but thorny stems up to 20 feet long. Spine curved and flattened. Leaves evergreen, usually 3-foliolate. Leaflets elliptic to ovate or slightly lanceolate, 2 to 3 inches long, dark green above, margin sharply serrate. Flower solitary on short lateral branches, white, 2 to 3½ inches in diameter, open nearly flat. Fruit pear-shaped, bristly. Native of China, escaped from cultivation. Widely distributed in Louisiana, a pest in many places. Also Texas, Arkansas, and Mississippi. Short bloom season, late March into April.

*R. setigera* Michx. is a native climbing rose with single, pink flowers. The outstanding feature is the united styles in the center of the flower. *R. carolina* L., is a native, pink-flowered shrub seldom over 3 feet tall.

## Southern Dewberry
*Rubus trivialis* Michx.
Rose family

Dewberries and blackberries have both primocanes and floricanes. Dewberries root at the tips of cane whereas blackberries do not. The flower and fruits are borne on the floricane. Dewberries have a single flower whereas blackberries have a many flowered cluster. Primocane erect at first, then trailing, densely covered with bright red glandular bristles and short stout recurved spines, leaves 5-foliolate. Floricanes (2-year-old canes) have 1-flowered peduncles and small 3-foliolate leaves. Flowers white, about an inch in diameter, petals clawed. Fruit about 1 inch long, an aggregate of fleshy nutlets, blackish. Widely distributed in Louisiana, abundant on alluvial soils. Also Texas, Arkansas, and Mississippi. February into March. Fruit ripe April into May.

L. H. Bailey named two other dewberries from Louisiana, *R. sons* and *R. clair-brownii*. The taxonomy of the blackberries is not yet stabilized. Many species occur in Louisiana.

### 72 Opopanax, Sweet-acacia, Huisache
*Acacia farnesiana* (L.) Willd.
Legume family

A large shrub to small tree with the numerous branches armed with paired spines. Leaves bipinnately compound with many small leaflets. Leaflets gray-green, less than ¼ inch long, linear-oblong. Flower head, globose, bright yellow, about ½ inch in diameter, many stamens per flower. Fruit nearly cylindrical, tapering at each end, about 3 inches long, leathery. Apparently native along the coast from Sabine Lake to Grand Isle, perhaps an escape at Mermentau and False River. Used as an ornamental. Also Texas and Mississippi. April to May.

### Lead Plant
*Amorpha fruticosa* L.
Legume family

A large shrub often 15 feet tall. Leaves more or less soft pubescent, alternate, odd-pinnately compound, 6 to 12 inches long. Leaflets 11 to 27, oblong, oval, about 1 to 1¼ inches long, glandular dotted below. Flower cluster spikelike, solitary to several, 4 to 8 inches long, opening from the base upward. Flower small, corolla purple with exposed golden stamens. Fruit a slightly curved pod about ½ inch long, glandular dotted. Common along streams and low wet woods, alluvial soils. Also Texas, Arkansas, and Mississippi. April to June.

## White Astragalus
*Astragalus soxmaniorum* Lundell
Legume family

Perennial, short ascending to erect stems about 1 foot long. Leaves pinnately compound, 1 to 4 inches long, short-petioled. Leaflets 13 to 19, obovate to oblong-obovate, notched, flat, about ½ inch long. Flower cluster short, compact. Flower cylindrical with greenish white to cream-white corollas. Fruit an inflated pod about ½ inch long, slightly curved. Adventive (?), Caddo Parish near Mira. Also Texas. April.

*A. distortus* T. & G. has prostrate stems, smaller flowers, blue, lavender, occasionally white. Sandy soil in Caddo, Natchitoches, and Cameron parishes.

## Hog Peanut
*Apios americana* Medic.
Legume family

A perennial plant with tuberous rhizomes. Stems tender, freeze back each year, 3 to 8 feet long, twining and high-climbing. Leaves alternate, odd-pinnately compound, 5- to 7-foliolate. Flower cluster short, compact, 3 to 6 inches long, flowers about ½ inch long. Calyx campanulate, corolla brownish purple. Standard rounded at summit. Keel strongly curved. Fruit a flat, linear pod 2 to 5 inches long. Widely distributed in moist woods and along streams. Weedy in nature. Also Texas, Arkansas, and Mississippi. June to October.

## 74 White Indigo
***Baptisia leucantha*** T. & G.
Legume family

Perennial herb with stout stem 3½ to 5 feet tall, glaucous. Leaves 3-foliolate, nearly sessile. Leaflets 2½ inches long, oblanceolate to obovate, upper leaves reduced. Flower cluster terminal or lateral, erect, blooms from bottom upward, elongates with maturity. Floral bracts shed readily. Flowers white, banner about ½ inch long. Fruit an inflated pod about 2 inches long. Entire plant turns black with maturity or drying. Widely distributed in prairie and pineland. Also Texas, Arkansas, and Mississippi. April to June.

## Nodding Indigo
***Baptisia leucophaea*** Nutt.
Legume family

Perennial herb, stems 12 to 18 inches tall, umbrellalike clumps. Leaves 3-foliolate. Leaflets ovate, lanceolate. Stipules large, persistent. Flower cluster drooping, usually below the level of the leaves, 10 to 16 inches long, strongly bracted. Flower yellow, pea-shaped, standard nearly 1 inch long. Fruit an inflated, rigid-walled pod about 2 inches long. Widely distributed and common in prairie and pineland. Also Texas, Arkansas, and Mississippi. April to June.

*Baptisia sphaerocarpa* Nutt.
(=B. *viridis* Larisey)
Legume family

Perennial, stems about 3 feet tall, much-branched, usually glabrous, compact masses, turning black at maturity. Leaves 3-foliolate to 1-foliolate on upper branches. Leaflets oblanceolate, to obovate, about 1 inch long. Flowers numerous, yellow, in terminal racemes that extend above the crown mass, about 1 inch long. Fruit a small, thick-walled, sphaerical pod less than ½ inch in diameter. Widely distributed and common. Prairie to pinelands. Also Texas, Arkansas, and Mississippi. April to June.

**Nuttall Indigo**
*Baptisia nuttaliana* Small
Legume family

Perennial herb, stems erect, much-branched, forming symmetrical masses, about 4 feet tall, pubescent, turning black on maturity. Leaves 3-foliolate, stipules very small if present at flowering. Leaflets broadly oval to obovate, about 2 inches long. Flower yellow, ½ to ¾ inch long, solitary in leaf axils or in short terminal clusters, not conspicuously above the leaf mass. Fruit a thickwalled, sphaerical pod, opening tardily, more than ½ inch in diameter. Widespread and abundant. Prairie and pinelands. Also Texas, Arkansas, and Mississippi. April to June.

**Partridge Pea**
*Cassia fasciculata* Michx.
Legume family

An erect annual herb, slender to branched, 3 to 5 feet tall. Leaves pinnately compound. Leaflets 8 to 15 pairs, linear to oblong, mucronate tip, about ¾ inch long. Petiole with a single short-stalked gland. Flower cluster short, 1 to 7 axillary flowers. Open in morning, wilting in afternoon. Flower irregular, about 1¼ inches in diameter, upper petal smaller, with 10 distinct stamens. Fruit a narrow flat pod about 2½ to 3 inches long with rhombic black seed. Plants are variable, and several species or varieties have been recognized. Widely distributed in Louisiana, abundant on alluvial soils. Also Texas, Arkansas, and Mississippi. July to October.

**Redbud**
*Cercis canadensis* L.
Legume family

A small tree 6 to 10 inches in diameter and about 35 feet tall, which is widely cultivated for its beautiful flowers in early spring. It has alternate heart-shaped leaves 3 to 6 inches in diameter. Clusters of pinkish to purplish blossoms appear before the leaves and consequently give the tree a striking and attractive appearance. The fruit is a flat pea-pod turning from green to bronze to brown. It is readily raised from seed, which need treatment to break dormancy, and plants 3 to 4 years old will bloom profusely. Widely distributed in Louisiana, but absent from the Mississippi floodplain. Also Texas, Arkansas, and Mississippi. It blooms from early February into March, and the fruit matures in May.

## Butterfly Pea
*Centrosema virginianum* (L.) Benth.
Legume family

A delicate twining herbaceous vine, often climbing to a height of 6 feet. Leaves alternate, 3-foliolate, 1 to 4 inches long. Leaflets quite variable from linear to ovate. Flowers usually solitary, bluish to pale violet or lavender, occasionally whitish, 1 to 1½ inches in diameter with a conspicuous standard. The fruit is a slender, rapier-like stiff pod. Widely distributed on acid soils of the blufflands and pinehills. Also Texas, Arkansas, and Mississippi. June to October.

## Red Rattlebox
*Daubentonia punicea* (Cav.) DC.
Legume family

A shrub 4 to 8 feet tall. Leaves pinnately compound, 8 to 10 inches long. Leaflets 12 to 40, about 1¼ inches long, linear-elliptic, mucronate. Flower cluster drooping, densely flowered. Standard dark red to orange-red, about 1 inch wide. Fruit a 4-angled, tardily dehiscent pod, 3 to 4 inches long. Widespread but not abundant in southern Louisiana marshes. Reported as an escape from cultivation. Also Texas and Mississippi. June to September. One author merges *D. texana* with this species, and another places it in the genus *Sesbania*.

## Rattlebox
*Daubentonia texana* Pierce
Legume family

A shrub 4 to 6 feet tall, small branches usually killed in winter. Leaves pinnately compound, 5 to 10 inches long. Leaflets 12 to 24 to as many as 60, about 1 inch long, linear to oblong, apiculate, silky below. Flowers in drooping clusters, pale yellow, sweetpealike, standard about ¾ inch wide. Fruit a dry stipitate, 4-angled pod about 3 inches long, which splits open tardily. Widely distributed in southern Louisiana from the Pearl River to the Sabine River margin of fresh-water marsh, often in standing water, on elevations in brackish and saline marshes. Extensive flooded areas in Cameron Parish are natural crawfish habitats. Seed reported as poisonous. Also Texas and Mississippi. June to September.

*Desmanthus illinoensis* (Michx.) MacM.
Legume family

A perennial herb with erect or ascending, spineless branches. Leaves bipinnately compound, 2 to 5 inches long. Leaflets very numerous about ⅛ inch long. Flower cluster sphaerical, white, less than ½ inch in diameter. Fruit a falcate, very flat pod, borne in clusters. Most abundant on Mississippi and Red river floodplain soils, in prairie soils, and elsewhere in wet sites. Also Texas, Arkansas, and Mississippi. May to September.

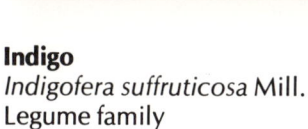

## Indigo
*Indigofera suffruticosa* Mill.
Legume family

Perennial with erect stems up to 6 feet tall. Leaves odd-pinnately compound, 2 to 4 inches long. Leaflets 7 to 9 pairs, elliptical to obovate, apiculate, about ½ inch long. Flower clusters elongate, blooming from base upward, a little longer than subtending leaves. Flowers small, reddish. Standard less than ½ inch long. Locally common on levees, in the marsh at Rockefeller Refuge, sandy cheniers of Grand Chenier to Cameron, Grand Isle, and in Natchitoche Parish. June. Fruit September to October. This plant was one of the sources of the dye indigo.

## Mamou, Coral Bean
*Erythrina herbacea* L.
Legume family

A perennial with tender stems up to 6 feet tall with dark red flowers about two inches long. This is a legume flower in which the banner is largest and folds over the smaller wing and keel petals. These are borne on annual stems about 5 feet tall. Some of the blossoms occur before the leaves, and others open after the leaves are fully developed. These are compound leaves with three leaflets alternately arranged on the stem with a few small prickles. The fruit is a typical bean pod which splits open at maturity to expose bright red seeds. It is widely distributed in Louisiana from the beach at Cameron Parish to the northern portion of the state. It is generally absent from the alluvial floodplain. Also Texas, Arkansas, and Mississippi. April to June.

## Bush Lespedeza
*Lespedeza capitata* Michx.
Legume family

Perennial herb up to 5 feet tall. Stem simple or occasionally branched. Leaves 3-foliolate, stalk of terminal leaflet longer than the petiole. Leaflets variable in shape, elliptic-linear, to lanceolate, about 2 inches long, pubescent. Flower cluster axillary and terminal at stem apex, very compact with many flowers. Peduncle shorter than subtending leaf. Flowers almost ½ inch long, pink. Widely distributed, most abundant in mixed pinelands. Also Texas, Arkansas, and Mississippi.

## Bluebonnet
*Lupinus texensis* Hook.
Legume family

These plants are very similar and often confused with *L. subcarinosa*. They can be distinguished by the acute, pointed tip to the leaflets. The flower cluster is larger, more crowded, and tips with unexpanded buds are whitish. This species is not only naturally widespread in eastern Texas but also extensively planted by the Highway Commission. It is illegal to pick in Texas. Escape (?) on Highway 8 near Leesville, Louisiana. Spring.

## Lady Lupine, Hairy Lupine
*Lupinus villosa* Willd.
Legume family

A perennial herb growing in dense clumps with a cluster of leaves at the base of the flowering stalk. Leaves entire, an unusual feature for lupines, elliptic to elliptical-lanceolate, 4 to 6 inches long, coated with a dense grayish pubescence. Flower cluster terminal, elongate, with many pea-shaped blossoms. Corolla a lavender-blue with a purplish spot in the standard. Fruit a flattish pea-pod 2 to 2½ inches long, coated with a dense tangle of hairs. Known only from the acid pineland soils in St. Tammany and Washington parishes. Also Mississippi. April to June.

### Texas Bluebonnet
*Lupinus subcarnosus* Hook.
Legume family

Seedlings produce a rosette of leaves in the fall and bloom the following spring. Stems branched at the base, 8 to 20 inches tall, coated with an appressed silky pubescence. Leaves composed of palmately lobed blades with usually 5 leaflets on a petiole about twice the length of the blade. The outstanding feature is the rounded to truncate leaflet tips. Flowers bright blue with a white center spot in the standard. The Texas legislature designated this species as the state flower. Present in Beauregard Parish near Merryville where it may be an escape from cultivation. March to April.

### Spotted Bur-clover, Spotted-medic
*Medicago arabica* (L.) Hudson
Legume family

An annual spreading over the ground. Stems usually glabrous. Leaves 3-foliolate. Leaflets marked with a reddish-purple inverted $V$, obovate to obcordate, apex finely toothed. Stipules conspicuous, lacerate. Flower clusters few-flowered, short racemes about 1 inch long. Flowers yellow, less than ¼ inch long. Fruit a spirally coiled pod with small spines. Widespread, weedy. Also Texas, Arkansas, and Mississippi. March to June.

CALIFORNIA BUR-CLOVER, *Medicago hispida* Gaertn., is a close relative, easily distinguished by the absence of a spot on the leaves early in the season and more toothed stipules. BLACK-MEDIC, *Medicago lupulina* L. has soft pubescent stems and foliage along with smaller flowers. The fruit, a small coiled pod, turns black very early.

**Yellow Sour Clover**
*Melilotus indica* (L.) All.
Legume family

An annual herb 12 to 30 inches tall. Leaves alternate, 3-foliolate, fleshy. Leaflets oblanceolate to obovate, about 1 inch long, remotely toothed on margin. Stipules lanceolate. Flower clusters numerous, short racemes 2 to 3 inches long with many flowers. Flower yellow, small, nearly ¼ inch long. Introduced, escape, widespread along roads and cultivated fields, more abundant on soils that are neutral to slightly alkaline. Also Texas, Arkansas, and Mississippi. March to May.

WHITE SWEET CLOVER, *M. alba* Desr., is a somewhat larger plant with longer clusters of slightly larger white flowers. Both are planted for soil improvement. Escape.

**Mimosa, Sensitive-plant, Shame-plant**
*Mimosa strigillosa* T. & G.
Legume family

A perennial with herbaceous, much-branched, spineless, prostrate stems to 6 feet long. Leaves bipinnately compound. Leaflets light green, 10 to 15 pairs per pinna, linear, about ¼ inch long, folding when touched. Flower clusters globose, pink. Pods flat, oblong, about 1 inch long. Abundant in Mississippi and Red river floodplains, prairie, and second growth pineland. Also Texas, Arkansas, and Mississippi. March to September. The genus *Mimosa* can be distinguished from the similar genus *Schrankia* by the absence of small spines.

**84** **Yellow Sensitive-plant**
*Neptunia lutea* (Leavenw.) Benth.
Legume family

A perennial, unarmed herb with procumbent stems, several feet long. Leaves bipinnately compound with 6 pinnae. Leaflets tiny, up to ¼ inch long by ¹⁄₁₆ inch wide, close rapidly when touched. Flower cluster axillary, globose to oblong, 1 inch in diameter. Flowers many, yellow, stamens, many per flower. Fruit oblong, very flat, smooth, 1 inch long by ½ inch wide. Prairie, calcareous soils, and longleaf pineland. June to September.

**Retama, Jerusalem Thorn, Horsebean**
*Parkinsonia aculeata* L.
Legume family

A small, much-branched tree with yellow-green, spiny branches. Leaves alternate, 2-compound, with flattened green rachis to each pinna. Leaflets tiny, very numerous, nearly ¼ inch long by ¹⁄₁₆ inch wide. Flowers in short clusters, more or less open, petals bright yellow, subequal in size. Fruit a constricted pod about 4 inches long. Widely planted as an ornamental. Also Texas. June to October.

### White Prairie Clover
*Petalostemum candidum* (Willd.) Michx.
Legume family

Stems procumbent to ascending in clumps. The alternate leaves, 1 to 1½ inches long, have 7 to 9 punctate leaflets which are oval to slightly obovate in shape. Flower cluster 1 to 3 inches long, cylindrical, blooms from the bottom upwards. Standard white, sepals strongly longitudinally ribbed. Widely distributed in prairie and pinelands. Also Texas, Arkansas and Mississippi. May to June.

PURPLE PRAIRIE CLOVER, *P. purpureum* (Vent.) Rydb., can be recognized by the smaller leaves, ½ inch long, and the purple standard to the flower.

### Kudzu
*Pueraria lobata* (Willd.) Ohwi
Legume family

A perennial, tender, high-climbing vine with hairy stems up to 60 feet long. Leaves alternate, 3-foliolate, petioles as long and longer than leaf blades. Leaflets ovate to rhombic, entire to 2- to 3-lobed. Flowers in axillary racemes blooming from the bottom upward. Corolla violet or reddish purple. Fruit produced occasionally, flat, linear-oblong pod. Widely planted for cattle, shade, and erosion control. Its vigorous, dense growth and its ability to choke out young forest trees makes it an outstanding pest. Experiments are now underway to control it. Also Texas, Arkansas, and Mississippi. April to June.

**Black Locust**
*Robinia pseudoacacia* L.
Legume family

A small tree in Louisiana but becoming a larger one in more northern areas. Branches with a pair of thorns at base of each branchlet. Leaves odd-pinnately compound, 4 to 8 inches long. Leaflets oval to oblong, ¾ to 1¾ inches long, stalked and with a point at the apex of the leaflet. Flower cluster white, compact, many flowers, drooping, 4 to 6 inches long. Flower pea-shaped, about 1 inch long, fragrant. Fruit flat, thin, 2 to 4 inches long. Widely planted in Louisiana. At times the excessive quantity of root suckers is a problem. Also Texas, Arkansas, and Mississippi. April to May.

*Rhynchosia latifolia* (Nutt.) T. & G.
Legume family

Stem slender to stout, erect, then arching and trailing, 2 to 4 feet long, densely pubescent. Leaves alternate, 3-foliolate, petiole portion shorter than the blade. Terminal leaflet, ovate, cordate, rhombic, broadly oval, palmately veined. Flower cluster axillary, elongate, 5 to 8 inches long, opening from the base upward. Flowers chrome yellow, about ½ inch long, calyx conspicuous. Fruit a flat pubescent pod. Widespread and abundant in pineland areas. Also Texas, Arkansas, and Mississippi. June to September.

## Snout Bean
*Rhynchosia minima* (L.) DC.
Legume family

A trailing, twining perennial several feet long. Leaves alternate, 3-foliolate. Terminal leaflet cordate to rhombic, 1 to 1½ inches long. Flower clusters axillary, short racemes 4 to 6 inches long. Flowers about ¼ inch long, chrome yellow standard. Fruit a flat, 2- to 3-seeded pod, about ½ inch long. Widespread and common, fields and pinelands. Also Texas, Arkansas, and Mississippi. May to September.

*R. reniformis* DC. has 1 round to reniform leaflet and slightly larger flowers and fruits.

## Sampson Snake Root, Congo-root
*Psoralea psoralioides* (Walt.) Cory
Legume family

Erect, bushy perennial up to 2 feet tall. Leaves 3-foliolate 2 to 3 inches long, lanceolate to broadly elliptic with a stalk about ½ inch long. Flower cluster axillary, strongly pedunculate up to 6 inches long, 1 to several, mainly near top of plant, compact, 1 to 1½ inches long. Flower purplish about ½ inch long. Pod small, less than ¼ inch long. Widely distributed, prairie, pinelands, along railroads. Also Texas, Arkansas, and Mississippi. March to June.

### Pink Sensitive Briar
*Schrankia microphylla* (Sm.) Macbr.
Legume family

Perennial with long trailing, procumbent, glabrous but prickled armed stems, branchlets, and peduncles. Leaves 2-pinnately compound, 6 pairs of pinna. Leaflets tiny, oblong, distinct midvein, apex apiculate ⅛ inch long. Flower cluster, globose, about 1 inch in diameter, pink. Fruit long, cylindrical, armed with prickles on ribs, 4 inches long by 3/16 inch in diameter. Widespread and abundant in pinelands. Also Texas, Arkansas, and Mississippi. April to June.

*S. hystericina* (Brit. & Rose) Standley and *S. uncinata* Willd. are very similar and have reticulate veins. *S. hystericina* has a short, thick pod about 1 inch long; *S. uncinata* pod is about 2 inches long.

### Pencil Flower
*Stylosanthes biflora* (L.) BSP.
Legume family

Perennial with erect stems to 2 feet tall, much-branched at base. Leaves 3-foliolate, 1 to 1½ inches long. Terminal leaflet linear, elliptic to oblanceolate. Flowers small, orange-yellow, erect standard less than ½ inch long. Pod 1-seeded, ovate, reticulate. Widely distributed in prairie and pinelands. Also Texas, Arkansas, and Mississippi. May to September.

**Goat's Rue**
*Tephrosia virginiana* (L.) Pers.
Legume family

A perennial herb 24 to 30 inches tall, in clumps, densely, silvery pubescent. Leaves odd-pinnately compound, 4 to 7 inches long. Leaflets 15 to 25, elliptic to linear-oblong, about 1¼ inches long. Flowers in erect racemes, pea-shaped, standard lemon to creamy yellow on the outside and cream to white on the inside, wings and keel rose. Fruit about 2 inches long, strongly white, villous. Abundant and widely distributed in pinelands, absent from the floodplain soils. Also Texas, Arkansas, and Mississippi. April to May.

**Rabbit Foot Clover**
*Trifolium arvense* L.
Legume family

An annual herb 8 to 18 inches tall, densely soft pubescent, with branching stems. Leaves 3-foliolate. Terminal leaflet lanceolate to narrowly oblong, about 1 inch long. Flower clusters dense, cylindrical to obovoid, about 1 inch long on peduncles about 1 inch long. Flowers numerous, sessile, bractless, pink or white, less than ¼ inch long, usually exceeded by the hairy calyx lobes. Adventive in Louisiana along roads, cultivated fields. Also Arkansas and Mississippi. April to June.

### Alsike Clover
*Trifolium hybridum* L.
Legume family

A perennial herb about 24 inches tall with erect, branching stems. Leaves 3-foliolate. Leaflets ovate to obovate, about 2 inches long, margin minutely toothed. Peduncles for flower clusters usually exceeding the subtending leaf. Heads globose about 1 inch in diameter. Flower nearly ½ inch long. Standard longer than wings and keel, white to pink. Introduced from Europe. Planted, it persists only a few years at a time under Louisiana conditions. Also Arkansas and Mississippi. April to June.

Similar in appearance to *T. repens* but differs by the erect aerial stem in contrast to the prostrate stem, rooting at the nodes.

### Crimson Clover
*Trifolium incarnatum* L.
Legume family

A winter annual. Plant with soft pubescence, 18 to 30 inches tall. Stipules adnate for half their length to the petiole base. Leaflets broadly obovate, rounded at apex and tapering toward base. Flower cluster elongate, cylindrical, 2 to 3 inches long, blooming from the base upward. Flower about ¾ inch long, crimson to dark red, almost black. Calyx pubescent. Native of Europe. Planted extensively. Does well in prairie and alluvial soils and on some pineland soils. Volunteer crops scant unless one plants a "self-reseeding strain." Also Texas, Arkansas, and Mississippi. March to June.

**Red Clover**
*Trifolium pratense* L.
Legume family

A perennial herb lasting only a few years. Stems decumbent near base, then ascending up to 30 inches tall, covered with a soft pubescence. Leaves 3-foliolate, stipules adnate to petiole. Leaflets sessile, ovate to elliptic, nearly 2 inches long, marked with an inverted whitened *V*. Flower head globose to ovoid, about 1¼ inches in diameter, many flowers, ½ to ¾ inch long. Magenta, definitely not red, occasionally pure white. Standard longer than wings and keel. Native of Europe, naturalized, widely planted on alluvial soils. Also Texas, Arkansas, and Mississippi. April to June.

**Buffalo Clover**
*Trifolium reflexum* L.
Legume family

Annual plant, spreading to erect, much-branched, about 18 inches tall. Leaves 3-foliolate, broad-ovate stipules at base of petiole. Leaflets all sessile, oval to oblong, or obovate. Flower head globose, about 1½ inches in diameter, flowers reddish or yellowish about ½ inch long, reflexed, and brownish with age. Common in prairie and scattered in forested areas. Also Texas, Arkansas, and Mississippi. April to July.

### White Dutch Clover, Ladino Clover
*Trifolium repens* L.
Legume family

A perennial with creeping stems which root at the nodes. Leaves 3-foliolate, size variable, stipules membraneous, sheathing stem. Flower heads about 1 inch in diameter on peduncles about 2 to 6 inches long, usually overtopping leaves. Flowers white to pinkish, short-stalked, ascending to erect, reflexed with age. Standard larger than the wings and keel. Widely distributed in Louisiana, making best growth on the floodplain soils. Also Texas, Arkansas, and Mississippi. An introduced species. Sporadic blooming, January to March, peak April to May. Most plants usually die down in hot summers, occasionally bloom on to November.

**Persian Clover**
*Trifolium resupinatum* L.
Legume family

Annual herb. Stems decumbent to ascending, 18 to 30 inches long, glabrous, lush development. Leaves 3-foliolate, with conspicuous stipules at petiole base. Leaflets sessile, about ¾ inch long, about 2 times longer than wide, glabrous or nearly so. Flower heads small, few-flowered. Standard rose to purple, longer than the wings and keel. Individual fruits thin, papery, inflated, pubescent, in mass about ¾ inch in diameter. Widespread on alluvial and terrace soils, became abundant following the 1927 flood. Seed impossible to mechanically separate from white dutch clover. Now widely planted. Also Texas and Mississippi. March to June.

**Narrow-leaved Vetch**
*Vicia angustifolia* L.
Legume family

Annual herb with decumbent to ascending climbing stems. Leaves pinnately compound with 4 to 10 leaflets plus terminal tendril. Leaflets linear to elliptic, truncate and mucronate at apex. Flowers usually 2, sessile in axils of leaves ½ to ¾ inch long, corolla purplish. Fruit a linear pod about 1½ inches long, turning black at maturity. Widely distributed in Louisiana. Also Texas, Arkansas, and Mississippi. March to June.

**94** **Purple Vetch**
*Vicia dasycarpa* Ten.
Legume family

Annual with ascending stems, climbing clinging by tendrils. Leaves pinnately compound, 5 to 10 pairs of oblong to linear-lanceolate leaflets, appressed, pubescent to glabrous. Flowers abundant on axillary peduncles, more or less secund, rose to purple, about ½ inch long. Widespread, introduced from Europe, planted, escape from cultivation. Also Texas, Arkansas, and Mississippi. April to June.

**Deer Pea, Wild Cowpea**
*Vigna luteola* (Jacq.) Benth.
Legume family

Perennial with annual stems twisting and trailing about 10 feet long strongly pubescent. Leaves alternate, 3-foliolate. Leaflets ovate to lanceolate, 2 to 3 inches long. Flower cluster axillary, on long peduncle, much longer than leaves, with few flowers at apex. Flowers yellow, about ½ inch in diameter. Fruit a pod 2 to 3½ inches long. Abundant in the coastal parishes, fresh marsh, cut-over cypress swamps, high ridges in saline marshes, and sand beaches. Important deer browse. Related to cultivated cowpea. Also Texas and Mississippi. April to June.

**Japanese Wisteria**
*Wisteria floribunda* (Willd.) DC.
Legume family

A high-climbing woody, twining vine with stems several inches in diameter, young branchlets pubescent. Leaves odd-pinnately compound, 15 to 19 leaflets, ovate to broadly elliptic, about 3 inches long. Flower cluster drooping racemes 6 to 15 inches long, blooming from the base toward the tip, usually before the leaves start to unfold. Flowers numerous, on slender pedicels about 1 inch long. Corolla blue, violet, occasionally white, standard ¾ inch long, ovary pubescent. Fruit a woody capsule 4 to 6 inches long, swollen near the basal end, pubescent, tardily opening. Seed round, flat, poisonous. Escape from cultivation, persistent at old house sites. Also Texas, Arkansas, and Mississippi. March to May.

This is usually distinguished from the CHINESE WISTERIA, *W. sinensis* (Sims) Sweet by the greater number of leaflets, 15 to 19 versus 7 to 13.

**Wild Wisteria**
*Wisteria macrostachya* T. & G.
Legume family

A high-climbing woody vine. Leaves odd-pinnately compound, alternate. Leaflets usually 9, 1 to 3½ inches long, broadly oval, acute base and apex, glaucous below. Flower cluster 4 to 6 inches long, many flowers, compact at apex of an almost naked peduncle. Flowers on pedicels about ½ inch long, blue to blue-violet, standard about ½ inch long, ovary naked. Fruit a torulose cylindrical pod with longitudinal wrinkles when dry. Thickets and woods along streams, widespread. Also Texas and Mississippi. March to May.

*W. frutescens* (L.) Poir., if specifically distinct, has smaller leaves and leaflets, smaller flowers, and usually a smaller flower cluster.

**96** *Oxalis rubra* St. Hil.
Wood sorrel family

A perennial herb from a woody crown with fleshy tubers. Leaves 6 to 12 inches tall, 3-foliolate. Leaflet broadly obcordate, 1½ inches wide, bright green. Scape pubescent, overtopping leaves. Flowers in compound cymes, pink to rose, about ½ inch long. Sepals pubescent and with orange glandular tips. Flowers and leaves close at night. An introduction from South America, escaped and now weedy. Widely distributed in Louisiana. Also Texas and Mississippi. February to frost.

*O. rosea* Jacq. is an Asiatic species with more compact growth, smaller leaves and flowers, flowers red, occasionally white.

**Violet Wood Sorrel**
*Oxalis violacea* L.
Wood sorrel family

An acaulescent, perennial herb from scaly, coated bulbs and slender stolons. Leaves 3-foliolate, petioles and scapes glabrous. Leaflets obcordate about ½ inch in length, usually marked with reddish pigments, partially expanded in shade. Scape overtopping leaves, 2 to 3 inches long. Flowers in simple umbels, one or two open at a time, violet to pinkish purple. Sepals glabrous with orange glandular tips. Widespread in Louisiana pinelands and mixed woods. Also Texas, Arkansas, and Mississippi. March to June.

**Yellow Wood Sorrel**
*Oxalis stricta* L.
Wood sorrel family

A decumbent to erect herb, 6 to 12 inches tall. Leaves 3-foliolate, frequently marked with reddish pigments. Leaflets ½ to ¾ inches long. Flowers umbellate, 1 to 4, overtopping leaves, yellow, about ½ inch in diameter. Fruit a prismatic, cylindrical capsule which splits open, borne on slender deflexed pedicels. A widely distributed weedy plant, fallow fields, lawns, and gardens. Also Texas, Arkansas, and Mississippi. March to May. Although the genus has been revised twice in the past few years, there are still problems in identification of the plants and the correct name.

**Wild Geranium**
*Geranium carolinianum* L.
Geranium family

A winter annual from a small taproot with a rosette of stems, procumbent to ascending, much-branched, forming large clumps, all densely pubescent. Leaves palmately lobed, 1½ to 2 inches in diameter. Flower solitary to 4-flowered corymbs, petals white, less than ¼ inch in diameter. Sepals with spine-like tips. Fruit open from base up with curled style segments. Widely distributed in lawns, waste places, idle fields. Also Texas, Arkansas, and Mississippi. March to May.

*G. dissectum* L. similar, but differs by the dichotomously forked leaf segments and small red petals.

## Candy Root
*Polygala cruciata* L.
Milkwort family

An annual with wing-angled stems, usually branched, up to 12 inches tall. Leaves 4, in a whorl, incurved, narrow. Flower cluster terminal, compact, cylindrical, 2 to 3 inches long. Flowers usually pink, occasionally white. Widely distributed from wet to dry pinelands. Also Texas, Arkansas, and Mississippi. April to June.

## Yellow Polygala
*Polygala ramosa* Ell.
Milkwort family

A biennial herb 8 to 12 inches tall with a basal rosette of leaves about 1 inch long, often dried up and dead at flowering time. Stem leaves reduced. Flower cluster much-branched, nearly flat-topped, bright yellow when fresh, drying dark green. Flowers highly modified, less than ⅛ inch long. Widely distributed in wet pinelands. Also Texas, Arkansas, and Mississippi. April into September.

*P. cymosa* Walt. is very similar, about 3 feet tall, basal leaves 3 to 4 inches long, grows in ditches and edges of ponds. Also Mississippi. April into October.

**Candy Root**
*Polygala incarnata* L.
Milkwort family

An annual herb with a smooth blue-green, slender, usually simple stem 12 to 18 inches tall. Leaves sparse or absent. Flower cluster terminal, about ¼ inch in diameter, and from 1 to 2 inches long, rose-purple. Widely distributed in pinelands. Also Texas, Arkansas, and Mississippi. April to September.

**Orange Candy Root,
Bog Batchelor Button**
*Polygala lutea* L.
Milkwort family

Plants up to 12 inches tall. Basal leaves spatulate, to obovate. Upper leaves linear. Flower cluster terminal, or frequently slightly tipped off-center, sphaerical to slightly cylindrical, about 1 inch in diameter, orange. Widely distributed in wet sites in the pine flatwoods of southeastern Louisiana. Also Mississippi. April to September.

**Candy Root**
*Polygala nana* (Michx.) DC.
Milkwort family

Plants grow in small tufts, annual or biennial. Leaves basal, spatulate to obovate, 2 inches long, rounded at apex. Flower stalks 4 to 6 inches long, terminal. Flower cluster yellow, compact, about 1½ inches long. Individual flowers small. Roots smell like wintergreen candy. Common, widely distributed in pinelands. Also Texas, Arkansas, and Mississippi. April to June with occasional plants into October.

**Bull Nettle**
*Cnidoscolus stimulosus* (Michx.) Engelm. & Gray
Spurge family

Herbaceous perennial covered with stinging hairs. Plants up to 24 inches tall. Leaves palmately 3- to 5-lobed, with margins entire to slightly dentate, alternate. Flower cluster terminal, composed of staminate and pistillate flowers (monoecious). Perianth of staminate flowers white, salverform, about 1 inch wide with perianth tube about an inch long. Pistillate perianth quickly deciduous, ovary developing into a 3-lobed capsule. Primarily east of the Mississippi River in deep, sandy soils. Also Mississippi. May to July.

**Texas Bull Nettle**
*Cnidoscolus texanus* (Muell. Arg.) Small
Spurge family

Densely set with conspicuous white stinging hairs, this is a more robust plant than *C. stimulosus*. Plants about 3 feet tall, several stems from same root system. Leaves fleshy, palmately lobed, 3 to 7 inches wide. Flower cluster with both staminate and pistillate flowers. Staminate perianth white, about 1½ inches broad, salverform. Pistillate flower produces a 3-celled capsule with seed ¾ inch long, looks like a fully gorged tick. Widely distributed west of the Mississippi River from Shreveport to DeRidder, on pineland soils. Also Texas. April to July.

**Snow-on-the-mountain**
*Euphorbia bicolor* Engelm. & Gray
Spurge family

Annual herb. Stems 3 to 4 feet tall, softly pubescent, with a milky juice. Stem leaves lanceolate, 2 inches long, margin slightly revolute, branchlet leaves 1 to 2½ inches long, sides parallel, with a white margin 1/16 to 1/8 inch wide. Flowers inconspicuous in a cyathium. Abundant in prairie in east Texas and western Louisiana. October to November. *E. marginata* Pursh, with the same common name, is frequently cultivated in Louisiana. The stem and branchlet leaves are wider, elliptical, without parallel margins. Locally abundant as an escape (?) in Vernon Parish. May cause dermatitis and has been reported to be poisonous when ingested.

## 102 Milk-weed, Wild Poinsettia
*Euphorbia heterophylla* L.
Spurge family

Annual herbs with milky sap up to 3 feet tall, much-branched. Leaves opposite at base, alternate for most of the plant, opposite again in the flower cluster, blades ovate to rhombic-ovate, uppermost reduced, fiddle-shaped, 3 to 5 inches long, marked with red and yellow near the base under the flower cluster. Stamens numerous, with 1 pistil in a cyathium with a stalked gland on the edge. Widely distributed on disturbed sites, sugarcane fields, alluvial and terrace soils. Also Texas, Arkansas, and Mississippi. October until frost.

*E. dentata* Michx. is similar but not always possible to distinguish. Leaves oblong to lanceolate, mainly opposite, marked whitish areas under the flower clusters.

## Poison Oak
*Rhus quercifolia* (Michx.) Steud.
(= *R. toxicodendron* L.)
Cashew family

A small shrub 12 to 18 inches tall growing only in dry pineland soils. The 3-foliolate leaves are leathery, lobed, suggestive of oak leaves, and toxic. Flowers greenish yellow. Fruit ¼ inch in diameter. Abundant and widespread in dry pineland. Also Texas, Arkansas, and Mississippi. May to July. Fruit until frost.

The name of the three poisonous species have been variously juggled. *R. glabra*, *R. copallina*, and *R. aromatica*, common in Louisiana, not described herein, are nonpoisonous.

**Poison Ivy**
*Rhus radicans* L.
Cashew family

A variable plant with slender stems until it finds something to climb. Then it produces a high-climbing vine, 50 feet or more long covered with aerial roots and holdfast disks. The 3-foliolate leaves, up to 2 feet long, are thin and quite variable in shape. Widely distributed in Louisiana. Seed spread by birds. Incorrectly called "poison oak." A contact poisonous plant. Severe cases of poisoning need medical attention. Also Texas, Arkansas, and Mississippi. Flowers inconspicuous. April to May. Fruit until frost.

**Poison Sumac**
*Rhus vernix* L.
Cashew family

A large shrub to small tree with light gray bark. The odd-pinnately compound leaves are from 8 to 12 inches long with 7 to 11 elliptic to oval, usually entire leaflets. The rachis is purplish (an important diagnostic character). Flower clusters paniculate, with small yellowish flowers which occur with leaf expansion. The fruits are ivory white, about ¼ inch in diameter. Widely distributed in pineland bogs or wet sites. Also Texas, Arkansas, and Mississippi. May to June. Fruits to frost. Extremely poisonous to sensitive individuals.

### 104 Titi, Cyrilla
*Cyrilla racemiflora* L.
Titi family

The titi is a large, nearly evergreen shrub or small tree with conspicuous racemes of tiny white flowers. The leaves are from 2½ to 5 inches long, elliptical to oblanceolate or obovate, shiny above. The flowers are about ¼ inch long, closely spaced on clusters of drooping or spreading racemes. A very good honey plant. Along streams and sloughs in the acid pinelands of southeastern Louisiana. Also Texas and Mississippi. April to June.

### Buckwheat Tree, Black Titi
*Cliftonia monophylla* (Lam.) Sarg.
Titi family

A large shrub or small tree with nearly evergreen leaves. Leaves 2 to 3 inches long, alternate, leathery, elliptical to oblanceolate, shiny green above, paler below. Flowers white, fragrant, small, in compact, short, terminal racemes, usually erect, at times nodding. Fruit about ¼ inch long with 4 distinct wings. Common in the acid pinelands, bogs, and wet sites in southeastern Louisiana. Also Mississippi. March to April.

## Deciduous Holly, Possum-haw
*Ilex decidua* Walt.
Holly family

A very bushy shrub to small tree especially noticeable when in fruit. Deserves more horticultural attention as an ornamental. Leaves alternate, deciduous, in clusters on spur shoots. Blades 1½ to 2 inches long, elliptic to obovate, tapering to a channeled petiole, margin crenate. Plants dioecious. Staminate and pistillate flowers small, inconspicuous, greenish white, solitary or in few-flowered clusters on spur shoots. Fruit bright red, globose, about ¼ inch in diameter, short-stalked. Widely distributed, common in thickets on alluvial soil as well as on older areas. Also Texas, Arkansas, and Mississippi. Fruit November to December to January.

*I. longipes* Chapm. is quite similar but can be distinguished by the longer pedicel for the fruit.

## Holly, American Holly
*Ilex opaca* Ait.
Holly family

This evergreen tree under Louisiana conditions usually has entire leaves on the fruiting branches, and spiny leaves on sterile branches or sprout growth. Leaves 2 to 4 inches long, broadly oval. Staminate flowers tiny, clusters on a common stalk. Pistillate or female flowers on a separate tree with individual stalks. Fruits ⅜ inch in diameter, red to yellowish, globose to ovoid or oblong. Many horticultural forms have been selected and named. Widely distributed but generally absent from the floodplain of the Mississippi and Red rivers. Fruit eaten by cedar waxwings. Also Texas, Arkansas, and Mississippi. April. Fruit ripe in November to December.

## 106 Yaupon
*Ilex vomitoria* Ait.
Holly family

A large shrub to small tree noted for the quantities of red fruits. The evergreen leaves ½ to 1¼ inches long, oval to elliptic with a crenate-serrate margin. Dark glossy green above. Flowers tiny, white, staminate, and pistillate on separate plants, occasionally perfect flowered forms. Fruit about ¼ inch in diameter, translucent, bright red. Dwarfed and weeping forms are known. Birds eat the berries of this species last. Widely distributed. Also Texas, Arkansas, and Mississippi.

Indian are supposed to have made a decoction of this to prove their suitability for the warpath. Strong decoctions are emetic.

## Drummond Red Maple
## Swamp Red Maple
*Acer drummondii* Hook. & Arn.
Maple family

A large tree, common in shallow swamps with cypress. Leaves opposite, palmately 3- to 5-lobed. Blade cordate at base, 3 to 6 inches long, about as wide, densely tomentose below, which usually persists, also glaucous. Flowers pedicellate, dioecious, but various combinations occur, some trees perfect-flowered. Fruit a double samara, bright red to bronze with age, wings convergent to divergent, 1½ to 2½ inches long. Widely distributed on alluvial soils, also along streams in the prairie. Also Texas, Arkansas, and Mississippi. February into March.

RED MAPLE, *A. rubrum* L., occurs in north Louisiana. TRIDENT RED MAPLE, *A. rubrum* var. *tridens* Wood, is more abundant than the species. It can be distinguished by the smaller leaves 2 to 3 inches long with rounded bases and fruits about 1 inch long. Along streams in pinelands and hill country.

## Red Buckeye
*Aesculus pavia* L.
Buckeye family

A large shrub or small tree. The opposite, palmately compound leaves have 5 leaflets on a stout petiole about as long as the leaflets. The leaflets are about 6 inches long, strongly veined above, with irregular serrate margins. The terminal flower cluster is 6 to 10 inches long with dark red flowers 1 to ½ inches long which consist of a thickened tubular calyx with a gibbous base and unequal petals. Common along streams in the hilly areas, usually absent from the floodplains. Also Texas, Arkansas, and Mississippi. March to May.

## New Jersey Tea
*Ceanothus americanus* L.
Buckthorn family

A low shrub usually under 3 feet, much-branched. Leaves ovate to ovate-oblong, 3-ribbed, green above, somewhat hairy below. Flower pedunculate on new growth, peduncles elongate, axillary, flower clusters terminal about 1¾ inches in diameter. Individual flowers white, small, petals clawed. Fruit 3-lobed capsule less than ¼ in diameter. Widespread in Louisiana on prairie, pineland soils, absent from the alluvial floodplain. Also Texas, Arkansas, and Mississippi. April to August.

### Virginia Creeper, Woodbine
*Parthenocissus quinquefolia* (L.) Plauch.
Grape family

A high-climbing woody vine with adhesive disks on the tendrils. The alternate palmately compound leaves are 5-foliolate, usually on a petiole about as long as the leaf blade. The leaflets are sharply serrate. The inflorescence is paniculate with many tiny flowers about 1/10 inch long. The fruit is a berry about 1/4 inch in diameter which is avidly eaten by birds. Widely distributed. Also Texas, Arkansas, and Mississippi. June to July with fruit into September. This has been mistaken for poison ivy but can be distinguished by the 5 leaflets instead of 3 leaflets for poison ivy.

### Poppy-mallow
*Callirhoe papaver* (Cav.) Gray
Mallow family

A sprawling, prostrate plant with stems 5 to 10 feet long from a taproot. Leaves variable, palmately lobed or 3 to 5 cleft, cordate to ovate. Lobes linear, often with secondary lobing. Flowers usually solitary, scattered, on long peduncles, red, 1 to 2 inches in diameter, with broad erose apex of petals. Calyx with stout bristles. Involucels under calyx, 3 small, about 1/4 inch long. Fruit a ring of alveolate carpels. Widely distributed in pinelands, calcareous prairies, roadsides, more abundant in north Louisiana. Also Texas, Arkansas, and Mississippi. March to July.

**Pineland Hibiscus**
*Hibiscus aculeatus* Walt.
Mallow family

A perennial herb with annual ascending to erect stems to 3 feet tall. Leaves alternate, palmately 3- to 5-lobed, about 2 to 4 inches long, irregularly cleft, with large sinuses between lobes. Stem and foliage densely covered with trichomes which feel rough to the touch. Flowers 2 to 3 inches wide, funnel-shaped, dark center, corolla yellow, turning purplish with age. Capsule about 1 inch in diameter, densely hairy. Confined to moist pinelands, along ditches, sloughs, and wet sites. Also Texas, Arkansas, and Mississippi. May to September.

**Woolly Rose-mallow**
*Hibiscus lasiocarpos* Cav.
Mallow family

Erect perennial with stems to 6 feet, stem and leaves more or less pubescent. Leaves simple, alternate, long-petioled, blades ovate, 4 to 6 inches long, sometimes slightly 3-lobed, margin crenate-serrate, densely white, stellate, tomentose below, pubescent to scabrous above. Flowers chiefly white, occasionally pink, 4 to 5 inches long, with a deep red center. Calyx more stellate on inside than outside. Bractlets as long as calyx. Fruit a capsule, very strigose. Widely distributed in wet sites, fresh marshes, alluvial soils. Also Texas, Arkansas, and Mississippi. May to September.

**Halberd-leaved Rose-mallow**
*Hibiscus militaris* Cav.
Mallow family

A perennial plant up to 6 feet tall with erect glabrous stems and leaves. Leaves ovate-triangular to halberd shape, with distinct sharp-pointed basal lobes at right angles to center vein, long-petioled. Flowers axillary, blooming from the base toward the apex, about 3 to 4 inches long, funnel-form corolla, pink, occasionally white, Calyx about 1 inch long, with slender bractlets. Fresh marshes, wet sites in Red and Mississippi river floodplains. May to October.

**Salt Marsh-mallow**
*Kosteletzkya virginica* (L.) Gray
Mallow family

A perennial herb to 6 feet tall, much-branched. Stems and leaves usually densely pubescent. Leaves broadly ovate, occasionally with slight lateral marginal lobes, margin serrate. Flowers mainly on axillary branches, opening wide, 1 to 2½ inches in diameter, pink. Fruit a flat ring of carpels about ½ inch in diameter, the major characteristic that distinguishes this from *Hibiscus*. Fresh to saline marshes, abundant in lower Louisiana. Also Texas and Mississippi. May to October.

**Carolina Mallow**
*Modiola caroliniana* (L.) Don.
Mallow family

A low, creeping, much-branched perennial herb with stems rooting at nodes, up to 24 inches long. Leaves petiolate, lower petioles longer than respective blade, upper shorter. Blade palmately dissected, ¾ to 1½ inches in diameter, lobes toothed. Flowers orange to purplish red, about ½ inch in diameter, opening flat. Fruit a ring of black, 1-seeded carpels, tardily separating, each with 2 small spines. A weed in lawns, gardens, disturbed soils, and marshes. Widely distributed and abundant. Also Texas, Arkansas, and Mississippi. Late February to June.

**Wild or Silky Camellia**
*Stewartia malacodendron* L.
Tea or Camellia family

A large open-branched shrub. Leaves alternate, deciduous, oval, elliptic to obovate, distinctly veined, 2 to 4 inches long, silky below. Flower white, sometimes streaked with red, 2 to 3 inches in diameter, cup-shaped to saucer-shaped, margin of petals crimped. Stamens numerous, conspicuous, purple with green tinges, surrounding a 5-lobed pistil. Fruit a capsule with shiny, lenticular seeds. Mixed woods, pinelands, along streams, on sandy, well-drained but occasionally flooded sites. Also Texas, Arkansas, and Mississippi. April to May.

### Loblolly Bay
*Gordonia lasianthus* (L.) Ell.
Tea family

A small tree with furrowed gray bark. Leaves evergreen, alternate, elliptic to oblanceolate, 4 to 6 inches long by 1 inch wide, margin finely appressed, serrate, nearly sessile, shiny above. Flowers white, solitary, about 2 inches wide, on peduncles nearly as long as the leaves. Sepals 5, pubescent, petals 5, stamens many, filaments fused. Rare. If native anywhere, St. Tammany Parish. Frequently planted. Also southern Mississippi. July to August.

### St. Peter's-wort
*Ascyrum stans* Michx.
St. John's-wort family

A small woody shrub. Leaves broadly oval, erect, slightly clasping, about 1 to 2 inches long. Flower about 1¼ inches broad. Corolla of 4 bright yellow petals, stamens many, in clusters. Sepals 4, the two outer broadly ovate to cordate, about ½ inch long, light green, turning brown with maturity, inner sepals small lanceolate. Widely distributed in pinelands as well as bluff and hill lands. Also Texas, Arkansas, and Mississippi. June to September.

**St. John's-wort**
*Hypericum densiflorum* Pursh
St. John's-wort family

Perennial woody shrub up to 5 feet tall, bushy, branched, foliage glandular-punctate. Leaves opposite, short-petioled, 2 inches long by ¼ inch wide, apex acute, base cuneate, margin revolute. Flower cluster mostly terminal, of compound cymes. Flower yellow, about ½ inch wide, many stamens in fascicles, styles tardily separating, usually into 3 styles. Widely distributed in longleaf pinelands. Also Texas and Mississippi. June to September.

**St. John's-wort**
*Hypericum cistifolium* Lam.
St. John's-wort family

A perennial up to 3 feet tall with stems semiwoody, sparingly branched near top. Foliage glandular-punctate. Leaves linear, 1½ inches long by ⅛ inch wide, sessile, subauriculate at base, margin enrolled, apex acute, midnerve of leaf extending to stem wing. Flower cluster of terminal and axillary racemes, with reduced bracts. Flowers numerous, less than ½ inch wide, many stamens. Pistil at first with a united style which splits into 3 styles on maturity. Common in prairie and pinelands. Also Texas and Mississippi. June to September.

### 114 French Tamarisk, Seaside Cedar
*Tamarix gallica* L.
Tamarisk family

A large shrub to small tree resembles, but it is unrelated to, a cedar. The multitude of tiny leaves about 1/16 inch long overlap each other. Flowers small, white to pink in short terminal racemes, often in compound clusters. It was introduced for windbreaks and erosion control and has escaped from cultivation. Common along the Gulf Coast, particularly Grand Isle, Pecan Island, Creole to Johnson Bayou in Cameron Parish. Also Texas and Mississippi. April.

### Langlois Violet
*Viola langloisii* Greene
(= *Viola affinis* LeConte)
Violet family

A stemless perennial with conspicuous rhizomes. Leaves ovate-triangular, 1½ to 3 inches long, glabrous, cordate base, margin near tip with 10 to 14 teeth. Flowers pale blue, ½ to ¾ inch wide, bilaterally symmetrical, flower stalks above the leaves, lateral petals bearded, lower petal spurred. Widespread in moist hardwood area. Also Texas, Arkansas, and Mississippi. March to May.

**Birds-foot Violet**
*Viola pedata* L.
Violet family

A perennial herb. The largest of the many kinds of violets which grow in Louisiana. Leaves divided into many narrow strips. Flowers irregular, 1 inch or more wide. Color variable, all petals a light violet, with darker veins, to a dark purple to a bicolored condition with the two upper petals a deep violet, and the 3 lower petals lighter. Widely distributed in Louisiana pinelands soils. Also Texas, Arkansas, and Mississippi. March to April.

**Primrose-leaved Violet**
*Viola primulifolia* L.
Violet family

Plants perennial with small cordlike white stolons. Leaves lanceolate to acute to obtuse tips. Blade tapering to petiole, somewhat winged, as long as blade. Flowers white, about ½ inch wide. Lower lip marked with bluish to brown veins. Fruit a capsule which splits into 3 valves. Common and widely distributed in wet sites, margins of ditches and streams, in both pine and hardwood areas. Most abundant violet in Louisiana. Also Texas, Arkansas, and Mississippi. March into May.

### 116 *Viola rosacea* Brainerd
### Violet family

A stemless acaulescent perennial herb in small tufts. Spring leaves with blades cordate-ovate, generally glabrous, crenate-serrate, 2 to 3 inches long. Summer leaves not lobed. Flower rose-purple, about ¾ inch wide, on stalks much longer than the leaves, later petals bearded, spur moderate. Cleistogamous flowers on horizontal pedicels. Common in rich, well-drained soils along streams and margins of swamps. Also Mississippi. Late February into April. Violets are difficult to identify. Botanists need cleistogamous flowers more than chasmogamous flowers. There are many hybrids.

### Maypop, Passion Flower
### *Passiflora incarnata* L.
### Passion Flower family

A perennial plant with annual, vine-like stems which climb over bushes and fences by means of tendrils. The leaves are alternate, deeply 3-lobed, with 2 conspicuous glands at the summit of the petiole. The beauty of the flower is not only in the colors of the floral parts but also in the delicate arrangement of parts. The flower, about 3 inches in diameter, has reflexed green sepals, 5 yellowish green petals, a mottled purple and white fringe, 5 drooping yellow stamens suspended around the pistil which has 3 to 4 reflexed stigmas and a conspicuous ovary. The fruit is a green berry, oval to sphaerical in shape, 2 to 3 inches long. Widely distributed in Louisiana. Also Texas, Arkansas, and Mississippi. May to September.

**Yellow Passion Flower**
*Passiflora lutea* L.
Passion Flower family

Annual, slender, tender stems, high-climbing with tendrils. Leaves thin, broader than long, 3 to 4 inches wide, obtusely 3-lobed at apex. Flower yellow, nearly an inch in diameter. Fringe short and stiff, yellow. Fruit a drooping, fleshy berry about ¼ inch in diameter. Widely distributed but not common, thickets along streams. Absent from the alluvial soils. Also Texas, Arkansas, and Mississippi. Late May into July.

**Prickly Pear Cactus**
*Opuntia compressa* (Salisb.) Mcbr.
Cactus family

Mat-forming, spreading over the ground, seldom over 2 or 3 joints or pads tall. Pads obovate to oblong-ovate, 4 to 6 inches long by 3 to 4 inches wide. Areoles with fine barbed bristles and some with a single spine about 1 inch long. Flowers about 3 inches in diameter, cup-shaped or wheel-shaped. Fruit pulpy, clavate to obovoid, dull purple. Washington Parish in deep sand along the Pushepetappa Creek. Also Texas and Mississippi. May to June.

### Fragile Cactus
*Opuntia drummondii* Grah.
Cactus family

A low-growing plant, often hidden in the grass and unnoticed until the easily disarticulating joints are found clinging to the clothing. The joints are small, 1 to 4 inches long, oval, elliptical to slightly obovate, with upper joints often subcylindrical with the usual aeroles and a single large spine 1½ to 2 inches long per areole. The petals are minutely mucronate. The fruit is clavoid to obovoid, fleshy, 1½ inches long, and purplish. Very abundant in the sandy soil of Bienville, Winn, and Vernon parishes. Also Texas and Mississippi. May to June.

### Lindheimer Cactus
*Opuntia lindheimeri* Engelm.
Cactus family

A robust plant forming clumps 3 to 5 feet high and several feet in diameter. The joints or pads are oval, elliptical to obovate, 12 to 18 inches long by 5 to 7 inches wide, bright green to glaucous. The subulate leaves about ¼ inch long occur at the areoles and are soon shed. The areoles are filled with fine, barbed bristles, (glochids) and 1 to 3 gray spines about an inch long. Many flowers develop on the margins of the joints. Flower yellow, with many petals and stamens, cup-shaped to rotate, 2 to 3 inches in diameter. Apex of the petals mucronate. Fruit fleshy, subgloboid, purplish when mature. Confined to the sandy cheniers of Cameron and Vermilion parishes where it is so abundant that it is a pest. Also Texas. May into July.

## Meadow Beauty
*Rhexia alifanus* Walt.
Melastoma family

Perennial erect herb, to 36 inches tall, with glabrous stems and leaves, somewhat glaucous. Leaves opposite, lanceolate to linear-lanceolate, about 3 inches long, 3-nerved, cuneate base and acute apex. Flowers purple, conspicuous, 4 large rhomboid petals, 1 to 1¼ inches wide, with 4 triangular sepals attached to the margin of the hypanthium. Stamens 8, with curved anthers, buds sharp-pointed. Fruit an urnlike structure with a globose setose base, a short, constricted neck and expanded margin. Widespread in moist pinelands. Also Texas and Mississippi. April to September.

*R. mariana* L. has smaller, light pink flower, with pubescent stems and is more abundant than the above species.

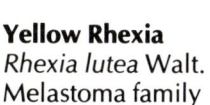

## Yellow Rhexia
*Rhexia lutea* Walt.
Melastoma family

Plants about 20 inches tall, bushy-branched and glandular-hirsute. Leaves elliptic, oblanceolate to obovate, about 1 inch long. Flower about 1 inch in diameter, yellow. Petals 4, shatter easily. Stamens straight, lacking typical melastoma attachment and curve. Fruit a glandular urn-shaped hypanthium. Common in moist pinelands. Also Texas, Arkansas, and Mississippi. May to June.

*R. petiolata* Walt. likewise has straight stamens, but pink flowers, broader leaves, with short petioles.

### 120 Evening Primrose
*Oenothera biennis* L. complex
Evening Primrose family

Erect branched biennial to 6 feet tall. Leaves lanceolate, elliptic, about 3 inches long, short-petioled, soft pubescent, margin serrate. Flower cluster terminal. Individual flower in the axils of bracts or leaves. Flowers about 1½ inches long, consisting of a slender perianth tube, more or less reflexed sepals, and 4 yellow petals about an inch wide. Fruit a cylindrical capsule. Widely distributed in disturbed soils, a weed. Also Texas, Arkansas, and Mississippi. May to frost.

### Drummond's Evening Primrose
*Oenothera drummondii* Hook.
Evening Primrose family

A perennial herb, decumbent to trailing, stems up to 2 feet long, densely pubescent. Leaves obovate, oblanceolate, elliptic, 2 inches long. Flowers bright yellow, about 2½ inches in diameter, turning towards the sun, on short erect stems. Fruit cylindrical capsule about 2 inches long. Common on sandy beaches above high-tide level, cheniers and prairie in southwestern Louisiana. Also Texas. April into June.

**Mexican Primrose**
*Oeonthera speciosa* Nutt.
Evening Primrose family

This is widely known in Louisiana as a buttercup in spite of its pink and white flowers. A perennial leafy herb, 8 to 20 inches tall. Leaves variable in shape. The nodding buds open into flowers which are pure white, pink, or white with pink lines. Early spring flowers are 3 inches in diameter and get progressively smaller to 1 inch in diameter as the soil moisture is reduced. Widely distributed, forming conspicuous colonies along roadsides, ditch banks, and idle fields. Also Texas, Arkansas, and Mississippi. March to June with occasional flower to October.

*Gaura lindheimeri* Engelm. & Gray
Evening Primrose family

Perennial, much-branched from an underground, woody stem, 6 to 8 feet tall, more or less strigose. Leaves oblanceolate to narrowly elliptic, 2 to 3 inches long, sessile, margin remotely and obscurely serrulate-dentate. Flower clusters terminal spikes, also on axillary branches. Flower consists of a slender perianth tube about ½ inch long including the subsessile hypanthium, sepals 4, reflexed, pinkish, petals 4, white, clawed, about ½ inch long, turning pink on drying, stamens 8 to 10 with long filaments which dangle from the open flower, and a long style. Fruit thick, fusiform, 4-angled. Widespread in prairie and pinelands. Also Texas. April into June.

**Hercules'-club,
Devil's-walking-stick**
*Aralia spinosa* L.
Ginseng family

A tall shrub, usually with simple, unbranched, spiny stem, about 2 inches in diameter. Leaves compound, 2-pinnate, large, 3 to 4 feet long, and about as wide, armed with slender spines. Leaflets many, ovate, 2 to 4 inches long. Flower cluster, crowning the stem, consists of umbellate clusters of tiny flowers in a large panicle. Fruit a juicy, blue berry about ¼ inch in diameter. Widely distributed in Louisiana, locally abundant, usually forms thickets. Also Texas, Arkansas, and Mississippi. Summer.

## Poison Hemlock
*Conium maculatum* L.
Parsley family

A stout, erect, much-branched herb, 5 to 10 feet tall from a stout, chambered taproot. Leaves 2-pinnate to 3-pinnate, divided, broadly ovate in outline, 12 to 18 inches long, segments 2 to 4 inches long, lanceolate to elliptic distinctly serrate. Upper leaves reduced. Flower cluster compound umbels, large, axillary, and terminal, exceeding the leaves. Flowers small, with white petals. Fruit small, flattened laterally. Widespread in wet sites, ditches, margin of Lake Ponchartrain and in north Louisiana. Also Texas and Mississippi. May to August. Very poisonous to man and livestock.

## Eryngo
*Eryngium integrifolium* Walt.
Parsley family

Perennial herb with slender, solitary stems, branched near the top, up to 30 inches tall. Basal leaves oblong-lanceolate, long-petioled, clasping, 5 to 6 inches long with serrate margin. Upper stem leaves smaller, needle-shaped. Flower cluster cymose with some branches nearly horizontal. Individual heads subtended by several linear bracts with spiny margins, about ½ inch long, longer than the globose flower head. Individual flowers bluish, numerous. Widely distributed in wet pineland and prairie soils. Also Texas and Mississippi. August to October.

**124** **Rattlesnake-master,
Button Snake-root**
*Eryngium yuccifolium* Michx.
Parsley family

A perennial herb, stem stout, glabrous, 24 to 30 inches tall, branched in the inflorescence. Leaves linear to broadly linear, rigid, 10 to 12 inches long by ¼ to 1 inch wide, raised parallel veins, margins remotely bristly with solitary bristles, sheath clasping stem. Inflorescence branched with dense pedunculate heads, globose to ovoid about ¾ inch in diameter. Flower tiny, greenish white, subtended by a stiff, subulate, pointed bractlet. Widely distributed and common in prairie and pinelands. Also Texas, Arkansas, and Mississippi. May to August.

**Salt Pennywort**
*Hydrocotyle bonariensis* Lam.
Parsley family

A low perennial herb from creeping stolons, 6 to 10 inches tall, fleshy. Leaves peltate, broadly oval to orbicular, 2 to 4 inches in diameter, margin undulate, Inflorescence a compound, much-branched umbel 2 to 3 inches in diameter. Individual flowers tiny, about 1/16 inch in diameter. Fruits conspicuous, about 3/16 inch in diameter. Abundant in sandy soils along the gulf from high tide level inland, common in saline to brackish marshes. Also Texas and Mississippi. March to May.

**Pennyworts, Dollar-grass**
*Hydrocotyle umbellata* L. (Right)
*Hydrocotyle verticillata* Thunb.
(Left)
Parsley family

Perennial, fleshy herbs from creeping stolons. Leaves peltate, smooth, up to 9 inches tall, blade 2 inches in diameter, margin lightly crenate. The foliage for both species is indistinguishable. *H. umbellata* has flowers in a terminal umbel whereas *H. verticillata* has from 2 to 7 whorls of flowers on the scape. Both grow together in moist soils, ditches, edges of ponds, and on lawns. Also Texas, Arkansas, and Mississippi. March to August.

**Mock Bishop's-weed**
*Ptilimnium costatum* (Ell.) Raf.
Parsley family

A perennial herb to 5 feet tall. Leaves alternate, 3 to 4 inches long, pinnately divided into many filiform segments which appear verticillate. Flower cluster a compound umbel, with the peduncles longer than the leaves. Bracts at the base of the umbel-rays filiform, short. Bracts at the base of the individual, umbels shorter than the pedicels. Flowers small, white, less than ⅛ inch wide. Fruit ovoid about ⅛ inch long. Wet sites in prairie, margins of swamps, and fresh marshes. Also Texas. August to October.

Closely allied to the more abundant *P. capillaceum* (Michx.) Raf. It is a smaller plant with fewer filiform leaf segments.

### Golden Alexanders
*Zizia aurea* (L.) Koch
Parsley family

A perennial herb with a basal rosette of leaves and later an erect stem up to 3 feet tall. Basal leaves 5 inches long, oval to ovate in outline, 2-pinnate, with pinnules sharply toothed, glabrous, base of petioles sheathing the stem. Upper stem leaves reduced. Flower cluster a compound umbel. Flowers yellow, tiny, less than ⅛ inch long. Fruit flat, dry, less than ¼ inch long. Widely distributed in prairie and pinelands. Also Texas, Arkansas, and Mississippi. April to June. Fruit to August.

### Flowering Dogwood
*Cornus florida* L.
Dogwood family

A medium-sized tree with bark divided into square plates with longitudinal and cross cracks. Leaves opposite, elliptical to broadly oval, strongly veined, 2 to 6 inches long. True flowers tiny, yellowish, about the size of a match head, surrounded by 4 white, apically notched bracts, which are often mistaken for petals. There are several strains with pink to reddish bracts. Fruits bright red berries. Widely distributed in Louisiana, but generally absent from the floodplain areas. Also Texas, Arkansas, and Mississippi. Earliest flowers in March before the leaves and with the leaves in April. Follow the dogwood trail in north Louisiana.

**Hairy Pepperbush, Clethra**
*Clethra alnifolia* L.
White-alder family

A shrub. The alternate, deciduous leaves are 1½ to 3½ inches long, elliptical to oval to obovate, deeply veined on top, densely hairy below, margin finely toothed. Flowers white, tiny, in terminal and auxillary racemes. Fruit a small pubescent capsule. Common in the cypress-black gum swamps around Lake Pontchartrain and in pineland sloughs of southeastern Louisiana. Also Texas and Mississippi. June to July.

**Tangleberry, Dangleberry**
*Gaylussacia frondosa* (L.) T. & G.
Heath family

A shrub to 6 feet tall with widespreading branches. Leaves alternate, deciduous, up to 3 inches long, elliptic to oblong or obovate, finely hairy to glabrous. Flowers in racemes, bracted, bracts small and tardily deciduous. Corolla bell-shaped, white, less than ½ inch broad. Fruit a glaucous blue berry about ¼ inch in diameter. Widespread in pinelands of southeastern Louisiana. Also Mississippi. April to May.

### 128 Mountain Laurel
*Kalmia latifolia* L.
Heath family

A large shrub with evergreen leaves and clusters of white to deep pink flowers. Look at the individual flower. It has a united corolla about the size of a nickle. It opens flat to wheel-shaped. As an unusual feature, the stamens have their anthers caught in a little pocket of the corolla. The weight of a bee on the corolla causes a stamen to pop out of the pocket and hit the bee with a load of pollen. When the bee visits the next flower the pollen is brushed off on the stigma, thus effecting pollination. Confined to the Pushepetappa Creek and tributaries in Washington Parish. Also Mississippi. Late April into June.

### Fetterbush
*Lyonia lucida* (Lam.) Koch
Heath family

An evergreen shrub with drooping, angled branches. Leaves stiff, leathery, elliptic to oval or obovate, dark green above, paler and glandular-dotted below, margin enrolled, thick. Flowers in axillary clusters of 3 to 10, about ⅜ inch long, white to pinkish, united corolla constricted beneath the apex. Stamen filaments with two awns. Capsule woody opening into seed cavity. Common in swamps and sloughs, sandy stream bottoms in the pinelands, most abundant in southeastern Louisiana. March and April.

SWAMP FETTERBUSH, *Leucothoë racemosa* (L.) Gray, is deciduous and bears its flowers in long racemes.

**Pinesap**
*Monotropa hypopithys* L.
Heath family

Plants 5 to 10 inches tall, lacking chlorophyll, growing in small clusters. Stems pubescent, many small, scalelike leaves, translucent yellow to reddish purple. Flowers several, apical, nodding at first, about ½ inch long. Mainly in mixed wood in north Louisiana. April to June.

**Indian Pipe**
*Monotropa uniflora* L.
Heath family

Perennial herb lacking chlorophyll, considered saprophytic. Plants solitary or in small clumps, 6 to 10 inches tall, white when fresh, occasionally flesh to light purplish, turning black when picked. Stems glabrous with many small, sessile, scalelike leaves about ½ inch long. Flower terminal, solitary, nodding, later becoming erect in fruit. Widely distributed in beech-magnolia woods and pine-hardwood areas. Also Texas, Arkansas, and Mississippi. September to October.

**130  Sourwood**
*Oxydendrum arboreum* (L.) DC.
Heath family

A small tree with distinctive bark consisting of deep furrows and heavy ridges. Leaves deciduous, 3 to 6 inches long, elliptic to oblong with a finely toothed margin. Stiff hairs present on the midrib below. Flowers white, small, ¼ inch long, constricted near the open end, on drooping racemes from the tips of branches. Widely distributed along stream bottoms in the pinelands of southeastern Louisiana. Less common elsewhere and absent from the floodplain. Sourwood honey is an outstanding delicacy. Also Mississippi. Flowers early in June.

**Squaw Huckleberry, Deerberry**
*Polycodium stamineum* (L.) Greene
Heath family

A deciduous shrub up to 8 feet tall. Leaves oval to elliptic, more or less fine hairy below, ¾ to 2½ inches long. Flowers axillary from smaller leaves, ½ to ⅜ inch long. Flowers drooping on slender stems, open bell-shaped. Corolla white with conspicuous anther tubes extending beyond the corolla. Fruit ⅜ inch in diameter, green to purplish, thick-skinned. Widely distributed in pinelands. Also Texas, Arkansas, and Mississippi. March to April.

**Orange Flowered Azalea**
*Rhododendron austrinum* (Small) Millais
Heath family

A large shrub with deciduous foliage. Leaf blades oval, obovate, or elliptic spatulate, finely pubescent. Flower cluster compact, several-flowered, appearing before the leaves unfold to half-grown leaves. Corolla tubular, opening at apex into a widespread limb about 1½ inches long, finely glandular-pubescent externally, shades of orange and yellow with some reddish tints. Woods, along streams in pinelands. Southern Mississippi. Cultivated in Louisiana. March to April.

**132** **Wild Azalea, "Honeysuckle"**
*Rhododendron canescens* (Michx.) Sweet
Heath family

A large shrub. Leaves deciduous, oblong to elliptic to slightly obovate, 1 to 2½ inches long, hairy above and below. Flower cluster compact, opening before and sometimes with the leaves. Flowers 1 to 2 inches with long exserted stamens and pistil. Corolla long, tubular, abrupt, flaring into 5 lobes, about 1 inch broad, white, pink, or pink and white, glandular sticky on corolla tube, fragrant. Widely distributed in moist pineland soils and occasional in hilly terrace soils, absent from the alluvial soil of the Red and Mississippi rivers. Also Texas, Arkansas, and Mississippi. March into April.

**Summer Azalea, Swamp Azalea**
*Rhododendron serrulatum* (Small) Mill.
Heath family

A large shrub distinguished from *R. canescens* by its habit of blooming in the summer after the leaves are formed and by its swamp habitat. Leaves elliptic to oblanceolate, 2 inches long, short-petioled, margin serrulate-ciliate, strongly incurved. Flower cluster few-flowered. Corolla white, tubular with a flaring limb of 5 petals, the lower 3 a little larger than the upper 2, tube glandular pubescent, sweet-scented. Fruit a woody capsule about ¼ inch long, on a pedicel about ½ inch long, both glandular-pubescent and strigose. Wet swamps and along sloughs in the pinelands of southeastern Louisiana. Also Mississippi. June to July.

**Tree Huckleberry,
Winter Huckleberry**
*Vaccinium arboreum* Marsh.
Heath family

A small tree with variable evergreen, usually glossy leaves. The alternate leaves are leathery, 1 to 2½ inches long, elliptic to oval or obovate, frequently hairy below. Leaves on the flower cluster ¼ to ⅝ inch long. Flowers very abundant, white, tiny, ⅜ inch long, constricted at open end. Fruit black, ⅜ inch in diameter, dry, poor flavor. Widely distributed in the pinelands of Louisiana, absent from the Mississippi River floodplain. Also Texas, Arkansas, and Mississippi. March to May.

**Sweetleaf, Horse Sugar**
*Symplocos tinctoria* (L.) L'Her
Sweetleaf family

A semi-evergreen shrub to small tree. Leaves all shed at times prior to blooming, at other times they remain on the tree. Leaves elliptic to oblanceolate, 2 to 6 inches long, with rough hairs on the veins on the under surface. Flowers yellow to orange, in dense clusters, ½ to ¾ inch long. Many conspicuous stamens and 5 petals about ¼ inch long. Fruit a small drupe, oblong, becoming reddish at maturity. Widely distributed in the small stream valleys. Also Texas, Arkansas, and Mississippi. Late February into April.

## 134 Snowbell
*Styrax americana* Lam.
Storax family

A large shrub to small tree. Leaves alternate, deciduous, elliptic, oval or oblanceolate, typically with acute apices and bases, margin minutely and remotely serrate. Blooming on both old and new wood, more or less pulverulent. Flowers axillary, white, 5-lobed corolla, about ½ inch long. Fruit a 1-seeded capsule about ¼ inch in diameter with capsule wall hard and pubescent. Widespread in moist soils, margins of cypress swamps, and along pineland streams. Also Texas, Arkansas, and Mississippi. March to April.

## Silver Bell
*Halesia diptera* Ellis
Storax family

A large shrub or small, slow-growing tree. The deciduous alternate leaves are elliptical to oval, 2 to 7 inches long. The white flowers, about 1 inch in diameter, consist of 4 waxy white petals with a tight cluster of stamens in the center, which resembles a candle in a candle holder. The fruits are 2-winged, green, and fleshy at first, later becoming hard and dry. They have a pleasing acidic flavor when green. It is widely distributed along branch bottoms of the small streams and absent from the Mississippi River floodplain. Also Texas, Arkansas, and Mississippi. February into March.

**Fringetree, Grancy-graybeard**
*Chionanthus virginica* L.
Ash family

A large shrub or small tree. Leaves deciduous, opposite, lanceolate, elliptic to oval with enrolled margins, densely hairy below. Flower cluster 5 to 10 inches long, compound. Flowers white, corolla composed of 5 strap-shaped petals about 1 inch long by 1/16 inch wide. Fruit nearly 1/2 inch long, ovoid, dark purple. Widely distributed in pinelands, absent from the Mississippi River floodplain. Also Texas, Arkansas, and Mississippi. April.

**Swamp-privet, Whitewood**
*Forestiera acuminata* (Michx.) Poir.
Ash family

A large shrub with opposite, deciduous leaves. Leaves ovate-oblong to ovate-lanceolate with acute to acuminate apices and bases, petioled. Flowers dioecious, staminate in dense, yellowish clusters of stamens, no petals. Pistillate flowers inconspicuous, producing a dark purple drupe, with a juicy layer surrounding a thin-walled stone. Abundant on the Mississippi River floodplain and along small streams and swamps. Also Texas, Arkansas, and Mississippi. February to March. Can withstand considerable flooding and is good for erosion control. Browsed by deer, and fruit eaten by birds.

**136 Yellow Jessamine**
*Gelsemium sempervirens* (L.) Ait.
Logania family

A high-climbing, twining, woody vine. Leaves opposite, lanceolate, base acute to rounded, margin revolute. Flower yellow, usually fragrant, trumpet-shaped with flaring lobes, 1 inch in diameter. Fruit a dehiscent, oblong capsule about ¾ inch long. Very abundant and widespread in Louisiana. Also Texas, Arkansas, and Mississippi. January to April. Some plants stay in blossom nearly every month of the year.

**Indian Pink**
*Spigelia marilandica* L.
Logania family

A tender, perennial herb, solitary or in clumps up to 2 feet tall. Leaves opposite, broadly lanceolate, sessile, 3 to 6 inches long. Flower cluster terminal, curved. Flowers secund, opening from bottom toward top. Corolla united, tubular, bright red externally, opening at tip into 5 sharp-pointed lobes which are yellow inside. Widespread in moist woods, usually absent from the floodplain of the Mississippi and Red rivers. A fine plant for the garden. The bloom season can be prolonged by removing the withering flowers. Also Texas, Arkansas, and Mississippi. Late March into May.

**Catchfly-gentian**
*Eustoma exaltatum* (L.) G. Don
Gentian family

Annual plant 20 to 30 inches tall. Stems 1 to several, branched above. Stem leaves oblong, about 3 inches long, sessile, strongly glaucous. Flowers on long pedicels, bluish to lavender, cup-shaped, about 1½ inches wide. Calyx lobes broad at base, abruptly tapering to slender lobes about midway. Saline to fresh marshes, Grand Isle west into Texas. Sandy cheniers and damp depressions. Very abundant near Beaumont. May to October.

**Bottle Gentian, Soapwort Gentian**
*Gentiana saponaria* L.
Gentian family

A perennial herb producing annual stems up to 3 feet tall. Leaves opposite, nearly sessile, perfoliate, dark green above, lighter below, 1½ to 2½ inches long, elliptical to lanceolate, with acute apices. Flowers usually blue, more or less tubular, 1½ inches long in compact clusters, closed at first and then opening slightly. Petals 5, alternate with membranaceous plaits, slightly toothed at apex, about equal to corolla lobes in length. Moist depressions and gullies in pinelands of southeastern Louisiana. Also Texas and Mississippi. Late October into November.

**Sampson's Snakeroot**
*Gentiana villosa* L.
Gentian family

A perennial herb about 18 inches tall with thick, fleshy roots. Leaves opposite, distinctly petioled, punctate below, 1½ to 3 inches long, elliptic-lanceolate, apices obtuse to acuminate. Flowers about 1½ inches long in dense clusters, tubular, gradually opening slightly. Corolla whitish with distinct green veins, lobes longer than the plaits. Occasional to locally abundant in upland or mixed woods in southeastern Louisiana. Also Mississippi. Late September into November.

**Pennywort**
*Obolaria virginica* L.
Gentian family

A perennial herb with annual, succulent, purplish green leafy stems, about 6 inches tall and scaly near the base. Leaves sessile, opposite, obovate, about ½ inch long. Flowers solitary or in small groups, both lateral and terminal, corolla white, petals 4. Rich woods. Scattered, not common, easily overlooked in early stages of growth. Also Texas and Mississippi. March to April.

**Rose-pink, Bitter-bloom**
*Sabatia angularis* (L.) Pursh
Gentian family

An annual herb, seldom over 8 inches tall, with alternate branching and slight wing-angled stems. Leaves ovate to lanceolate, about ½ inch long, thin, sessile, somewhat clasping. Flowers few, terminal on the branches, pink, ¾ inch in diameter, petals obovate. Calyx lobes lanceolate, longer than the ovary, nearly as long as the corolla, acuminate. Calyx ribbed at junction of 2 calyx lobes. Common in grass in the pine flatwoods and in the prairie. Also Texas, Arkansas, and Mississippi. June to July.

**Rose-gentian**
*Sabatia brachiata* Ell.
Gentian family

Annual, stems wing-angled, up to 3 feet tall, opposite abundant branching in top. Lower leaves ovate, to broadly oval 1½ inches long, thin, glabrous, opposite, sessile, upper stem leaves smaller. Flower cluster paniculate branched. Flowers pink, corolla ½ to ¾ inch wide, sepal lobes dilated, linear, longer than calyx proper. Widespread in prairie and pinelands. Also Mississippi. June to September.

**Rose-gentian**
*Sabatia gentianoides* Ell.
Gentian family

Herbaceous plants to 18 inches tall, slightly branched above. Basal leaves about 1 inch long, obovate to oblanceolate. Stem leaves linear, opposite, appressed to spreading, 3 inches long by ⅛ inch wide. Flowers 1 to 1½ inches in diameter, opening nearly flat, with 9 pink to rose obtuse petals. Usually several flowers at stem apex and solitary in upper axils. Widely distributed in moist areas, fresh marshes, prairie, and pinelands. Also Texas and Mississippi. June into August.

Closely allied to *S. dodecandra* (L.) BSP. which usually has a larger flower at the stem apex and broader stem leaves.

*Sabatia macrophylla* Hook.
Gentian family

A perennial herb to 3 feet tall, branched at the summit. Leaves ovate-lanceolate to elliptic-lanceolate, 2½ to 3 inches long, apex acute. Flower cluster, umbrellalike many-flowered. Flowers white about ½ inch in diameter. Bogs and wet pinelands, southeastern Louisiana and Mississippi. June to July.

**Floating Heart**
*Nymphoides aquatica* (Gmel.) Ktze.
Gentian family

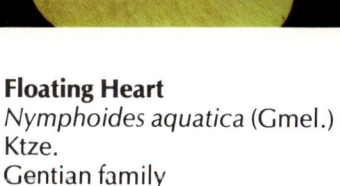

Submerged aquatic with floating leaves. Petioles long, ⅛ inch in diameter with flower cluster or tubers close to sinus of leaf blade. Leaf blades cordate to orbicular, peltately attached, 3 to 6 inches wide, sinus large, basal lobes rounded, smooth, light green above, roughened and purplish below. Flower clusters single or compound. Flowers many, erect at water level, white, wheel-shaped rotate corolla, ½ inch in diameter. Buds and spent flower deflexed. Widespread in fresh marshes, ponds, and sluggish bayous. Texas and Mississippi. May to September.

**Yellow Floating Heart**
*Nymphoides peltata* (Gmel.) Ktze.
Gentian family

An introduced aquatic herb which can take over shallow ponds similar to the agressiveness of water lettuce and water hyacinth. Plants are rooted under water, stems semifloating, creeping, and branching. Leaves opposite, nearly orbicular in shape, about 2 inches in diameter with the petiole at the base of a deep sinus. Leaves subtend an umbel of many flowers. Pedicels up to 4 inches long with a large terminal bud which opens into a deep yellow, almost wheel-shaped corolla about 1¼ inch in diameter. Flower is fragile. Texas and Mississippi. July to September.

### Blue-star
*Amsonia tabernaemontana* Walt.
Dogbane family

A perennial herb up to 3 feet tall, growing in clumps. Leaves alternate, lanceolate to broadly lanceolate, 2 to 3 inches long, glabrous above and below, margin revolute. Flower cluster terminal, many-flowered. Flowers blue externally and light bluish to white internally. Corolla salverform about ½ inch in diameter, glabrous externally. Calyx minute. Fruit a follicle, in pairs, slender, cylindrical, 4 to 6 inches long. Common and widespread, wet sites in alluvial pineland and prairie soils.

*A. ludoviciana* Vail has corolla pubescent externally, and leaves tomentose below.

### Swamp Milkweed
*Asclepias incarnata* L.
Milkweed family

A perennial herb with milky juice, stems up to 6 feet tall, branched above. Leaves opposite, ovate-lanceolate to elliptic-lanceolate, membranous, apex acute to acuminate, base somewhat cordate about 6 inches long. Flower clusters more or less globose umbels, axillary and terminal, many-flowered. Corolla pink to red, reflexed, hood less than ¼ inch long, horn longer and incurved. Fruit a smooth follicle 4 to 5 inches long on erect pedicels. Occasional in swampy places. Also Texas, Arkansas, and Mississippi. July to October.

**Red Milkweed**
*Asclepias lanceolata* Walt.
Milkweed family

Herbaceous perennial with milky juice. Stems slender, 4 to 5 feet tall. Leaves opposite, linear, 3 to 8 inches long, about ¼ inch wide, 3 to 6 pairs. Flowers in umbels, mainly terminal. Corolla reflexed, dull red, about ½ inch long, horn basal, acicular, shorter than the hood. Fruit erect on deflexed pedicels. Fresh to brackish marshes, wet sites in pinelands. Also Texas and Mississippi. May to August.

**Red Milkweed**
*Asclepias rubra* L.
Milkweed family

Perennial. Stem slender, erect to sprawling, juice milky. Leaves opposite, glaucous below, lanceolate, 4 to 6 inches long by ½ to 1 inch wide. Flower cluster umbellate, terminal, and axillary in top nodes. Corolla reflexed, red with tinges of yellow-orange, about ½ inch long, hood lanceolate, about ¼ inch long, horn acicular, shorter than the hood. Follicles erect on deflexed pedicels, smooth. Bogs, marshes, and wet pineland sites. Also Texas, Arkansas, and Mississippi. May to September.

**144**    **Butterfly-weed or Orange Milkweed**
*Asclepias tuberosa* L.
Milkweed family

Herbaceous perennial, stems ascending to erect, 2 to 3 feet tall, strongly hairy. Leaves lanceolate, 2 to 4 inches long, nearly sessile, bright green above and silvery pubescent below. Flowers complex, reflexed sepals and petals, bright orange or yellow, erect hoods and horns in many flat-topped clusters on side of stem. Widespread in the drier upland soils. Generally absent from the alluvial floodplain. It is difficult to transplant. However, it can be propagated by root cuttings and by seed. Also Texas, Arkansas, and Mississippi. May into July.

**White-flowered Milkweed**
*Asclepias variegata* L.
Milkweed family

Perennial. Stem stout, simple, solitary or in small clumps, 30 to 36 inches tall, juice milky. Leaves opposite, ovate to broadly oval, petioled, 4 to 6 inches long, glabrous to scantily pubescent. Flower cluster, large globose umbels 2½ to 3 inches in diameter. Corolla about ½ inch long, bright white with purple area at junction of corolla and hoods. Hoods shorter than horns with an incurved apex. Follicle 5 to 7 inches long, erect on deflexed pedicels. Mixed woods, occasional to locally abundant. Also Mississippi. May to June.

*A. humistrata* Walt. has decumbent to ascending stems with clasping leaves which are infused with pink to lavender colors. Sandy soil, Washington Parish. Also Mississippi.

**Green-flowered Milkweed**
*Asclepias viridiflora* Raf.
Milkweed family

Perennial. Stems usually simple, solitary, 24 to 30 inches tall, juice milky. Leaves opposite, variable, linear to lanceolate to suborbicular, 2 to 5 inches long, leathery. Flower clusters terminal and lateral, subglobose, many-flowered. Corolla yellowish green, reflexed, about ¼ inch long. Hood erect, horns absent. Follicle erect, 4 to 6 inches long. Pinelands, nowhere abundant. Also Texas, Arkansas, and Mississippi. April to August.

**Spider Milkweed**
*Asclepias viridis* Walt.
(= *Asclepidora viridis* (Walt.) Gray)
Milkweed family

Perennial, decumbent to ascending. Stems stout 2 to 3 feet long, solitary but more often in dense clumps, juice milky. Leaves oblong, lanceolate, 3 to 6 inches long, short petiolate, essentially glabrous. Flower cluster usually terminal, 3 to 4 inches broad, occasionally with smaller lateral umbels. Flowers about 1 inch wide, corolla greenish, hoods purplish. Common in prairie, fresh marshes, and mixed woods, pinelands. Also Texas, Arkansas, and Mississippi. March to September.

**Hedge Bindweed**
*Calystegia sepium* (L.) R.Br.
(= *Convolvulus sepium* L.)
Morning-glory family

A variable perennial plant with annual stems which twine into small trees, shrubs, and crops. Leaves triangular, about 2 to 5 inches long, sagittate at base, sharp-pointed at apex. Flower solitary in axils of the leaves, white, 2 to 3 inches in diameter. This has two linear stigmas whereas species of *Ipomoea* have globose stigmas. Occasional on cheniers from Pecan Island to Johnson Bayou and north tier of parishes in Louisiana. Also Texas, Arkansas, and Mississippi. June to September.

**Dodder, Love-vine**
*Cuscuta gronovii* Willd.
Morning-glory family

Plants a tangle of yellow, filamentous, twining stems about $1/16$ inch in diameter. Leaves reduced to minute scales. Seedlings green at first but turn orange after the haustoria or absorbing organs penetrate the host. Flowers white, minute, about $1/8$ inch in diameter, normally with 5 corolla lobes. Capsule globose, not beaked. Seeds black with minute hooks. Widespread on a variety of hosts. Also Texas, Arkansas, and Mississippi. August to October.

Several species occur in Louisiana, one a parasite on white Dutch clover, another, which is a perennial, occurs in the woody stems of *Iva frutescens*.

**Common Morning-glory**
*Ipomoea lacunosa* L.
Morning-glory family

Annual climbing, twining vine with slender stems several feet long. Leaves membranous, alternate, ovate to cordate, entire or with 2 major basal lobes, 1 to 3 inches long, base cordate, apex acute, essentially glabrous. Flower clusters in axils of leaves, usually 3-flower peduncles. Corolla funnel-formed, pink to purplish or white, about 1 inch long by ¾ inch wide. Sepals broadly lanceolate with papillose-based hairs. Widely distributed in Louisiana, especially in disturbed soils and along fence rows. Also Texas, Arkansas, and Mississippi. June to frost.

**Wild-potato, Man of Earth**
*Ipomoea pandurata* (L.) Mey.
Morning-glory family

This morning-glory produces a large, underground tuber. The early colonists had many superstitions about it. Leaves thin, ovate, occasionally fiddle-shaped, 3 to 6 inches long. Flowers white, funnel-formed with a purple tube, 3 to 4 inches in diameter. The ridged sepals distinguish this from close relatives. Widely distributed, usually on upland soils. Louisiana specimens seldom set seed. A host for the sweet potato weevil. Also Texas, Arkansas, and Mississippi. Summer into fall.

### 148 Goat-foot Morning-glory, Railroad Vine
*Ipomoea pes-capre* (L.) Sweet
Morning-glory family

This creeping vine has stems up to 20 feet long. The alternate, thickened leaves are 4 to 6 inches long, nearly orbicular, slightly notched at the apex, hence the common name. The funnel-formed, united corolla is purplish, 2 to 3 inches in diameter. Common but confined to sandy coastal soil above normal high tide. Absent from the interior. Also Texas and Mississippi. May to November.

### Cypress Vine
*Ipomoea quamoclit* L.
Morning-glory family

This is a vigorous annual whose tangled stems twine over the adjoining vegetation. The pinnately divided, ovate leaves are 1½ to 2½ inches long with many threadlike divisions about $\frac{1}{16}$ inch in diameter. The salverform crimson flower is about 1 inch in diameter. Widely distributed, frequently a weed in cultivated fields. Also Texas, Arkansas, and Mississippi. Summer to frost.

*I. coccinea* L. is quite similar but has entire leaves.

**Morning-glory**
*Ipomoea sagittata* Poir.
Morning-glory family

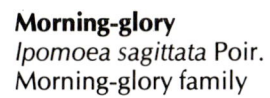

The stems twine over the surrounding vegetation. One of the outstanding features is the sagittate to sagittate-hastate leaves, 2 to 4 inches long. Flower large, purplish, funnel-formed, united corolla, about 3 to 4 inches in diameter. Frequent along streams in the prairie and common on slight elevations in the coastal marshes from the Sabine River to the Pearl River. Also Texas and Mississippi. April into October.

**Beach Morning-glory**
*Ipomoea stolonifera* (Cyrill.) Poir.
Morning-glory family

The trailing stem has thick, fleshy leaves about 2 inches long, elliptic to ovate in shape, conspicuously lobed. The large white, funnel-shaped flower, about 2½ to 3 inches in diameter has a yellowish center. Confined to the sandy beach along the Gulf above high tide level, from the Sabine River to Pearl River. Also Texas and Mississippi. April into November.

### 150 Morning-glory
*Ipomoea hederacea* Jacq.
Morning-glory family

An annual trailing vine with stems several feet long. Leaves alternate, very variable in shape and size, usually broader than long, entire with a cordate base or 3- to 5-lobed, "butterfly"-shaped with apex of central lobe acute and constricted near the junction with the other lobes, up to 5 inches wide by 3 inches long. Flowering peduncle 1 to 3 inches long. Flowers pink, 1½ to 2 inches long, funnel-shaped. Ovary pubescent with long yellow hairs. Sepals linear, about ½ inch long. Widely distributed in disturbed soils, alluvial, prairie and pinelands. Also Texas, Arkansas, and Mississippi. June to frost.

### Tie Vine
*Jacquemontia tamnifolia* (L.) Griesb.
Morning-glory family

The common name refers to the tangle the annual stems make in row crops. Leaves ovate, 4 to 6 inches long. Flower cluster compact, 2 to several light blue flowers about ½ inch in diameter. The long slender sepals are densely covered with hairs which are whitish when fresh but which turn brownish in the herbarium. Widely distributed in cultivated fields and roadsides. Also Texas, Arkansas, and Mississippi. July until frost.

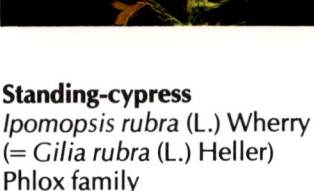

**Standing-cypress**
*Ipomopsis rubra* (L.) Wherry
(= *Gilia rubra* (L.) Heller)
Phlox family

A biennial from a rosette the first year and a coarse stem the second year, up to 8 feet tall. Leaves many, pinnately divided into linear segments about $1/16$ inch wide by $2\frac{1}{4}$ inches long. Flower cluster slender, about 2 feet long above the stem leaves. Flowers numerous, showy, salverform, 1 to $1\frac{1}{4}$ inches long, red on outside, marked with red spots in a yellow background inside the corolla. Sandy soil in roadside thickets. There are no Louisiana records of this plant. Texas and Mississippi. April.

**Blue Phlox**
*Phlox divaricata* L.
Phlox family

Herbaceous perennial with decumbent semievergreen shoots and erect flower stems in clumps, up to 2 feet tall. Leaves sessile, elliptic to ovate, about 2 inches long by ¾ inch wide, pubescent and minutely glandular. Flower cluster flattish, blooms from the center toward the margin. Flowers have a slender tube and a limb about 1 inch wide, color variable, blue to lavender, pinkish or nearly white. Scattered in well-drained, deciduous, mixed woods. Also Texas, Arkansas, and Mississippi. Late March into May.

### 152 Downy or Prairie Phlox
*Phlox pilosa* L.
Phlox family

An herbaceous perennial with ascending to erect stems 1 to 2 feet tall. Leaves linear to lanceolate with rolled margins, opposite near the base of the plant and alternate near the inflorescence. The leaf stems and calyx lobes are coated with soft, usually glandular, hairs. The corolla is about 1 inch in diameter with a conspicuous limb, which is quite variable in color—pink, lavender, bluish. Common and widely distributed in the pine flatwoods as well as the pinehills. Also Texas, Arkansas, and Mississippi. April into May.

### Blue Waterleaf
*Hydrolea ovata* Nutt.
Waterleaf family

A gregarious, perennial herb with spiny stems up to 30 inches tall. Stems and foliage covered with fine, soft pubescence. Leaves alternate, entire, ovate to ovate-lanceolate or elliptic, 1 to 3 inches long, very short petioles with a spine at each leaf node. Flower cluster both terminal and lateral, the latter often long peduncled. Flowers bright blue to purplish, with a rotate corolla about 1 inch in diameter. Sepals less than ½ inch long. Common and widely distributed in wet sites, often in standing water for weeks, fresh marshes, prairie, alluvial, and pineland soils. Also Texas, Arkansas, and Mississippi. August to October.

## Puccoon
*Lithospermum caroliniense* (Gmel.) MacM.
Borage family

Perennial from a woody root, up to 24 inches tall, bushy-branched. Leaves linear to lanceolate, 2 to 3 inches long, rough hirsute with papillose base to hairs. Flower cluster compact then elongating. Flowers bright orange-yellow, gamopetalous with corolla lobes spreading. Fruit white, shiny nutlets. Sandy dry pinelands, occasional. Also Texas, Arkansas, and Mississippi. March to May.

## Narrowleaf Gromwell
*Lithospermum incisum* Lehm.
Borage family

Perennial herbs 8 to 12 inches tall. Leaves 2 to 2½ inches long, linear to lanceolate, petiolate, margin rolled, appressed, strigose, reduced in size up the stem. Flower cluster terminal, occasionally branched. Corolla lemon yellow, tube 1 inch long, limb of 5 lobes, crisped and erose. A Texas species reaching its easternmost distribution on cheniers between Sabine Lake, Cameron, and Pecan Island. April.

**154** **Bluebell**
*Mertensia virginica* (L.) Pers.
Borage family

A perennial herb in small clumps, about 2 feet tall. Basal leaf blades orbicular to broadly, oblong, smooth, on petioles 2 to 5 inches long. Stem leaves reduced, sessile, elliptic 1½ to 2 inches long, glaucous. Flowers blue with shades of pink in buds, corollas 1½ inches long, limb ½ inch in diameter. Grows near Ash Flat, Arkansas. Not reported for Louisiana.

**Black-mangrove, Honey-mangrove**
*Avicennia germinans* (L.) L.
(= *Avicennia nitida* Jacq.)
Black-mangrove family

A large evergreen shrub, occasionally a small tree. Leaves opposite, 1½ to 2½ inches long, elliptic to obovate, dark green above, pale gray tomentose below. Flowers irregular, white with dark spots in corolla. Produces cylindrical pneumatophores after 4 years old. The fruit is flattened, ellipsoidal. The seed coat cracks and exposes a pair of thick green seed leaves and a tiny stem, all ready to grow. Saline to brackish soils along Gulf. Also Texas. July.

**French Mulberry,
American Beauty Berry**
*Callicarpa americana* L.
Vervain family

A large shrub. Leaves opposite, 3 to 10 inches long, ovate to elliptic, petioled, margin crenate-toothed, upper surface rugose, characteristic odor when crushed. Flower cluster axillary, composed of many small flowers with pinkish corollas. Fruit about ¼ inch in diameter, globose, conspicuous red-purple. Widely distributed, more abundant in but not confined to cutover pine-oak-hickory woods along streams. Flowers May to June. Ripe fruit September to November. There is a form with white fruit.

**Rose Vervain, Verbena**
*Verbena canadensis* (L.) Brit.
Vervain family

Perennial with decumbent to erect stems, rooting at the lower nodes, about 20 to 24 inches tall. Leaves opposite, palmately veined, petioled. Blade about 2 inches long, ovate, cleft, double-toothed, upper half of petiole winged, margined. Flower cluster terminal, bracted, many-flowered, flat-topped at first, elongating with age. Corolla united, tube slender, limb about ½ inch in diameter, lavender to purple, occasionally white, corolla tube about twice as long as calyx. Calyx lobes filiform, bracts shorter than calyx. Widely distributed, alluvial to pineland and hill soils. Also Texas, Arkansas, and Mississippi. March to June.

### Tuber Vervain
*Verbena rigida* Spreng.
Vervain family

Perennial with decumbent to ascending stems up to 2 feet tall, forming large colonies. Leaves opposite, sessile, 2 to 3½ inches long, lanceolate to oval, margin coarsely toothed, rough to the touch. Flower clusters terminal and axillary, spikelike, about 2 to 3 inches long. Corolla tube slender, ½ inch long, 2 to 3 times the length of the calyx, limb about ¼ inch wide, deep purple. Widespread, naturalized from South America. Also Texas, Arkansas, and Mississippi. April to October.

### Moss Verbena
*Verbena tenuisecta* Briq.

Perennial with creeping stems, rooting at nodes, forming low, dense mats with short erect flower clusters. Leaves opposite, sessile, triangular, 1 to 1½ inches long, 3-pinnatifid with filiform segments. Flower clusters terminal, short and dense, spreading with maturity. Flowers showy, purple or white with limb about ½ inch wide. Extensive colonies along road shoulders in prairie and pinelands. Naturalized from South America. Also Texas, Arkansas, and Mississippi. March to July.

**Henbit, Dead-nettle**
*Lamium amplexicaule* L.
Mint family

A low annual herbaceous plant up to 18 inches tall. Leaves of two types, basal-petioled, suborbicular, crenately lobed whereas upper stem leaves subtending the flower clusters are sessile. Flowers purple, 2-lipped, upper lip arched and pubescent externally, lower lip spotted, stamens 4. Corolla falling entire, leaving 4 nutlets in a 5-lobed sessile calyx. A winter annual usually killed by hot weather. Abundant in cultivated soils, gardens, and common in lawns. Also Texas, Arkansas, and Mississippi. Late February into May. Considered toxic to livestock in Australia. Seldom grazed here.

**Lemon Beebalm**
*Monarda citriodora* Cerv.
Mint family

Plants to 3 feet tall, branching near the top. Leaves petioled, blades linear, lanceolate to oblong, 2 to 3 inches long by ¼ inch wide, margin finely serrate-punctate. Inflorescence terminal and axillary, a series of compact, more or less sphaerical heads 1½ inches in diameter, placed one above another. Bracts conspicuous, purple-tinted, partly reflexed, terminated with a filiform bristle. Flowers white to pink, dotted with purple spots, extending beyond the bracts, upper lip arched. Widely distributed in Louisiana but not common. Also Texas and Mississippi. May to July.

**158**    **Bergamont, Beebalm**
*Monarda fistulosa* L.
Mint family

Perennial with long rhizomes, stems up to 6 feet tall. Leaves opposite, petioled, ovate-lanceolate, sharply toothed, base rounded, apex acuminate. Flower cluster terminal on all branches, 2 inches in diameter, subtended by leafy bracts ¾ to 1 inch long, marked with purple. Flowers irregular, 2-lipped, about 1½ inches long, lavender, upper lip hairy at apex. Common, widespread in variety of habitats from dry sand to moist pinelands. Also Texas, Arkansas, and Mississippi. May to August.

**Horsemint**
*Monarda punctata* L.
Mint family

A perennial herb about 3 feet tall with opposite branching and leaves. Leaves linear-lanceolate 1½ inches long, serrate, glandular-punctate. Inflorescence consists of several globose heads in an interrupted spike. Bracts lanceolate, about 1 inch long, purplish, apex acute, more conspicuous than the flower. Corolla yellow, strongly arched, distinctly purple-spotted. Widely distributed. Also Texas and Mississippi. July to October.

Closely related to *M. citridora* Cerv. but differs by its yellow corolla, acute bract apex, and the late bloom season.

**Obedient Plant**
*Physostegia digitalis* Small
Mint family

Perennial herb. Stems stout, to 6 feet tall, conspicuously square with prominent margins. Basal leaves, when present, have a broadly winged petiole. Middle stem leaves opposite, clasping, 3 to 4 inches long, becoming smaller up the stem. Flower cluster simple to branched, blooms from the base upwards. Flowers about 1½ inches long, pink with deeper colored spots or lines on the throat of the united bilabiate corolla. Corolla lobes with definite reddish spots and lines. Most abundant in the prairie and longleaf pinelands of western Louisiana. Also Texas. June into July.

**Obedient Plant**
*Physostegia virginiana* L.
Mint family

Plants perennial. Stems 4-angled, 36 to 40 inches tall. Midstem leaves linear to lanceolate, 3 inches long, opposite, clasping base, apex acute, margin sharply serrate. Upper leaves reduced to bracts. Flower cluster elongate, spike-like racemes about 10 inches long, blooms from bottom up. Flower pink, united corolla, 2-lipped, marked with purple spots, ¾ inch long, calyx about ¼ inch long. Common in moist habitats, roadside ditches, open fields, pinelands. Also Texas, Arkansas, and Mississippi. March to May.

### 160 Self-heal, Prunella
*Prunella vulgaris* L.
Mint family

A perennial in large clumps, creeping to decumbent to erect stems up to 24 inches tall. Lower leaves opposite, petioled, blades lanceolate to ovate, margin entire, at times obscurely toothed. Upper leaves sessile, subtending the flower cluster. Flower cluster compact, cylindrical, about 2½ inches long by 1 inch in diameter. Flowers bracted. Corolla 2-lipped, upper lip arching, lower lip 3-lobed, color variable, violet, pink, white, at times bicolored. Widely distributed in Louisiana, absent from the alluvial floodplains. Also Texas, Arkansas, and Mississippi. Late March into June.

### Rough Skullcap
*Scutellaria integrifolia* L.
Mint family

A perennial herb 12 to 20 inches tall with slender, angled stems, simple or branched. Leaves opposite, lower petioled, elliptic-lanceolate, toothed, 1 to 1½ inches long, upper leaves about 1 inch long, linear. Flowers apical, blue-lavender, upper lobe of calyx with a horizontal projection, corolla united, bilabiate, ¾ to 1 inch long, hood and throat enlarged. Widely distributed in moist to dry sites and common in pinelands, but not confined to them. Also Texas, Arkansas, and Mississippi. March to May. Note: the flower appears bluish, but photographs lavender.

### Blue Sage
*Salvia azurea* Lam.
Mint family

A perennial herb, erect to spreading, about 6 feet tall. Basal leaves usually lacking. Lower stem leaves opposite, oblanceolate to narrowly lanceolate, 1 to 2 inches long, petioled, cuneate base, margin minutely serrate, lightly pubescent below. Flower cluster elongated, spikelike, with crowded whorls of flowers. Flowers irregular, bilabiate, deep blue, pure white, or intermediate shades, ¾ inch long, glandular-pubescent externally, tube exserted from 2-lipped calyx. Calyx green, strongly veined, glandular. Common in prairie and pinelands. The white-flowered plants more abundant south of Lake Charles; the blue are more abundant between Lake Charles and Many. Also Texas, Arkansas, and Mississippi. May to October.

**Tuberous Hedge-nettle**
*Stachys floridana* Shuttlw.
Mint family

Perennial from an intermittently constricted, elongate tuber 4 to 6 inches long. Stems decumbent to erect about 2 feet tall. Leaves opposite, petioles reduced in length up the stem, blade ovate-lanceolate, base truncate to cordate, margin distinctly serrate, apex acute. Flower clusters terminal and axillary in the top 4 to 6 nodes. Corolla white to light lavender, irregular, about ½ inch long, upper lip straight, lower lip 3-lobed. Widely distributed as a weed in flower beds. Easily recognized by the white, wormlike tubers. Also Texas and Mississippi. March to June.

*S. tenuifolia* Willd. is very similar, has very short petioles on lower leaves, and lacks the tuber.

**Mountain-mint**
*Pycnanthemum tenuifolium* Schrad.
Mint family

A perennial herb. Stem 4-angled, 24 to 30 inches tall, branched in the upper half, grows in dense colonies. Leaves opposite, linear, 1 inch long by 1/16 inch wide, punctate, strong mint odor. Flower cluster flat-topped. Flower head about ¼ inch long, compact, containing several flowers. Corolla small, white with occasional purple spots, hirsute externally. Calyx with rigid spinelike tips. Widely distributed, roadside, open pine woods. Also Texas, Arkansas, and Mississippi. May to August.

**Wood Sage**
*Teucrium canadense* L.
Mint family

A perennial herb with simple or branched stems 3 to 4 feet tall. Stem leaves opposite, lanceolate, sharply serrate, 3 to 5 inches long, pubescent below. Flower cluster compacted, bracted spike, white, at times with pink lines, glandular pubescent externally. Calyx ribbed, pubescent. Flower unusual, about ¾ inch long, irregular, lower lip conspicuously 3-lobed. Stamens and stigma arch over the lower lip. A polymorphic species, widely distributed on alluvial soils, margins of fresh marshes. Also Texas, Arkansas, and Mississippi. July to October.

**Jimson-weed**
*Datura stramonium* L.
Nightshade family

An erect, much-branched annual, usually glabrous, up to 6 feet tall. Leaves petioled, ovate to elliptic, about 8 inches long, margin wavy, toothed. Flower white, united corolla with 5 short lobes, about 4 inches long and 2 inches broad. Calyx about 2 inches long, reflexed, with the basal portion forming a ring under the fruit. Fruit a spiny capsule, subglobose, about 2 inches long, splits open at apex into 4 parts. Widely distributed, locally common in barnyards, idle areas, and roadsides. Poisonous to man and beast. Also Texas, Arkansas, and Mississippi. July to September.

**164** **Salt Matrimony Vine**
*Lycium carolinianum* Walt.
Nightshade family

Woody shrub with vinelike trailing branches several feet long, with spiny branchlets. Leaves succulent, linear or club-shaped, about 1 inch long, sessile. Flowers wheel-shaped to bell-shaped, lavender to purple about 1 inch in diameter. Fruit a fleshy, red berry about ½ inch in diameter. Common in saline marshes at normal water level onto small elevations. Also Texas and Mississippi. Some flowers nearly every month of the year.

**Ground Cherry**
*Physalis angulata* L.
Nightshade family

A fleshy annual about 2 feet tall, much-branched with angled stems, glabrous. Leaves petioled, 2 to 4 inches long. Blades ovate to ovate-lanceolate, 2 to 4 inches long, margin entire or irregularly toothed. Flower yellow, small, less than ½ inch in diameter, bell-shaped, at times with dark spots at base of petals. Fruiting calyx inflated, 10-ribbed, about 1½ inches long by 1 inch wide, containing a fleshy berry about ½ inch in diameter. A common weed in cultivated fields, roadsides, and fence rows. Also Texas, Arkansas, and Mississippi. June to frost.

### Horse-nettle
*Solanum carolinense* L.
Nightshade family

A perennial herb up to 2 feet tall, armed with coarse yellow prickles on stem and midrib of leaf. Leaves linear to oblong-lanceolate, sinuately lobed, 2 to 3 inches long, stellate-pubescent. Flower cymes few-flowered. Corolla united, wheel-shaped, about 1 inch in diameter, usually white, slightly tinged with purple. Stamens prominent, with short filaments and 2-pored yellow anthers around the stigma. Fruit globose, yellow, about ½ inch in diameter. Widely distributed in disturbed soils, waste places. Also Texas, Arkansas, and Mississippi.

There are several other species. The SILVERLEAF NIGHTSHADE, *S. elaeagnifolium* Cav., has silvery foliage and a distinctly violet corolla. The BUFFALO BUR, *S. rostratum* Dunal, has a yellow corolla, and the plant is copiously armed with straight prickles.

### Jerusalem-cherry
*Solanum pseudocapsicum* L.
Nightshade family

A small, much-branched, leafy shrub, seldom over 2 feet tall. Leaves short-petioled, blades narrowly lanceolate to oblong, 2 to 4 inches long, entire or with wavy margin. Flower solitary in axils of reduced leaves or in few-flowered clusters, wheel-shaped, white about ½ inch in diameter with conspicuous yellow stamens. Fruit a globose, orange to red berry about ¾ inch in diameter. Highly poisonous. Cultivated as a pot plant. Naturalized from Old World, widely distributed, waste places, fence rows, thickets. Also Texas and Mississippi. March to June.

**166** **Pink Foxglove**
*Agalinis fasciculata* (Ell.) Raf.
Figwort family

An annual herb, branched above, up to 24 inches tall, usually a root parasite on grasses. Leaves filiform, needlelike, curved, alternate, about 1 inch long with fascicles of smaller leaves in their axils. Flower pedicel shorter to a little longer than the calyx. Corolla pink, about 1 inch long, campanulate, swollen a little on lower side, corolla lobes spreading, edges pubescent. Widespread and abundant in pineland areas. Also Texas, Arkansas, and Mississippi. August to frost.

*A. purpurea* (L.) Pennell is similar but lacks the fascicles of leaves. *A. maritima* Raf. is quite fleshy and is confined to brackish to saline marshes. *A. oligophylla* Pennell has small flowers less than ½ inch long.

**False Foxglove**
*Aureolaria dispersa* (Small) Pennell
Figwort family

Parasitic on roots of oaks. Stems decumbent to erect, branched above, glaucous, and minutely pubescent. Lower leaves opposite, pinnatifid, coarsely lobed, ovate to lanceolate, 3½ inches long. Stem leaves elliptic-lanceolate, petioled, about 2 inches long, bracteal leaves elliptic to oval, ½ to ¾ inch long. Flowers axillary. Corolla yellow, funnel-formed, limb spreading, about 1 inch wide. Calyx about ¼ inch long, lobes deltoid-lanceolate, erect or reflexed, pedicels about ¼ inch long. Mixed woods, southeastern Louisiana and Mississippi. May to October.

### Indian Paint Brush
*Castilleja indivisa* **Engelm.**
Figwort family

An annual herb with slender taproot. These plants are supposed to be parasitic on grasses. Stems 8 to 12 inches tall. Leaves on lower half of the plant, 2 to 2½ inches long, linear with long attenuate tips, hairy. Dwarfed, proliferating leaves in lower axils. Flower cluster a bracted, apical spike. Bracts about 1 inch long, broadly obovate, tapering to a narrow green base, more conspicuous than the subtended flower. Calyx ovate, tapering to a constricted neck. Corolla relatively small, red. Plants with yellow bracts and corollas are known. Very abundant in east Texas. Featherman reported the only known Louisiana collection from Calcasieu Parish in the 1870's.

### Blue Toadflax
*Linaria canadensis* **(L.) Dumont**
Figwort family

A winter annual with usually simple stems 18 to 24 inches tall. Basal leaves elliptic, about ½ inch long on procumbent basal stems 4 to 6 inches long. Stem leaves linear to needlelike, alternate, about 1 inch long. Flowers in apical racemes, blue, irregular, about ½ inch long, lower lip arched to close throat. Spur slender about ½ inch long. Fruit a many-seeded capsule about ⅛ inch in diameter. A common weed in disturbed soils, flower beds, and idle areas. Also Texas, Arkansas, and Mississippi. March into May.

### Hedge-hyssop
*Gratiola brevifolia* Raf.
Figwort family

Perennial with erect stems 12 to 18 inches tall, usually shorter. Leaves opposite, sessile, clasping, linear-lanceolate, ½ to ¾ inch long by ⅛ inch wide, when toothed, teeth opposite near apex. Flowers 2-lipped, small, about ½ inch long, somewhat funnel-shaped, open end about ¼ wide, white with yellow center. Aquatic in roadside ditches, ponds, and depressions in longleaf pine flatwoods. Also Texas, Arkansas, and Mississippi. April to July.

### Flame Flower
*Macranthera flammea* (Bartr.) Pennell
Figwort family

Stems in compact clumps, 5 to 6 feet tall, much-branched in top. Leaves opposite, pinnatifid, 2 to 3 inches long, margins enrolled. Flower cluster paniculate, individual flowers on deflexed pedicels, with spreading calyx lobes about ½ inch long. Tubular bud opens into an irregular orange-yellow corolla about 2 inches long, which opens near the apex and exposes 4 large stamens with very pubescent filaments and a threadlike style. Locally abundant in pineland bogs and wet sandy soil is southeastern Louisiana and southern Mississippi. August to September. Like other members of this family, it is a root parasite.

## Empress Tree, Princess Tree
*Paulownia tomentosa* (Thunb.) Steud.
Figwort family or Bignonia family

A medium-sized tree, with stout, spreading branches forming an open crown. Mature branches with prominent white lenticels. Leaves deciduous, opposite, cordate-ovate, 4 to 6 inches long, on petioles 2 to 5 inches long, densely tomentose below, scant, simple pubescence above. Flower cluster a pyramidal panicle. Flowers on branching, tomentose peduncles. Calyx large, ½ inch long, tomentose, persistent. Corolla 2-lipped, 1½ to 2 inches long, violet-blue with yellow stripes inside, more or less glandular-pubescent. Fruit a miniature cotton boll, subglobose, about 1 inch long, containing many small papery, winged seeds. Introduced from Asia, escaping from cultivation. More abundant north of a line from Natchez, Mississippi to Natchitoches, Louisiana. Also Texas, Arkansas, and Mississippi. April to May.

## Lousewort
*Pedicularis canadensis* L.
Figwort family

Perennial in clumps with basal rosette of leaves, stems about 12 inches tall. Basal leaves 3 to 5 inches long, irregularly 2-pinnatifid, petioled. Stem leaves smaller in size. Flower cluster terminal, bracted, compact, about 1 to 2 inches long. Corolla 1 inch long, yellow, at times with tints of lavender, irregular, strongly arched, upper lip beaklike. Widely distributed in pine-hardwood areas, generally absent from the alluvial floodplains. Also Texas, Arkansas, and Mississippi. March into May.

### Red Penstemon
*Penstemon murrayanus* Hook.
Figwort family

A perennial herb with 1 to several erect stems up to 6 feet tall. Basal leaves sessile, strap-shaped, 3 inches long. Mid-stem leaves cordate-perfoliate, 3 inches long by 2 inches wide, gradually reduced up the stem. Leaves glaucous with purplish colors. Flowers bright red, about 1 inch long, with an open throat and distinct lobes. A rare plant known only from Winn Parish in Louisiana. Most attempts to transplant this species have failed. It requires a deep, sandy soil. A Texas species which has its eastern limits in Louisiana. April to June.

### Beard-tongue
*Penstemon laxiflorus* Pennell
Figwort family

Perennial herb with slender stems branched in the inflorescence, about 24 inches tall. Basal leaf blades obovate to oval, 1 to 2 inches long, petioled with a winged margin. Stem leaves opposite, sessile, lanceolate. Margin toothed. Flower about ¾ inch long, tubular to slightly widened above, white with tints of lavender. Sterile stamen lightly bearded, exserted from corolla, lying in groove between 2 purple lines. Lips not spreading. Fruit a conical capsule. Common and widespread, prairie, pinelands, terrace soils, wooded areas. Also Texas, Arkansas, and Mississippi. April into May.

*P. tubaeflorus* Nutt. and *P. digitalis* Nutt. are quite similar, both more robust than this species.

## Beard-tongue
*Penstemon tubaeflorus* Nutt.
Figwort family

Perennial. Stems slender about 30 inches tall, branching in top. Stem leaves opposite, sessile, clasping to perfoliate, oblanceolate, oblong, ovate-lanceolate, 3 to 4 inches long, glabrous, membranous, margin entire to slightly serrate. Successive pairs of leaves placed at right angles to each other. Flowers irregular, white with tints of lavender toward base. Corolla trumpet-shaped, abruptly enlarged near base of corolla tube, lobes spreading. Sterile stamen with yellow beard included. Abundant in Louisiana terrace soils, pinelands. Also Texas, Arkansas, and Mississippi. April to June.

## Crossvine
*Bignonia capreolata* L.
Bignonia family

A high-climbing woody vine. Leaves opposite, compound, consisting of a pair of leaflets about 4 inches long with a branching tendril by which the vine climbs. Flowers axillary in clusters, pedicels about 1 inch long, corolla united, 2-lipped with flaring lobes, dark red outside, red to yellow inside with yellowish lobes. Fruit a capsule about 6 inches long, flattened, splits open to release thin papery seeds. Widely distributed in thickets and woods. Also Texas, Arkansas, and Mississippi. April into June.

## 172 Trumpet-creeper, Cow-itch
*Campsis radicans* (L.) Seem.
Bignonia family

A deciduous woody vine with opposite, odd-pinnately compound leaves. Flowers in apical clusters. Corolla tubular to funnel-formed, orange to red, about 4 inches long with 5 spreading or slightly reflexed lobes. Fruit is cigar-shaped, with 2 conspicuous ridges and contains many flattened seeds. Widely distributed in Louisiana. Many erroneously consider it to be poisonous to touch because it is sometimes near hidden poison-ivy. It is frequently cultivated for its attractive flowers, but it is too much a pest in Louisiana to be recommended wholeheartedly. Also Texas, Arkansas, and Mississippi. Late May into November.

## Hardy Catalpa, Northern Catalpa
*Catalpa speciosa* Engelm.
Bignonia family

A large tree with alternate heart-shaped leaves. Leaf blades 6 to 12 inches long, with a petiole about as long as the blade, pubescent below, leaf tips long acuminate. Flower cluster paniculate, several-flowered. Corolla white, united, about 2 inches wide, 2-lipped with 2 yellow strips and several purple-brown spots inside. Fruit a capsule, 16 to 20 inches long. Once extensively cultivated for fenceposts and shade. Escaped from cultivation. Also Texas, Arkansas, and Mississippi. March to April.

SOUTHERN CATALPA, *C. bignonioides* Walt., has larger clusters with many smaller flowers. Blooms about 2 weeks to a month later than the above species.

## Unicorn-plant
*Proboscoidea louisianica* (Mill.) Thell.
(= *Martynia louisianica* Mill.)
Unicorn-plant family

An annual herb, ascending opposite branching near the base, up to 3 feet tall. Stems and leaves sticky, pubescent. Leaves opposite near the base and alternate in the top, cordate to reniform, 1½ to 6 inches wide, margin entire to sinuate. Petioles stout on large leaves. Flowers gamopetalous, bell-shaped, about 2 inches long, lateral, color variable, white to purplish, often spotted with red. Fruit ovoid when green, about 3 inches long, single beak about 4 inches long, hooked apex, drying into a black, dehiscent capsule with 2 curved "claws" from the split beak. Occasional in Louisiana gardens, sandy soils. Also Texas and Mississippi. May to September.

## Pale Blue Butterwort
*Pinguicula caerulea* Walt.
Bladderwort family

Perennial, basal rosette of leaves, flat on the ground, scape terminated with a single flower. Leaves strap-shaped about 2 inches long. Scape filiform 6 to 8 inches long. Flowers light blue to white, ½ to ¾ inch long, lower petal spurred. Scattered in moist branch bottoms. Southern Mississippi. April.

DWARF BUTTERWORT, *P. pumila* Michx., has a pale blue flower ¼ to ½ inch long and a scape seldom over 4 inches long. Widely distributed in Louisiana, moist ditches in prairie, and boggy sites in the pinelands, frequently with pitcher plants. Also Texas and Mississippi. April to October.

**Yellow Butterwort**
*Pinguicula lutea* Walt.
Bladderwort family

Perennial herb with a basal rosette of leaves, up to 3 inches in diameter and a glandular pubescent scape 10 to 12 inches long. Leaves broadly ovate, 1 to 2 inches long, rolled margin, upper surface sticky. Scape terminated with a single yellow flower about 1 inch in diameter. Corolla lobed, united, spurred. Frequent in moist, sandy pinelands, at times in dry sites, southeastern Louisiana. Also Mississippi. February to April. This is an insect-trapping plant.

**Floating Bladderwort**
*Utricularia inflata* Walt.
Bladderwort family

A floating aquatic with 8 radiating, inflated branches, each terminated with tiny ends. Submerged leaves much-divided into filiform segments, with tiny bladders which trap microscopic animal life. Flower scape arises from the center of the radiating floats and bears several yellow flowers about ½ inch in diameter. Most abundant in fresh-water marshes, lakes, and streams in lower Louisiana, but not restricted. Also Texas and Mississippi. May to June.

**Ruellia, Wild Petunia**
*Ruellia caroliniensis* (Walt.) Steud.
Acanthus family

Perennial herb 12 to 14 inches tall. Leaves opposite, on short petioles, blades ovate to elliptic-lanceolate, hirsute, veins distinct, about 4 inches long. Flowers axillary, trumpet-shaped, visually bluish, photographing lavender, occasionally pure white, readily shed when picked. Corolla tube slender, about 1 inch long, limb at right angles to tube, about 1 inch in diameter. Widely distributed in the pinelands. Also Texas, Arkansas, and Mississippi. April to June.

**Buttonbush**
*Cephalanthus occidentalis* L.
Madder family

A much-branched shrub usually under 10 feet tall. Leaves 4 to 6 inches long, opposite or whorled in 3's or 4's, ovate to oblong, dark green above, veins conspicuously depressed. Flower cluster globose, 1 to 2 inches in diameter, composed of radially attached small flowers. Corollas white, stamens exserted like pins in a pincushion. Common, widely distributed, usually in standing water at least part of the year. Also Texas, Arkansas, and Mississippi. June to September.

## Buttonweed
*Diodia virginiana* L.
Madder family

A perennial herb with creeping herbaceous stems which root at the nodes and climb on other plants. Leaves opposite, narrowly linear-lanceolate, 1½ to 2 inches long. Flowers white, tiny, about ½ inch wide. Corolla united with 4 spreading, pubescent lobes. Two or three flowers occur in the axils of each leaf, and the inferior ovary develops into a green somewhat hardened fruit about ¼ inch long which breaks into two segments. Widely distributed. A weed. Also Texas, Arkansas, and Mississippi. June to October.

POOR JOE, *D. teres* Walt., has a smaller pink flower about ⅛ inch in diameter, linear leaves. Also a widespread weed in row crops.

## Tea Berry, Partridge Berry
*Mitchella repens* L.
Madder family

An evergreen, trailing herb. Leaves opposite, petioled, round to broadly ovate, leathery, ½ to ¾ inch in diameter. Flowers in pairs, white, fragrant. Corolla tube slender, slightly longer than the spreading limb of 4 lobes, densely bearded on inside. Fruit a twin berry, red, edible, about ½ inch in diameter. Widely distributed in the mixed woods on drier sites, absent from the Mississippi floodplain. Also Texas, Arkansas, and Mississippi. May to July.

## Bluets
*Houstonia caerulea* L.
Madder family

A perennial plant with very slender rhizomes which produce gregarious masses of slender erect stems. Stems 6 to 8 inches tall. Leaves mostly basal, ovate to oblong, about ¼ inch long, upper reduced. Flower solitary, about ½ inch in diameter, pale blue with a yellow eye, 4-lobed limb. North Louisiana in grassy areas. Also Arkansas and Mississippi. April.

*H. patens* Ell. is a smaller plant, seldom 4 inches tall, and the flower is less than ¼ wide. Common in lawns, and widespread. *H. purpurea* has opposite-ovate, sessile leaves 1 to 2½ inches long with few-flowered terminal clusters. Flowers white sometimes pale purple.

### Japanese Honeysuckle
*Lonicera japonica* Thunb.
Honeysuckle family

A fast-growing twining woody vine widely distributed by birds who have eaten the black fruits. Leaves opposite, ovate to oblong-elliptic, 3 to 4 inches long, generally evergreen. Flowers borne in pairs in axils of leaves. Flowers tubular at base, splitting into 2-lipped irregular lobes at apex, white, fragrant, often with lavender tints on exterior, turning yellow on the second or third day. Fruit in pairs, black berries about ¼ inch in diameter. Introduced from Asia, escaped, and now widely distributed. So abundant that it crowds out native plants. Also Texas, Arkansas, and Mississippi. March until frost.

### Coral Honeysuckle, Trumpet Honeysuckle
*Lonicera sempervirens* L.
Honeysuckle family

A twining woody vine. Leaves opposite, linear-oblong to obovate, dark green above and conspicuously whitened about 3 inches long. Leaves just under the flower cluster perfoliate, elsewhere petioled. Flower cluster with 2 to 6 coral-red, trumpet-shaped corollas, 1½ to 2 inches long. Fruit red, about ¼ inch in diameter. Woods and fence rows, widely distributed. March to November, in mild winters all year. Also Texas, Arkansas, and Mississippi.

## Ash's Arrow-wood
*Viburnum ashei* Bush
Honeysuckle family

A woody shrub with sparse branching, up to 10 feet tall. Leaves simple, opposite, long-ovate to lanceolate, 1½ to 2½ inches long, margin coarsely toothed, 4 to 6 teeth per side. Flower cluster compact, compound cyme. Flowers white, small. Fruit a small spindle-shaped drupe. Widespread and common along streams. Also Texas and Mississippi. Flowers May to June. Fruit July to September.

## Arrow-wood
*Viburnum dentatum* L.
Honeysuckle family

A large shrub about 15 feet tall. Leaves opposite, broadly oval to orbicular, 1½ to 3 inches in diameter, base cordate to truncate, margin coarsely toothed with 7 to 11 sharp-pointed teeth per side, lateral veins conspicuous. Flower cluster a compound cyme. Flowers white, small, stamens exserted. Fruit ovoid to globose, blue-black. Widespread along streams to dry hillsides. Also Texas, Arkansas, and Mississippi. Flowers May to June. Fruit July to September. There is no unanimity among botanists as to the limits and status of the species that grow in Louisiana.

**180** **Possum Haw**
*Viburnum nudum* L.
Honeysuckle family

A woody shrub to about 20 feet tall. Leaves opposite, evergreen, variable in size, oval to oblong or oblanceolate, 2 to 3 inches long, and often on the same branch leaves lanceolate to oblanceolate to 6 inches long. Both sets are petioled, margin revolute, shiny above and glandular-dotted below. Flower cluster flat-topped, compound, about 4 inches wide. Flowers white, small, less than ¼ inch wide, stamens exserted. Fruit a fleshy obovoid drupe, blue to black, a little longer than wide, about ¼ inch long. Common along streams. Also Texas, Arkansas, and Mississippi. Flowers May to June. Fruit September to December.

**Elderberry**
*Sambucus canadensis* L.
Honeysuckle family

A large shrub with a large-diameter white pith in the stems. Leaves pinnately compound. Leaflets 5 to 11, ovate to elliptic, about 10 inches long, fleshy, sharply serrate on margin. Flower cluster compound, on tender growth of season, flat at first, later with drooping sides, up to 12 inches wide. Flowers small, nearly ¼ inch wide, white, conspicuous stamens. Fruit purple-black nearly ¼ inch in diameter. Common all over the state, distributed by birds who eat the fruits. Also Texas, Arkansas, and Mississippi. May to July.

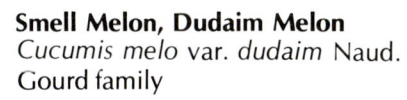

**Smell Melon, Dudaim Melon**
*Cucumis melo* var. *dudaim* Naud.
Gourd family

An annual plant with trailing angular stems several feet long. Stems, petioles, and major veins of leaves covered with bulbous-based bristles. Leaves alternate, broadly deltoid, ovate-oblong, petioled, membranous, about 2 inches long, rough above and below, margin finely toothed. Petioles about 2 inches long with axillary simple tendrils. Flowers both staminate and pistillate axillary, yellow, about ½ inch in diameter. Fruit globose to oblong, 1 inch in diameter, about 2 inches long, yellow when mature, odoriferous. Widespread, most abundant on alluvial soils but not confined, weedy at times. Cultivated for perfumed fruit. Also Texas and Mississippi. August to frost.

**Cardinal Flower**
*Lobelia cardinalis* L.
Bluebell family

A perennial herb 2 to 5 feet tall. Leaves elliptic to lanceolate, 4 to 10 inches long, serrate to crenate, reduced in size upwards. Flowers in a terminal raceme, compact to open, scarlet with a dark anther mass. Corolla tube about 1 inch long, opening into an irregular tip about 1 inch long, 2-lipped with 2 petals in upper lip and 3 in lower lip. United stamens and anthers at stigma level. Widespread in moist sites, stream banks, cypress swamps. Also Texas, Arkansas, and Mississippi. September until frost.

**Pale Lobelia**
*Lobelia appendiculata* A. DC.
Bluebell family

Stem slender, erect, 14 to 24 inches tall, simple or with a few branches. Stem leaves few, sessile, thin, oblong to ovate, 1 to 1½ inches long. Flowers pale blue to white, small, ⅜ inch long, lower lip 3-lobed, longer than the corolla tube. Calyx acuminate, shorter than corolla tube. Widely distributed in pinelands and prairie. Also Texas and Mississippi. April to June.

**Big Blue Lobelia**
*Lobelia siphilitica* L.
Bluebell family

Perennial. Stem erect, with basal offshoots. Leaves thin, variable, ovate, oblong, lanceolate, 3 to 4 inches long, margin irregularly serrate. Flowers in racemes, bracted, blue with white lines in throat, open, ¾ inch long, lower lip spreading. Calyx with leaflike lobes. Widely distributed but not common, alluvial soils. Texas and Mississippi. September to October.

## Venus' Looking-glass
*Triodanis perfoliata* (L.) Nieuwl.
(= *Specularia perfoliata* (L.) DC.)
Bluebell family

Annual herb, stem hairy below, rough to touch above, usually simple, up to 2 feet tall. Leaves ovate, clasping, broader than long, about 1 inch wide. Flowers axillary, about ½ inch wide, purplish with rotate 5-lobed corolla. Fruit a capsule with ellipsoid pore in lower third of capsule. Widely distributed in disturbed soils. Also Texas, Arkansas, and Mississippi. April into May.

*T. biflora* (R. & P.) Greene is similar with smaller leaves, nonclasping, longer than broad, and smaller flower. Apical pores in fruit.

## Yarrow
*Achillea millefolium* L.
Sunflower family

A perennial herb in small clumps, about 2 feet tall. Stems and foliage more or less silky pubescent. Leaves finely 3-pinnately divided into short, slender segments, alternate, 2 to 3 inches long. Flower cluster terminal, flat-topped. Flower head about ¼ inch long. Rays white, disk white. A weed in disturbed soil. Also Texas, Arkansas, and Mississippi. May to July.

### Mayweed, Dog Fennel, Camomile
*Anthemis cotula* L.
Sunflower family

A bushy-branched annual with a strong, distinctive, unpleasant odor. Leaves 3-pinnately divided, divisions threadlike. Flower heads hemisphaeric, about 1 inch wide, with white rays and yellow disk flowers on a conical receptacle. This weed is widely distributed in Louisiana, most abundant on alluvial soils but not confined to them. Common in pastures, levees, and roadsides. Also Texas, Arkansas, and Mississippi. April to July.

## Pussy's Toes
*Antennaria plantaginifolia* (L.) Richardson.
Sunflower family

Perennial from creeping stolons several inches long. Lower leaves about 3 inches long, spatulate to broadly obovate, long-petioled, conspicuous veins, lower surface white from a densely packed pubescence. Flower stalk with greatly reduced leaves, stolon for next year's flower stalk with reduced leaves and at apex expanded leaves. Flower cluster compact 5 to 7 flower heads, each about ⅜ inch wide with all tubular flowers. Pinelands of north Louisiana, colonies scattered but not abundant. Also Texas, Arkansas, and Mississippi. April.

*A. solitaria* Rydb. is distinguished by the presence of one terminal flower head. Rare.

## Lazy Daisy
*Aphanostephus skirrobasis* (DC.) Trel.
Sunflower family

An annual, bushy-branched plant, 14 to 16 inches tall, usually broader than tall, stems and foliage soft pubescent. Leaves numerous, alternate, oblong to obovate, essentially sessile, about 1 inch long, margin entire, apex rounded. Flower heads numerous, solitary on axillary to terminal peduncles, about 3 inches long, head about ½ to ¾ inch in diameter. Ray flowers numerous, white, about ½ inch long by 1/16 inch wide. Disk flowers yellow. Very abundant on sandy beach above high-tide level and cheniers from Grand Isle to Sabine River. Also Texas. March to June and sporadically to frost.

### Fall or Frost Aster
*Aster ericoides* L.
Sunflower family

Plants 24 to 30 inches tall, much branched, erect to reclining. Upper stem and pedicel leaves tiny, ⅛ inch long by ¹⁄₁₆ inch wide, spreading to recurved. Flower heads in racemes or solitary, about ½ inch in diameter, rays white, disk yellow. Widely distributed in Louisiana. Also Texas, Arkansas, and Mississippi. September into November.

### White Aster
*Aster lateriflorus* (L.) Britt.
Sunflower family

A perennial with stems up to 3 feet tall. Basal rosette leaves elliptic to oval, toothed, petiole winged, about 2 inches long. Stem leaves broadly elliptic, 4 inches long, sharply toothed petiole so winged as to be sessile. Inflorescence paniculate, with short axillary branches, and many flower heads. Flower heads bell-shaped, ¼ inch long. Rays white, about twice as long as involucral bracts, disk flowers yellowish. Involucral bracts in several series, marked with spindle-shaped green blotches. Widespread in Louisiana. Also Texas, Arkansas, and Mississippi. September to frost.

## Chain-leaf Aster
*Aster adnatus* Nutt.
Sunflower family

A much-branched perennial herb, 19 to 24 inches tall. Basal leaves about ¾ inch long, practically sessile. Branch and peduncle leaves reduced to tiny scales about ⅛ inch long, rough-setulose, tightly appressed to stem or slightly spreading at tip, chainlike arrangement. Flower head usually terminal with occasional side heads, about ½ inch in diameter. Rays bluish to lavender, disk flowers yellow. Common in pine flatwoods, widely distributed in Louisiana. Also Mississippi. October.

### Aster
*Aster praealtus* Poir.
Sunflower family

A perennial growing in large colonies with much-branched stems up to 8 feet tall. Lower leaves missing. Stem leaves elliptic-lanceolate with single vein ending as a sharp point. Inflorescence leaves ½ to ¾ inch long with bract about ¼ inch long. Flower heads about ½ inch wide with the ray flowers blue at a distance, lavender close-up, about twice as long as the bell-shaped involucre. Involucral bracts marked with fusiform green areas. Abundant and widespread, not confined to any soil type. Also Texas, Arkansas, and Mississippi. September to frost.

### Asters
*Aster* sp.
Sunflower family

The genus *Aster* is a complex genus in which the identification of species is difficult for several reasons. The shape of the basal leaves is important, and these are usually withered and gone by the time the plants are in flower under Louisiana conditions. Botanists have different concepts on the delimitation of species. J. K. Small's *Manual of the Southeastern Flora* lists some 106 species. More recent manuals list fewer. Some names have been placed as synonyms, some have been assigned the status of a variety to another species. It is well known that natural hybridization is occurring, thus producing individuals which are similar to but different from either of the parents. No one knows how many species occur in Louisiana.

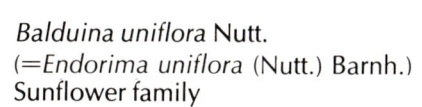

*Balduina uniflora* Nutt.
(=*Endorima uniflora* (Nutt.) Barnh.)
Sunflower family

Perennial 3 to 6 feet tall, usually with a solitary, terminal, daisylike flower head. Leaves alternate, narrowly linear, up to 3 inches long, glandular-punctate, with acute apices. Flower heads long-stalked with yellow ray and disk flowers. Ray flowers 3-toothed. Involucral bracts in several series with individual bracts acute to acuminate. Receptacle honeycombed, compact. Disk flowers pappus of membranaceous scales. Widely distributed in the wet pinelands of southeastern Louisiana. Also Mississippi. August to October.

**Sticktight, Beggar Ticks**
*Bidens aristosa* (Michx.) Britt.
Sunflower family

Annual, stems erect to 4 feet tall, much-branched, glabrous. Leaves opposite, about 3 inches long, pinnate with pinnules toothed, finely strigose. Flower heads numerous, axillary to terminal, 2 per node, 1½ inches broad, opening flat. Ray flower yellow, disk flower dark. Involucre in 2 series, outer green with ciliate margin and some pubescence on back, shorter than the inner. Inner series with a yellow scarious margin. Fruit an achene with an erose and ciliate margin, tapering from top downward. Chaffy bracts with scarious margin. Weedy, ditches, roadsides, and idle fields, marshes, prairie, and pinelands, occasional. Also Texas, Arkansas, and Mississippi. October to frost.

**Nodding Sticktight**
*Bidens cernua* L.
Sunflower family

Plants forming dense, sprawling, decumbent to ascending masses about 3 feet tall. Stems fleshy, rooting at the nodes. Lower stem leaves opposite, connate-clasping, petiole 2 inches long, winged. Blade ovate-lanceolate to linear-lanceolate, about 6 inches long. Upper stem leaves linear to elliptic, 1½ to 2 inches long. Flower head 1½ inches wide, nodding, not erect, disk portion about ½ inch wide. Ray and disk flowers yellow. Fruit an achene with 2 to 4 awns at apex. Widely distributed in wet sites on alluvial soils. Also Texas, Arkansas, and Mississippi. September to frost.

*B. laevis* (L.) B. S. P. is very similar and distinguished by the erect flower head.

**Shepherd's-needle**
*Bidens pilosa* L.
Sunflower family

A much-branched herb up to 6 feet tall with squarish stems and opposite branching. Leaves opposite, 2- to 3-pinnatifid, simple at the base of the plant, petioled, winged. Flower head ¾ inch in diameter with 5 to 8 white rays about ¼ inch long. Disk flowers yellowish. Fruit columnar, 4-angled, with 2 retorsely barbed awns. Locally abundant in orange groves in south Louisiana, along railroad in Baton Rouge. Also Texas and Mississippi. April to October. It differs from most of its relatives by its white rays.

**Rayless Goldenrod**
*Bigelowia nudata* (Michx.) DC.
(= *Chondrophora nudata* (Michx.) Brit.)
Sunflower family

A perennial herb about 2 feet tall with a flat-topped inflorescence, resinous, dotted, and sticky. Basal leaves spatulate, about 3 inches long, long-petioled. Stem leaves linear-spatulate to filiform. Flower heads 1/8 inch long, numerous, no ray flowers, disk flowers yellow, few. Involucral bracts acute to obtuse. Moist pinelands on both sides of the Mississippi River floodplain. Also Mississippi. September to October.

*B. virgata* (Nutt.) DC. has filiform basal leaves and is confined to the Miocene strata in Louisiana, in particular the contact of Fleming siltstone and Catahoula sandstone. This plant was lost for over 100 years.

*Boltonia asteroides* (L.) L'Her.
Sunflower family

Perennial herb up to 4 feet tall with profuse branching. Leaves alternate, 3 to 4 inches long, linear to narrowly lanceolate, apex acute, tapering to the base. Inflorescence leaves linear, about 1 inch long. Flower heads numerous, 3/4 inch in diameter. Ray flowers white to faintly lavender. Disk flowers yellow. Widely distributed in Louisiana, common on alluvial soils but not confined to them. Also Texas, Arkansas, and Mississippi. September to frost.

*B. diffusa* Ell. is similar. The leaves are linear to filiform, about 2 inches long by 1/16 inch wide.

### 192 Sea Ox-eye
*Borrichia frutescens* (L.) DC.
Sunflower family

A woody stoloniferous shrub, forming extensive colonies with usually simple stems 2 to 3 feet tall. Leaves opposite, petioled, obovate to oblanceolate, 2 inches long by 1 inch wide, thick, somewhat fleshy, gray-green, minutely pubescent below. Branched specimens, with smaller leaves 1½ inches long by ¼ inch wide. Flower head terminal on short pubescent peduncle. Ray flower yellow, pistillate. Disk flowers yellow, perfect. Involucral bracts in several series, ovate to deltoid, apiculate. Chaffy bracts with short, rigid spine tip. Common and widely distributed, in the coastal parishes, saline to brackish marshes, wet depressions and on sand ridges. Also Texas and Mississippi. April to June and on to frost.

### Indian Plantain
*Cacalia plantaginea* (Raf.) Shinners
Sunflower family

A stout perennial up to 6 feet tall, glabrous, and more or less glaucous. Basal leaves long-petioled, clasping, with petiole as long as the ovate blades, blades about 7 inches long. Upper stem leaves variable, about 6 inches long by 2 inches wide, short-petioled, margin remotely sinuately toothed. Flower cluster flat-topped, greenish white. Individual flower heads about ½ inch long, all disk flowers, barely opening at apex. Widely distributed, locally abundant, prairie and pineland. Also Texas, Arkansas, and Mississippi. Normal bloom season April to June, out-of-season blooming August to October.

LANCE-LEAVED INDIAN PLANTAIN, *C. Lanceolata* Nutt., has leaves only ½ inch wide.

**Nodding or Musk Thistle**
*Cirsium nutans* L.
Sunflower family

Plants biennial, stems over 6 feet tall, covered with pinnatfid, decurrent-winged leaf bases, with spines on each lobe. Lower leaves up to 16 inches long, glabrous. Upper leaves 4 to 6 inches long, and seminaked scape, lanate-pubescent. Flower head about 3 inches in diameter, consists of several rows of short, broadly lanceolate, stiff involucral bracts, each tipped with a spine. Erect at first, later nods just below the head. Disk flowers only, numerous. Corolla lobes slender, lavender-blue, occasionally white. It is apparently a recent introduction and is most abundant on the Red River alluvial soils. One pasture in Red River Parish has over 100 acres infested with this pest. Also Texas. May to June and sporadically until frost.

**Swamp Thistle**
*Cirsium muticum* Michx.
Sunflower family

Biennial. Stems 3 to 4 feet tall. Lower leaves lanceolate, about 6 inches long, conspicuously spiny, toothed, reduced in size up the stem. Under surface of leaves conspicuously arachnoid. Flower heads 2 to 3 inches long on a seminaked stem. Involucral bracts tight, sticky, with tiny appressed spines. Disk flowers are light lavender with extra long stigmas. Pineland bogs in southeastern Louisiana. Also Texas and Mississippi. August to frost.

### 194 Spiny Thistle
*Cirsium horridulum* Michx.
(= *Carduus spinosissimus* Walt.)
Sunflower family

A winter annual with basal rosettes often 2 feet in diameter. Stems usually solitary, compacted at top, gray, pubescent and about 2 feet tall in prairie and pineland soils. Stems on alluvial soils 6 feet tall, by 2 inches in diameter, hollow, and glabrous. Stem leaves linear to lanceolate, irregularly pinnatifid, spiny on all divisions, 6 to 8 inches long. Flower heads large, terminal, up to 2½ inches long by 3 inches wide, a little smaller on lateral branches in congested clusters. Heads subtended by spiny bracts about 2 inches long. True involucral bracts linear with a weak spine tip. Corolla and stamen color varied, corolla lobes ivory, white, yellow, lavender to red. Stamens white, lavender, yellow, in different combinations with the corolla lobes. Widely distributed in Louisiana pastures, roadsides, idle land. Also Texas, Arkansas, and Mississippi. March into June.

### False Liatris
*Carphephorous pseudo-liatris* Cass.
Sunflower family

Perennial with persistent fibers of old leaf bases. Stems up to 2 feet tall, pubescent. Basal leaves needlelike, 6 to 12 inches long by $1/16$ inch wide. Stem leaves tightly appressed, 1 to 1¼ inches long with ciliate margins. Flower cluster compact, flat-topped, umbellike, or occasionally elongate. Heads bell-shaped, about ½ inch long by ⅜ inch wide. All disk flowers, purple. Involucral bracts strigose-pubescent, lanceolate. Confined to pine flatwoods of southeastern Louisiana and Mississippi. August into November.

## Basket Flower, Star-thistle
*Centaurea americana* Nutt.
Sunflower family

Annual. Stems 6 to 8 feet tall, branched above. Lower stem leaves narrowly obovate, rough, upper stem leaves lanceolate, about 3 inches long, nearly glabrous. Flower heads solitary at ends of branches, 2 to 3 inches wide, bell-shaped. Involucral bracts firmly appressed, several series, outer short fimbriate, inner longer with base entire and apex fimbriate. Corollas pink to white, outer disk flowers larger than inner. No rays. Showy. Occasional in Louisiana. Common in Texas. April into July.

## Sunbonnet
*Chaptalia tomentosa* Vent.
Sunflower family

This plant has the curious habit of closing and nodding the flower head during the night. The next morning it opens to face the sun. Leaves basal, 3 to 6 inches long, elliptic to oblanceolate, green above with a white tomentose lower surface. Scape 3 to 10 inches tall, with terminal flower head. Ray flowers whitish within, often stained purplish on the outside. Disk flowers inconspicuous, whitish to cream colored. Abundant in wet pine flatwoods and in the drier pinehills. Also Texas, Arkansas, and Mississippi. One of the earliest blooming spring flowers, middle of February into April.

### Silk-grass, Golden-aster
*Chrysopsis graminifolia* (Michx.) Ell.
(= *Heterotheca graminifolia* (Michx.) Shinners)
Sunflower family

A perennial herb in small clumps, about 3 feet tall, bushy branched above, stems and foliage densely coated with a silvery white, silky pubescence. Basal leaves linear, clasping, 10 inches long. Upper stem leaves 2 inches long. Flower cluster an open panicle with many flower heads. Flower heads about ½ to ¾ inch wide. Ray flowers yellow. Disk flowers yellow. Involucral bracts with green stripe at apex where it is glandular-pubescent. Frequent in grassy pinelands. Also Texas, Arkansas, and Mississippi. July to frost.

### Tickseed, Coreopsis
*Coreopsis lanceolata* L.
Sunflower family

Perennial, growing in small clumps but forming extensive colonies, stems branching near base, up to 24 inches tall. Basal leaves petioled, blades 3 to 4 inches long, oblanceolate to elliptic to linear. Upper stem leaves 3-pinnatifid or simple, essentially sessile. Flower clusters on long, naked peduncles, solitary, 1 inch in diameter, constricted under the ray flowers. Ray flowers yellow, 3-toothed at apex, disk flowers yellow. Outer involucral bracts shorter than inner. Achenes curved, ⅛ inch long, winged. Chaffy bracts linear. Common along roadsides, widespread in Louisiana prairie and pinelands. Also Texas, Arkansas, and Mississippi. April into June.

*Coreopsis major* Walt.
Sunflower family

An erect perennial herb to 3 feet tall, branched above. Midstem leaves consist of 4 to 6 whorls of 4 to 6 sessile leaflets, lanceolate, occasionally obovate, about 2 inches long, glabrous above and below, margin minutely ciliate. Branches of the flower cluster dichotomously branching with a single flower head per peduncle. Flower heads small, open flat, about 1 inch in diameter. Ray flowers yellow, about ½ inch long. Disk flowers yellow at the apex and reddish near the base. Involucral bracts in two series, the outer strap-shaped, green, the inner narrowly ovate, yellow, obtuse at apex, with thin scarious margin. Relatively rare but found in pinelands. Also Mississippi. May to June.

**Coreopsis**
*Coreopsis tinctoria* Nutt.
Sunflower family

An annual, much-branched herb to 5 feet tall. Leaves opposite, nearly sessile, about 4 inches long, 2-pinnate, with linear segments. Flower heads numerous, about 1¼ inches in diameter. Ray flowers yellow, usually with a basal red blotch, 3-toothed at apex. Disk flowers dark purplish-red. Achenes about ⅛ inch long, wingless. Involucral bracts in 2 series, small. Widespread in disturbed soils. Also Texas, Arkansas, and Mississippi. May into June.

**Purple Cone-flower**
*Echinacea pallida* Nutt.
Sunflower family

Perennial from a taproot, stems usually simple, occasionally branched, up to 3 feet tall, strigose. Basal rosette leaves oblanceolate, petioled, 2 to 3 inches long. Lower stem leaves numerous, linear to narrowly lanceolate, 6 to 8 inches long by ¼ inch wide, strigose, midrib prominent, lateral veins indistinct, petiole winged, sessile. Flower head solitary, hemisphaerical, 1 inch in diameter. Disk flower bracts stiff, sharp-pointed, longer than the disk flowers. Ray flowers drooping, 2 inches long by ⅛ inch wide, lavender to white. Widespread in pinelands and prairie. Also Texas, Arkansas, and Mississippi. May into June.

*E. purpurea* (L.) Moench. has ovate, petioled leaves more than 1 inch wide, and ray flowers have broader, deep purple rays nearly ¼ inch wide.

**Daisy Fleabane**
*Erigeron philadelphicus* L.
Sunflower family

Basal leaves start growing in October to November, and stems up to 30 inches tall are produced from December on, all depending upon the winter freezes. Basal leaves oblanceolate, 5 inches long, petiole winged, semiclasping, blade coarsely toothed, pubescent. Upper stem leaves ovate-lanceolate, 2 to 3 inches long. Flower cluster apical and axillary, buds nodding. Flower heads many, ½ inch in diameter. Ray flowers numerous, white to pink. Disk flowers yellow. Lawns, gardens, idle fields, roadsides, an abundant and widely distributed weed. Also Texas, Arkansas, and Mississippi. December to May.

**White Thoroughwort**
*Eupatorium album* L.
Sunflower family

Perennial, with stems 2 to 3 feet tall. Leaves opposite, elliptic to lanceolate, 2 to 4 inches long, usually folded, coarsely toothed with conspicuous veins on under surface, also punctate and strigose. Flower cluster flat-topped. Individual flower heads nearly ½ inch long with white acuminate involucral bracts and 5 disk flowers per head. Widely distributed in dry pinelands. Also Texas, Arkansas, and Mississippi. August to September.

**Mist-flower, Wild Ageratum**
*Eupatorium coelestinum* L.
Sunflower family

Perennial usually under 3 feet tall. Stems in clumps, ascending to erect, purplish, or greenish. Leaves opposite, petioled, blades ovate to deltoid, about 2 inches long, margin crenate-serrate. Inflorescence much-branched, nearly flat-topped. Heads about ¼ inch long, numerous, bell-shaped with all disk flowers. Styles filiform about twice the length of the corolla, which is conspicuous, bluish, photographing lavender. Involucral bracts green, very small. Common in disturbed soils, margins of wet sites. Also Texas, Arkansas, and Mississippi. August to frost, occasionally April.

### Joe-pye Weed
*Eupatorium fistulosum* Barratt
Sunflower family

Perennial with stems up to 10 feet tall, purplish, hollow, up to ½ inch in diameter. Leaves 4 to 7 in whorled clusters, elliptic in shape, petiolate, 10 to 12 inches long, coarsely serrate, lower surface with tiny yellow glands. Flower cluster paniculate, 3 to 4 or more whorls high, purplish when fresh turning brown with maturity. Involucral bracts in several series, the inner with 2 to 3 conspicuous veins. Widely distributed in Louisiana, along branch bottoms. Also Texas, Arkansas, and Mississippi. July to September.

*E. purpureum* L., also called JOE-PYE WEED, usually has a solid stem with purple coloration only at the nodes.

### Boneset, Thoroughwort
*Eupatorium perfoliatum* L.
Sunflower family

Perennial herb with erect stems to 6 feet tall, opposite branching near the top. Leaves opposite, basally united around the stem, narrowly lanceolate, about 4 inches long, pubescent below. Margin finely crenate-serrate. Flower cluster flat-topped. Heads numerous, small, less than ¼ inch long, crowded. Corolla white. Involucral bracts imbricate, pubescent. Widespread in Louisiana. Also Texas, Arkansas, and Mississippi. August to October.

## False-hoarhound, Roundleaf Eupatorium
*Eupatorium rotundifolium* L.
Sunflower family

Perennial herb usually 3 to 4 feet tall, stems pubescent, opposite branching in flower cluster. Leaves opposite, sessile, or with a very short petiole, ovate-deltoid, 1½ inches long, margin crenately toothed, base generally truncate, 3 major veins. Flower cluster more or less flat-topped, white. Flower heads cylindrical, about ¼ inch long. Widely distributed and abundant, in pinelands and elsewhere. Also Texas, Arkansas, and Mississippi. June into October. Very variable, closely related to *E. sessilifolium* L.

## White Snakeroot
*Eupatorium rugosum* Houtt.
Sunflower family

Perennial in clumps, stem simple to much-branched above, up to 5 feet tall. Leaves opposite, long-petioled, blades 4 inches long, ovate to lanceolate, thin, glabrous, cuneate base, acuminate apex, margin coarsely serrate, smaller up the stem. Flower clusters both terminal and axillary, more or less paniculate. Flower heads small about ¼ inch long, few-flowered. Ray flowers white, disk flowers white. Involucral bracts in one series. Poisonous to livestock, transmissible to humans in milk. Widely distributed in disturbed soils, fields, woodlands. Also Texas, Arkansas, and Mississippi. July to October.

### Yankee-weed, Cypress-weed
*Eupatorium capillifolium* (Lam.) Small
Sunflower family

Perennial, erect stems to 6 feet tall, often in dense clumps. Stem much-branched with a panicle-like arrangement of cascading arched branches. Leaves crowded, 1- to 2-pinnate, divided into many filiform segments about 1 inch long. Flower cluster occupying top ⅓ to ½ of plant. Flower heads small, few-flowered about ⅛ inch long, greenish to white. A common weed in disturbed soils, idle fields, and roadsides. Also Texas, Arkansas, and Mississippi. June to November.

### Indian Blanket
*Gaillardia pulchella* Foug.
Sunflower family

Plants with a definite taproot, perennial(?), branched at base, very leafy with peduncles 12 to 16 inches long. Leaves highly variable, pinnatifid to entire, oblanceolate, up to 3 inches long. Flower head terminal, 2 inches in diameter. Flower color variable, typical rays purple at base with yellow toothed tips. Disk flowers dark purple. Corolla lobes acuminate, glandular, pappus scalelike at base, abruptly tapering to a filiform bristle about as long as corolla tube. Achene hirsute. Very abundant in saline, sandy soils along the Gulf Coast. Also Texas and Mississippi. April to frost.

*G. aestivalis* (Walt.) Rock is similar with yellow or purple disk, ray flowers often absent, leaves linear to spatulate. Pineland in interior. Also Texas and Mississippi.

**Narrow-leaved Sunflower**
*Helianthus angustifolius* L.
Sunflower family

A perennial herb, solitary or growing in dense clumps, with leafy stems to 6 feet tall. Leaves alternate, or occasionally opposite, about 4 inches long, linear, 1/16 inch wide to narrowly lanceolate about ¼ inch wide, surface rough, margins enrolled. Flower heads few, about 2 inches in diameter, terminal on branchlets. Rays yellow, shallowly toothed at apex. Disk flowers dark. Involucral bracts linear, acute to acuminate. Widely distributed, generally absent from the alluvial floodplains. Also Texas, Arkansas, and Mississippi. September into November.

**Sunflower**
*Helianthus annuus* L.
Sunflower family

Annual, stem often 1½ inches in diameter up to 10 feet tall, single or much-branched. Leaves alternate, petioled, shorter to longer than the blade. Blade broadly ovate, 3 to 6 inches long, apex acute, base cordate to cuneate, margin coarsely serrate. Flower head 3 inches in diameter (certain cultivated strains much larger). Ray flowers yellow, oblong, 1½ inches long, numerous. Disk flowers dark. Involucral bracts ovate to lanceolate with ciliate margin and long filiform apex. This crosses with other native species. Widespread, locally abundant in prairie. Also Texas, Arkansas, and Mississippi. May to frost.

## 204 Sunflower
*Helianthus mollis* Lam.
Sunflower family

Perennial herb to 8 feet tall from stout creeping rhizomes, stem and foliage scabrous-hirsute. Leaves opposite below, subalternate above, sessile, ovate-lanceolate to broadly ovate, margin entire, occasionally minutely serrate. Flower head hemisphaerical, pedunculate, axillary. Involucral bracts broadly ovate, ½ to ¾ inch long, pubescent with ciliate margins. Ray flowers yellow, 1 inch long. Disk flowers yellow, each subtended by chaffy scale, pubescent and acute at apex. Achene top-shaped, about ⅛ inch long. Widely distributed and common in prairie and pineland. Also Texas and Mississippi. June to September.

## Cucumber Leaf Sunflower
*Helianthus cucumerifolius* T. & G.
Sunflower family

A perennial herb, stems erect, up to 6 feet tall, leafy to the top, scabrous-hirsute. Leaves alternate, deltoid to ovate-lanceolate, petioled, palmately 3-veined, up to 6 inches long by 3½ inches wide at base. Flower head 2 to 3 inches wide, scattered along top portion of stem. Rays yellow, disk flowers dark purple. Marginal row of involucral bracts ovate with long filiform tips up to ½ inch long. Scattered, prairie and roadsides. Also Texas. July into September.

**Sunflower**
*Helianthus divaricatus* L.
Sunflower family

Perennial with long rhizomes. Stems 3 to 5 feet tall, simple to branched, glabrous to pubescent. Leaves opposite, short-petioled, lanceolate to ovate-lanceolate, glaucous and resin-dotted below to pubescent, rough above. Margin entire to serrate, apex acuminate. Flower heads solitary, about 2 inches in diameter. Rays yellow up to 1½ inches long, distinctly veined. Disk flowers yellow. Involucral bracts in several series, lanceolate with ciliate margin. Common in the pinelands of southeastern Louisiana. Also Mississippi. June to August.

**Sunflower**
*Helianthus heterophyllus* Nutt.
Sunflower family

A perennial herb up to 3 feet tall. Basal leaves, usually 2 pair, opposite, linear to linear-lanceolate or oblanceolate, petioles winged, rough hirsute, margins enrolled strigose, upper leaves on stem reduced, topmost scalelike and alternate. Flower head 3 inches wide, solitary, terminal, on naked stems 6 to 10 inches long. Involucral bracts ovate-lanceolate, apex acuminate, about ½ inch long. Ray flowers yellow, disk flowers dark purple. Widely distributed in pinelands. Also Mississippi. September to November.

**206** **African Daisy, Sunflower**
*Helianthus simulans* Watson
Sunflower family

Perennial, vigorous and aggressive with stems up to 12 feet tall, branched near the top. Lower stem leaves numerous, alternate, 6 inches long by 1 inch wide, rough, hairy above and below, margins usually enrolled, entire. Upper stem leaves narrower, linear to narrowly lanceolate, about ½ inch wide. Flower heads numerous, showy, nearly 3 inches in diameter. Ray flower yellow, disk flowers dark. Involucral bracts long, acuminate. Locally cultivated and escaping from cultivation. Also Mississippi. September to frost.

Determined by C. Heiser.

**Sunflower**
*Helianthus strumosus* L.
Sunflower family

A perennial, much-branched plant up to 10 feet tall, with glaucous stems ½ inch or more in diameter. Cauline leaves 6 inches long on short petiole, scabrous, pubescent, and minutely glandular below, scabrous above, remotely serrate. Upper stem leaves opposite to alternate, about 2 inches long. Flower heads single on peduncles, about 1 inch in diameter. Ray flowers yellow, 1 to 2 inches long, disk flowers yellow. Pubescent-tipped bracts subtending flowers. Weedy, disturbed soils, pinehills. Also Mississippi. August to October. Determined by C. Heiser.

## Bitterweed
*Helenium amarum* (Raf.) Rock
(= *H. tenuifolium* Nutt.)
Sunflower family

A much-branched winter annual or biennial herb 6 to 30 inches tall. Seedling rosette with pinnatifid leaves. Mature plant leaves very numerous, mostly linear not decurrent, 1 to 3 inches long, about ⅛ inch wide, strong odor. Flower heads numerous, ¾ inch in diameter, yellow. Ray flowers toothed at apex, receptacle of disk flowers essentially flat. Widely distributed and very abundant, alluvial as well as hill soils, pastures, idle fields, and fence rows. Imparts a bitter taste to milk when grazed. Also Texas, Arkansas, and Mississippi. June until frost.

## Sneezeweed
*Helenium autumnale* L.
Sunflower family

Perennial herb with stems to 30 inches tall, much-branched, conspicuously winged. Leaves numerous, alternate, linear, elliptic, to ovate, narrowed to a sessile base, and decurrent on stems as wings. Inflorescence leafy. Flower heads numerous, about 1 inch in diameter. Ray flowers 3-toothed at apex, usually drooping. Disk flowers yellow. Involucral bracts narrow, acuminate. Widespread in Louisiana, somewhat weedy. Also Texas, Arkansas, and Mississippi. September to frost.

**208** **Camphor-weed**
*Heterotheca subaxillaris* (Lam.) Brit. & Rusby
Sunflower family

A polymorphic, much-branched, perennial herb up to 4 feet tall, erect or reclining, with scabrous, hispid foliage. Basal leaf blades oval to ovate, 1 to 2 inches long, petiole 1 inch long. Upper stem leaves 1 inch long, short, winged petioles, reduced to short bracts on peduncles. Flower cluster a panicle. Flower head 1 inch in diameter, ray flowers yellow, disk flowers yellow. Widely distributed in disturbed soils, weedy habitats. Also Texas, Arkansas, and Mississippi. March to frost.

*Hymenopappus scabiosaeus* L'Her.
Sunflower family

Perennial with a taproot. Stems solitary, occasionally in small clumps, erect, branched near top. Stems and lower surface of leaves with matted, whitish pubescence. Basal leaves petioled, blades 2 to 3 inches long by ¾ inch wide, entire to pinnatifid. Stem leaves lanceolate to oblanceolate, about 3 inches long, pinnatifid, segments narrow with terminal lobe lanceolate. Inflorescence branched, flower heads at ends of branches, about ½ inch in diameter. Involucral bracts enlarged, conspicuous petallike, white. Disk flowers only, with reflexed corolla lobes. These and the exserted stamen tube purplish. Widely distributed in northern and western Louisiana, pinelands in particular. Also Texas, Arkansas, and Mississippi. April into June.

**Dwarf Dandelion**
**Potato Dandelion**
*Krigia dandelion* (L.) Nutt.
Sunflower family

A low perennial herb from a rhizome, bearing a small tuber, sap milky. Leaves about 3 inches long, forming a flat basal rosette, lanceolate, linear, entire, or dentate to irregularly lobed. Flower scape 3 to 12 inches tall with solitary head. Flower head yellow, about 1 inch in diameter, composed of all ray flowers. Fruit a dark achene about ¼ inch long, ribbed, pappus of capillary bristles. Widespread and common, roadsides, gardens, prairie, pinelands, alluvial soils, frequently in large colonies. March to May.

**Blazing-star, Gay Feather**
*Liatris elegans* (Walt.) Michx.
Sunflower family

A perennial herb from a small corm. Stem pubescent, 3 to 5 feet tall. Lower stem leaves glabrous, punctate, sessile, linear, about 6 inches long, usually deteriorated. Upper stem leaves linear, about 1 inch long, margin thickened, apex apiculate. Flower cluster a spikelike raceme up to 2 feet long. Flower heads about ½ inch long. Corolla purple or white, resinous-dotted. Pappus plumose. Involucral bracts in two series, the outer short, the inner about ½ inch long, dilated at the apex and sides into a petaloid, fringed tip, purplish, midrib strigose. The petaloid bracts are more conspicuous than the corollas. Widely distributed in prairie and pinelands. Also Texas, Arkansas, and Mississippi. August to October.

### Blazing-star
*Liatris squarrosa* (L.) Michx.
Sunflower family

Perennial from a blackish, globose tuber with stems up to 3 feet tall. Basal leaves linear, stiff, 6 inches long by ¼ inch wide, sheathing base. Stem leaves 5 inches long by ⅛ inch wide, spreading, progressively smaller into inflorescence, margin revolute, under surface punctate. Flower cluster spicate, mainly axillary. Flower heads about 1 inch long, few-flowered, corolla and filiform stigmas purple. Outer involucral bracts about ½ inch long, green, spreading, with a sharp acuminate tip (the most distinctive feature). Inner bracts with splashes of purple, margin scarious. Widespread and common in open woods, longleaf pine in particular, and prairie soils. Texas, Arkansas, and Mississippi. July to September.

### Blazing-star
*Liatris squarrulosa* Michx.
Sunflower family

Perennial from a small subglobose corm, 24 to 36 inches tall. Basal leaves oblanceolate, 6 inches long, petioled, margin enrolled, punctate. Upper stem leaves much reduced, linear bracts ½ to 1¼ inches long. Flower cluster spike-like, 20 or more pedunculate heads. Flower heads more or less globose with 15 to 25 disk flowers, purplish corollas, nodding at times. Involucral bracts imbricate, obtuse, recurved, deep purple. Widespread in prairie and pinelands. Also Texas and Mississippi. September to October.

**Blazing-star**
*Liatris pycnostachya* Michx.
Sunflower family

Perennial 4 to 6 feet tall from a corm. Lower leaves linear, 12 inches long by ¼ inch wide, conspicuously reduced below the spikelike purplish inflorescence. Stem usually densely pubescent. Flower heads about ½ inch long, 5 to 7 disk flowers. Stigmas extend beyond the purplish corollas. Involucral bracts reflexed at the purplish tips and ciliate on the margin. The pappus is distinctly barbulate. Widely distributed in the pinelands, absent from alluvial soils. Also Texas, Arkansas, and Mississippi. August to September.

**Climbing Hempweed**
*Mikania scandens* (L.) Willd.
Sunflower family

Annual stems from perennial rootstalks, many feet long, twining and climbing over other vegetation. Leaves opposite, petioled. Blades 2 to 3 inches long, deltoid, ovate, base cordate, glabrous to lightly pubescent. Flower clusters flat-topped to convex, blooming from the outside toward center, sweet-scented. Flower heads small, about ¼ inch long with white to pinkish corollas. Abundant, widespread. Also Texas, Arkansas, and Mississippi. July to frost.

**Bear's-foot**
*Polymnia uvedalia* L.
Sunflower family

A rank perennial herb, 8 to 10 feet tall in favorable habitats. Leaves palmately 3- to 5-lobed, 6 to 12 inches long and nearly as wide. Flower cluster paniculate. Flower heads about 1½ inches in diameter. Ray and disk flowers yellow. Fruit nearly sphaerical, without a pappus. Widely distributed in alluvial and terrace soils. Also Texas, Arkansas, and Mississippi. July to October.

**False Dandelion**
*Pyrrhopappus carolinianus* (Walt.) DC.
Sunflower family

Annual herb to 30 inches tall with basal leaves 10 inches long by 3 inches wide. Stem leaves, 1 or 2, 5 inches long, elliptic-lanceolate, coarsely and remotely toothed. Scape portion solitary or branched. Flower head on long peduncle, all ray flowers yellow, open in morning close by 1 P.M., no disk flowers. Achene long-necked, pappus white when fresh, turning brown with age. A weed of disturbed soils, gardens, and lawns, widely distributed. Also Texas, Arkansas, and Mississippi. March into May, and a few may persist to June.

**Cone-flower**
*Ratibida pinnata* (Vent.) Barnh.
Sunflower family

Perennial with stems up to 3 feet tall, leafy at the base, scapelike at the top, with a few branches. Stem and leaves appressed, pubescent, and glandular-dotted. Basal leaves long-petioled, 6 inches long, pinnate, with 5 to 7 segments. Apical segment lanceolate, 2 to 3 inches long, margin toothed, upper stem leaves reduced to 3 segments. Flower head solitary at ends of branches. Receptacle of disk flowers elongate, ¾ inch long by ½ inch wide, subsphaerical, disk flowers greenish to brown. Ray flowers yellow, spreading to drooping, about 1½ inches long, occasionally toothed at apex. Occasional in black soil prairies in Louisiana. Also Mississippi and Alabama. June to August.

**Cone-flower, Mexican Hat**
*Ratibida columnaris* (Sims) D. Don
Sunflower family

Perennial from a taproot with several stems up to 2 feet tall, foliage confined to lower half, upper portion naked. Leaves alternate, pinnatifid to 2-pinnatifid, middle lobe lanceolate, 3 inches long, lateral lobes linear, appressed-pubescent, margin revolute. Flower cluster terminal, ¾ to 1 inch long. Ray flowers yellow or marked with red-brown near the base, ¾ to 1 inch long, drooping. Disk flowers dark, a trifle longer than the subtending bracts which are white, pubescent at apex. Receptacle erect, cylindrical. Widely distributed in prairie and pinelands. Also Texas, Arkansas, and Mississippi. June to October.

**Clasping-leaf Cone-flower**
*Rudbeckia amplexicaulis* Vahl
Sunflower family

Annual with a taproot. Stems to 5 feet tall, branched above. Leaves sessile, clasping, 6 inches long, reduced above, pale green, elliptic, margin entire to coarsely toothed. Flower cluster solitary at ends of branches, 2 to 2½ inches in diameter. Ray flowers yellow with a red spot at base, occasionally dark maroon to nearly black. Disk flowers on an elongated axis which increases in length with maturity, dark brown. Common and widely distributed on alluvial soils. Also Texas, Arkansas, and Mississippi. April to June.

**Black-eyed Susan**
*Rudbeckia hirta* L.
Sunflower family

Perennial but often flowering the first year, single-stemmed, 18 to 24 inches tall. Second-year plants branched. Stem leaves linear-lanceolate, 3 to 4 inches long, petiole winged, sessile, strongly rough hirsute. Upper ⅓ of stem naked. Flower head terminal, solitary, 1½ to 2 inches in diameter. Rays yellow, radiating to drooping. Receptacle raised hemisphaeric, with dark disk flowers. Involucral bracts green, about ½ inch long, shorter than the rays. Widely distributed in prairie and pinelands, absent from the Mississippi floodplain. Also Texas, Arkansas, and Mississippi. April into July.

**Giant Cone-flower**
*Rudbeckia maxima* Nutt.
Sunflower family

Perennial, over 6 feet tall, leafy at the base, reduced upward to a naked scape. Foliage not glandular-dotted. Lower leaves alternate, with winged petioles about 2 inches long. Blade elliptic-lanceolate, 6 inches long by 2 inches wide. Upper stem leaves sessile, clasping, grading into leaflike bracts 1 to 2 inches long. Flower head terminal, occasionally with a side branch, 2 inches long by 1 inch in diameter. Ray flowers yellow, 1½ inches long, several, shorter than the elongated conical receptacle. Disk flowers dark brown to black, slightly longer than the subtending chaffy bracts. Widespread, prairie and pineland. Also Texas and Arkansas. June to September.

**Bracted Cone-flower**
*Rudbeckia fulgida* Ait.
Sunflower family

Perennial up to 36 inches tall, branched, upper ⅓ naked, leafy below. Stem and leaves copiously hirsute. Lower stem leaves with winged petiole. Upper stem leaves almost sessile, elliptic-lanceolate, 2 to 3 inches long, margin remotely toothed. Flower head solitary at apex of naked stem. Rays yellow, disk dark. Involucral bracts reflexed, longer than ray flowers, ¾ inch long by ⅛ inch wide, apex acute. Occasional, terrace and prairie soils. Also Texas and Mississippi. May into July.

**Yellow Top, Butterweed**
*Senecio glabellus* Poir.
Sunflower family

The color of a few scattered plants is conspicuous, but does not compare to the sheet of gold when one sees acres of them in bloom. A fleshy annual 1 to 3 feet tall. The leafy stem which arises from the basal rosette of leaves may be single or clustered. Leaves irregularly cut and toothed. Flower head nearly an inch in diameter with a single marginal row of yellow rays surrounding a yellow disk. Abundant and widely distributed in alluvial soils, swamps, fresh marshes, cultivated fields, and roadside ditches. Also Texas, Arkansas, and Mississippi. December into May.

*S. aureus* L. has basal leaves which are entire, usually densely woolly. This species occurs in the dryer pinelands in central to north Louisiana. Also Texas, Arkansas, and Mississippi. March into May.

**Rosin Weed**
*Silphium asperrimum* Hook.
Sunflower family

Perennial with stems up to 4 feet tall. Stems and foliage copiously rough strigose. Stem leaves alternate, sessile, 2½ to 4 inches long, ovate-lanceolate, margins entire to lightly toothed. Flower head terminal on stem branches, large, 2 to 3 inches in diameter, opening flat. Ray flowers, about 20, yellow, 1 inch long. Disk flowers yellow. Involucral bracts broadly ovate, ½ inch long, with ciliate margins. Occasional in pinelands of western Louisiana. Also Texas. May to July.

**Compass-plant**
*Silphium laciniatum* L.
Sunflower family

Perennial with coarse stems up to 6 feet tall. Leaves alternate, chiefly near the base of the stem, deeply pinnatifid, longer than broad, 12 to 18 inches long, rough to the touch. Cut stems exude a clear resinous compound. Flower cluster elongate. Flower head, up to 3 inches in diameter, consists of large green ciliate involucral bracts with papillose-based cilia. Ray flowers marginal, yellow, numerous, disk flowers yellowish. Common in prairie soils and extending into longleaf pinelands of central Louisiana. Also Texas, Arkansas, and Mississippi. June to August.

**Rosin Weed**
*Silphium gracile* Gray
Sunflower family

Perennial herb up to 36 inches tall with basal rosette of petioled leaves, scapose stem with 1 or 2 opposite reduced leaves or bracts. Leaf petioles 2 to 3 inches long, blade about 6 inches long, broadly ovate-lanceolate to elliptic, very scabrous, margin obscurely serrate. Flower heads solitary, about 2 inches in diameter, or elongated on peduncles. Involucral bracts broadly ovate about ½ inch long. Ligulate flowers yellow, in two rows, disk flowers numerous, dark. Achene broadly oval, about ½ inch long, surrounded by a marginal wing except for the notched apex. Setae on inner face. Scattered in prairie and longleaf pineland, at times in colonies. Also Texas. April to July.

### Common Goldenrod
*Solidago altissima* L.
Sunflower family

Perennial herb with abundant rhizomes, up to 8 feet tall. Stems and foliage rough to touch. Stem leaves 3 to 4 inches long, narrowly to broadly lanceolate, midnerve prominent, side veins less so, margins serrate in the upper half of the blade. Flower cluster a panicle of curving, more or less secund branchlets, about as wide as long. Stem tip injuries result in multiple, smaller panicles. Flower heads tiny, about 1/8 inch long, yellow. Very common throughout Louisiana, occupying idle land, roadsides. Also Texas, Arkansas, and Mississippi. September to October, and at times until a freeze.

### Sweet Goldenrod
*Solidago odora* Ait.
Sunflower family

Perennial with glabrous, purplish stems 24 to 36 inches tall. Leaves linear to lanceolate, 1¼ to 3 inches long, drooping and twisting, glabrous, fragrant, margin minutely rough. Upper stem leaves and bracts linear, greatly reduced, sometimes with axillary leaves. Flower clusters terminal and axillary, 1-sided, gracefully branched. Flower heads 1/8 to 3/16 inch long, yellow with minute ray and disk flowers. Involucral bracts top-shaped, appressed with dark midrib. Widespread and abundant in pinelands. Also Texas, Arkansas, and Mississippi. September to frost. It is easily recognized by the drooping, slightly twisted leaves. Good deer browse.

### Elm-leaf Goldenrod
*Solidago rugosa* Ait.
Sunflower family

Perennial. Stems pubescent, occasionally unbranched, more often with spreading branches up to 6 feet tall. Midstem leaves elmlike, ovate to lanceolate, up to 2½ inches long by 1 inch wide, deeply rugose above, reticulate and pubescent below, margin serrate. Inflorescence leaves greatly reduced in size, ¼ to ½ inch long, branches slender, spreading. Flower heads secund, about ¼ inch long, yellow ray and disk flowers. Widely distributed and very variable. Also Texas, Arkansas, and Mississippi. August to frost.

### 220 Seaside Goldenrod
*Solidago sempervirens* L.
Sunflower family

Perennial with extensively creeping rhizomes. Stems up to 6 feet tall, glabrous. Flower clusters as solitary wands or much-branched as result of injury to stem tip, glaucous. Lower stem leaves linear, fleshy, 6 inches long with winged petiole, distinct midrib, glabrous. Upper stem leaves appressed, linear to lanceolate, 1¼ inches long with acute to acuminate apices. Bracteal leaves linear, about ½ inch long. Flower cluster elongate, compact, tip curved. Flowers about ¼ inch long, ray and disk flowers yellow. Widespread and abundant along the Gulf Coast from the Pearl River to the Sabine in fresh to saline marshes. Out-of-season blooming in April. Normal blooming, August to November.

### Goldenrod
*Solidago* sp.
Sunflower family

This goldenrod was considered a different species and was chosen to show a branched, spreading inflorescence. The plant has leaves similar to those of *S. altissima*. A restudy of the voucher specimen shows a swollen, gall-like structure just below the point of branching which has been determined as an insect gall. Nearly all the plants in the vicinity had this branching. Identification is complicated because goldenrods are known to hybridize freely, and botanists are not in agreement as to the number of species, synonyms, hybrids, or varieties.

## Goldenrod
*Solidago tenuifolia* Pursh
Sunflower family

Perennial, stem glabrous, 24 to 30 inches tall. Leaves linear to narrowly lanceolate, about 2 inches long by ¼ inch wide, distinct midrib and two indistinct lateral veins, glabrous, margins minutely ciliate, apex long acuminate. No axillary fascicles of leaves. Inflorescence much-branched, flat-topped. Flower heads about ¼ inch long. Ray and disk flowers yellow, ligules small. Involucral bracts in 2 to 3 series, obtuse to acute. Roadsides, widespread in pinelands. Also Mississippi. September to frost.

*S. microcephala* (Greene) Bush is very similar, but has fascicles of tiny leaves in the axils of the stem leaves.

## Blackleaf Goldenrod, Flat-topped Goldenrod
*Solidago nitida* Torr. & Gray
Sunflower family

Perennial, smooth-stemmed plant to 3 feet tall. Basal leaves linear-lanceolate, 6 to 8 inches long, winged petiole, clasping base, glabrous. Upper stem leaves reduced, linear, 1 to 1½ inches long, more or less revolute margin. Inflorescence terminal and axillary, flat-topped, branchlets strigose. Flower heads ¼ inch long, yellow ray and disk flowers. Involucral bracts, 2 to 3 series, appressed, obtuse, distinct midnerve. Widespread in sandy pinelands. Also Texas, Arkansas, and Mississippi. August to frost.

### Sow-thistle
*Sonchus asper* (L.) Hill
Sunflower family

A winter annual with a rosette of spinose margined, usually entire leaves in November. Stem fleshy with a milky juice, single or in clumps, 24 inches tall. Leaves entire to pinnatifid, clasping, obovate to oblanceolate, very variable. Lobes of the blades rounded at the base, margin spinose. Flower cluster of few heads. Flower heads glandular, about ½ inch long, composed of all ray flowers, yellow. Achene ribbed but not rugulose, with a dense white pappus of capillary bristles. Common weed in disturbed soils, abundant in sugarcane and cotton soils. Also Texas, Arkansas, and Mississippi. December to May.

*S. oleraceus* L. has acute blade lobes and achenes with transverse rugulose marking as well as obscure longitudinal ribs.

### Creeping Spilanthes
### Creeping Spot Flower
*Spilanthes americana* (Mutis) Hieron.
Sunflower family

Stems of this perennial herb creep over the ground and root at the nodes. Leaves opposite, petioled, serrate margins, about 2 to 4 inches long. Flowering branches ascending. Flower heads hemisphaeric to campanulate about ¾ inch in diameter. Ray and disk flowers yellow, disk receptacle conical. Very abundant in moist sites, occasional as a weed in gardens and lawns. Also Texas, Arkansas, and Mississippi. April until frost.

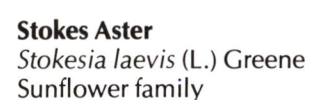

### Stokes Aster
*Stokesia laevis* (L.) Greene
Sunflower family

Perennial in compact clumps. Basal leaves leathery, glandular-punctate, 5 to 12 inches long, petioled. Flower heads from 1 to several on leafy peduncles, 2 to 3 inches in diameter subtended by leaflike bracts. Involucral bracts spinulose, punctate. Ray and disk flowers present, the rays 5-lobed. Color varies from whitish, faint lavender, to deep blue-violet. Very difficult to reproduce on color film. Common in the pinelands of the Florida Parishes. Also Mississippi. May into September. Strains of this have been introduced into cultivation.

### Dandelion
*Taraxacum officinale* Wiggers
Sunflower family

Perennial from a strong taproot. Leaves 4 to 8 inches long, forming a basal rosette, oblanceolate, sharply incised with the segments pointing toward the base. Scapes hollow, elongating in fruit, sap milky. Flower head solitary 1 to 1¼ inches in diameter, yellow, all ray flowers. Fruithead globose with a long-beaked achene and a white pappus parachute. For many years local and not common, now widespread on lawns, roadsides, and idle areas. A bad weed. Leaves edible. Also Texas, Arkansas, and Mississippi. February to June, with an occasional plant in blossom nearly every month of the year.

## 224

**Deer's-tongue, Vanilla-plant**
*Trilisa odoratissima* (Walt.) Cass.
Sunflower family

A perennial herb with stems 4 to 5 feet tall, much-branched in the top. Basal leaves petioled, winged, linear to oblanceolate, 12 inches long. Stem leaves sessile, with winged petiole reduced to small bract in top half of stem. Flower cluster flat-topped, many-flowered. Flower heads small, less than ¼ inch long. Disk flowers only, with purplish corollas. Involucral bracts unequal, with some purple color. Widely distributed in the longleaf pine flatwoods of southeastern Louisiana. Also Mississippi. September to frost. The fragrant foliage is used as a flavoring agent.

**Yellow Crownbeard**
*Verbesina helianthoides* Michx.
Sunflower family

A perennial with erect, sparsely branching stems to 3 feet tall. Stem pubescent, winged. Leaves alternate, subsessile, lanceolate, narrowly ovate, rough on both surfaces, 3 to 6 inches long. Flower heads few, about ¾ inch in diameter. Rays yellow, drooping, up to 1½ inches long. Occasional in pinelands of north Louisiana. Also Texas, Arkansas, and Mississippi. August to October.

**Virginia Crownbeard**
*Verbesina virginica* L.
Sunflower family

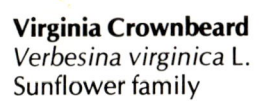

A perennial herb to 10 feet tall, with the stem branched near the summit, pubescent and winged. Leaves alternate, broadly ovate to lanceolate, 7 inches long by 2 inches wide, petioles long, winged. Inflorescence a compact flat-topped cluster. Individual heads about ¼ inch long. Ray flowers, 4 to 5 per head, white, entire, or with slight notch in apex. Disk flowers white with dark stamens. Widely distributed on alluvial and terrace soils, weedy. Also Texas, Arkansas, and Mississippi. August to October.

**Wing-stem Crownbeard**
*Verbesina walteri* Shinners
Sunflower family

Perennial herb to 10 feet tall, branching near the top. Lower stem leaves alternate, broadly elliptic, petioled, 6 inches long. Upper stem leaves essentially sessile, 3 inches long, linear-lanceolate, scabrous above and below, both types with membranaceous wings extending down the stem. Flower cluster paniculate. Flower head ½ inch in diameter, whitish, all disk flowers, no ray flowers. Alluvial soils, somewhat weedy, widespread. Also Mississippi. August to October.

### Ironweed
*Vernonia altissima* Nutt.
Sunflower family

A perennial herb to 8 feet tall with branching near the top. Stem leaves lanceolate, 4 to 6 inches long, base cuneate, apex acuminate, margin serrate, slightly roughened above and essentially glabrous below. Infloresence much-branched, nearly flat-topped, blooming from the center outward. Flower heads campanulate, disk flowers purplish, no ray flowers. Involucral bracts in several series, strongly imbricate, purplish, margin soft, pubescent. Outer pappus scalelike, short, inner of capillary bristles, tawny in color. Widespread and abundant. Alluvial, terrace, and pineland soils. Also Texas, Arkansas, and Mississippi. August to October.

### Ironweed
*Vernonia missurica* Raf.
Sunflower family

A perennial herb, stem stout, much-branched in top portion. Stem leaves 3 to 4 inches long, broadly elliptical, rough above, tomentose below, margin serrate, sessile to short-petioled. Upper stem leaves smaller. Flower cluster essentially flat-topped. Flower heads about ½ inch long, campanulate. Disk flowers only, purplish. Involucral bracts, imbricate, several series, margins soft pubescent and purplish. Pappus of 2 series, outer of small scales and inner of purplish capillary bristles. Locally abundant in prairie and pinelands from Cameron Parish into north Louisiana. Also Texas and Arkansas. August to October.

# Glossary

*Acaulescent.* Stemless or apparently so.

*Achene.* A small, dry, indehiscent, one-seeded fruit.

*Acuminate.* Tapering to a prolonged point.

*Acute.* Distinctly and sharply short pointed.

*Adnate.* Fusion of unlike structures.

*Adventive.* An introduction locally established.

*Alveolate.* Honeycombed.

*Anther.* The pollen-bearing part of a stamen.

*Apical, apicies.* Pertaining to apex or tip, commonly of leaves.

*Arachnoid.* Cobwebby; composed of soft, slender, entangled hairs.

*Awn.* A bristle or slender, stiff appendage, usually terminal.

*Axil.* The upper angle formed between the axis and any organ that arises from it.

*Axillary.* Situated in the axil.

*Banner.* The topmost petal in a legume family flower. Also called standard and vexillum.

*Bi-.* A prefix signifying two, twice or doubly.

*Bifid.* Forked.

*Bipinnate, 2-pinnate.* Twice pinnate, twice divided.

*Blade.* The expanded portion of a leaf or petal.

*Bract.* A reduced leaf. Specialized bracts under the flower head of the Sunflower family are called involucral bracts or phyllaries, and within the heads chaffy bracts are termed *pales* in some books.

*Calcareous.* Pertaining to soil rich in calcium.

*Calyx.* The outer layer of the floral envelope, usually green.

*Cambium.* A layer of dividing tissue that produces wood on the inside and bark on the outside.

*Carpel.* A simple pistil, or one unit of a compound pistil.

*Cauline.* Pertaining to the stalk or stem.

*Chaffy bracts.* Small, thin, specialized bracts subtending the flowers in the Sunflower family, often called *pales*.

*Chasmogamous.* Applies to flowers that open for pollination.

*Cilia.* Marginal hairs.

*Ciliate.* A fringe of marginal hairs, applicable to leaves, bracts, calyx, corolla, and chaffy bracts.

*Clasping.* One structure partly surrounding another, as leaves clasp stems.

*Clavate, clavoid.* Club-shaped. A long structure thickened near the apex.

*Cleistogamous.* Applies to unopened flowers in which self-pollination and fertilization occur.

*Clone.* Vegetatively produced offspring from a single individual.

*Connate.* Similar structures joined together, such as united stamens, united corolla.

*Cordate.* Heart-shaped.

*Corolla.* Inner floral envelope, collective term for petals.

*Corymb.* A short, broad, more or less flat-topped, indeterminate flower cluster, opening from the outside toward the center.

*Crenate.* Applies to blunt or rounded teeth.

*Crisped.* Curled, twisted, or wavy margins.

*Culm.* The jointed stem of grasses and sedges.

*Cultivar.* A cultivated variety, usually by hybridization or selection, abbreviated CV.

*Cyathium.* A specialized, cup-shaped structure bearing stamens and pistil; in the Spurge family.

*Cyme.* A flat-topped flower cluster, blooming from the center to the outside.

*Decumbent.* Lying on the ground, with the top end ascending.

*Decurrent.* Extending downward from point of attachment of leaf, forming a wing or ridge on stem.

*Deflexed.* Turned abruptly downward.

*Dehiscent.* Opens along sutures to shed pollen or seed.

*Dentate.* Having sharp teeth pointing outward on margin.

*Dioecious.* Staminate and pistillate flowers on different plants.

*Discoid.* Shaped like a disc.

*Disk flowers.* The tubular flowers in the center of a flower head in the Sunflower family.

*Entire.* Without lobes or teeth on margin.

*Erose.* Finely lacerate, or minutely and irregularly eroded.

*Escape.* To run wild from cultivation.

*Exserted.* Projecting from; stamens extending beyond corolla.

*Falcate.* Sickle-shaped.

*Falls.* The sepals in the Iris family.

*Fascicle.* A close cluster or bundle of flowers, leaves, stems, or roots.

*Filiform.* Threadlike, very long, and slender.

*Flabelliform.* Fan-shaped.

*Floricane.* The flowering stems of dewberries and blackberries.

*3-foliolate.* Having three leaflets on a compound leaf.

*Follicle.* A dry fruit developing from a simple ovary which opens along one suture.

*Fusiform.* Spindle-shaped. Tapering each way from the center.

*Gamopetalous.* Petals united into one unit and fall entire.

*Glabrous.* Smooth, devoid of any hairs.

*Glaucous.* A thin waxy layer, easily rubbed off, causes stems and leaves to be gray-green or bluish green.

*Hastate.* Arrowhead-shaped, with two divergent basal lobes.

*Haustoria.* Specialized structure for absorbing food from a host by some parasitic plants.

*Head.* A dense flower cluster, composed of sessile flowers crowded on a short axis.

*Hispid.* Pubescent with stiff spreading hairs.

*Horn.* A specialized structure associated with the hood and pistil in the Milkweed family.

*Imbricate.* Overlapping, like shingles on a roof.

*Inflorescence.* A complete flower cluster, including axis and bracts.

*Involucel.* A diminutive term; bracts subtending a definite part of the inflorescence in contrast to the involucre which subtends the whole.

*Involucre.* A cluster of bracts subtending an inflorescence or flower.

*Keel.* The two lower petals in legume flowers. Also a sharp longitudinal ridge.

*Lanceolate.* Lance-shaped; narrow, tapering to both ends with the broadest part below the middle.

*Lenticel.* A small corky spot on the bark of young, woody twigs. Functions in gas exchange.

*Ligule, ligulate.* A strap-shaped corolla in the Sunflower family.

*Linear.* Elongate and narrow with parallel sides.

*Linear-lanceolate.* Intermediate between linear and lanceolate.

*Margin.* The edge of a blade.

*Monoecious.* Stamens and pistil in separate flowers on the same plant.

*Naked.* Wanting in the usual covering, such as without leaves, bracts, perianth, or pubescence.

*Naturalized.* Established in a region in which it is not native.

*Ob-.* Prefix signifying in a reverse direction, attached to adjectives referring to shape.

*Obcordate.* Inversely heart-shaped, with notch at apex.

*Oblanceolate.* Reverse lanceolate, with broadest part near apex.

*Obovate.* Reverse ovate, broader near the apex.

*Ocrea.* A sheath around the stem

just above the leaf, derived from the stipules. Chiefly in the Smartweed family.

*Ovate.* Egg-shaped, widest below the middle, broader than lanceolate.

*Palmate.* With three or more lobes arising at same point.

*Pandurate.* Fiddlelike.

*Panicle.* A bushy, branched inflorescence type in which the primary branches are racemose and the flowers pedicellate.

*Papilla- ae.* Nipple-shaped projections.

*Papillose.* Bearing papillae.

*Pappus.* The modified limb of the calyx in the Sunflower family, consisting of bristles, awns, crown, and scales.

*Pedicel.* The stalk supporting a single flower.

*Peduncle.* The stalk supporting a flower cluster.

*Perfect* (flower). Having stamens and pistil.

*Perianth.* A collective term used when the sepals and petals closely resemble each other.

*Petiole.* The stem of a leaf.

*Phyllaries.* The modified bracts subtending the flower head in the Sunflower family.

*Pilose.* Having long soft hairs.

*Pinna.* Part of a pinnatifid or pinnately compound leaf.

*Pinnate.* Having leaflets on two sides of a rachis.

*Pinnatifid.* Partly divided. Divisions not extending to the midrib of the leaf.

*2-, 3-pinnate.* Pinna divided the second or third time.

*Pinnules.* Diminutive of pinna, applied to segments of a 2-pinnate leaf or 2-pinnatifid leaf.

*Pistil.* The central reproductive organ, usually composed of stigma, style, and ovary. Develops into fruit.

*Pistillate.* Having only pistils. Unisexual.

*Pneumatophores.* A structure developing on or from roots. Associated with gas exchange.

*Pollen.* The fertilizing dustlike powder produced in anthers.

*Polymorphic.* Having several or many forms.

*Primocane.* The first-year stem of dewberries and blackberries.

*Puberulent.* Minutely pubescent.

*Pubescence.* Hairiness, without reference to structure.

*Pubescent.* Covered with short, soft hairs.

*Punctate.* Marked with tiny dots or translucent glands.

*Raceme.* An unbranched axis with pedicelled flowers.

*Rachis.* An axis bearing leaflets or flowers.

*Raphides.* Needle-shaped crystals found in some plants.

*Ray flowers.* Flowers with strap-shaped corolla found in the Sunflower family.

*Receptacle.* The expanded apex of a floral axis that bears flower parts. Diagnostic in the Sunflower family.

*Reniform.* Kidney-shaped. Applies

to leaves.

*Retorsely.* Bent backward or downward.

*Revolute.* Leaf margin rolled toward the lower side.

*Rhombic.* Quadrangular in shape with the lateral angles obtuse.

*Rotate.* Wheel-shaped, circular, and flat.

*Rugose.* Roughened or wrinkled with sunken veins.

*Rugulose.* Finely wrinkled.

*Saggitate.* Arrow-shaped, lanceolate to ovate with two basal lobes nearly at right angles to the long axis.

*Salverform.* Having a slender gamopetalous corolla tube and an expanded corolla limb.

*Saprophyte.* A plant which lacks chlorophyll and lives off decaying organic matter.

*Scape.* A leafless peduncle from the ground, possibly having scales or bracts.

*Scarious.* Thin, dry, membranous, not green.

*Secund.* One-sided. Flowers so arranged that they appear to have originated on one side of an axis.

*Sepal.* One separate segment of the calyx.

*Serrate.* Forward-pointing, sharp teeth; like a handsaw.

*Sessile.* Lacking a petiole or stalk.

*Sinus.* The space between two lobes of a leaf.

*Spadix.* A thick, fleshy spike bearing flowers, chiefly in the Arum family.

*Spathe.* A large, fleshy bract surrounding the spadix.

*Spicate.* Arranged in a spike.

*Spike.* An elongate inflorescence with sessile flowers.

*Spinulose.* Having little thorns.

*Spur.* A hollow appendage on calyx or corolla.

*Standard.* The uppermost petal of the flower in the legume family. Also the petals of iris.

*Stellate.* Star-shaped, radiating like points of a star.

*Sterile.* Barren. Applies to staminate and neuter flowers.

*Stigma.* The terminal portion of a pistil for reception of pollen.

*Stipitate.* Having a stalk or stipe.

*Stolon.* A horizontal stem which develops new plants at apex or nodes.

*Strigose.* Having straight, stiff, appressed hairs.

*Style.* A portion of the pistil between the stigma and the ovary.

*Sub-.* A prefix meaning more or less, nearly, somewhat.

*Subauriculate.* With nearly earlike appendages.

*Subglobose.* Nearly ball-shaped.

*Suborbicular.* Almost circular in outline.

*Subtend.* Attached below.

*Subulate.* Awl-shaped.

*Tendril.* A stringlike modification of a stem, leaf, or stipule used for support.

*Tetrad.* A group of four objects.

*Tomentose.* Matted, soft, woollike hairiness.

*Torulose.* A condition of expanded areas alternating with constricted areas, as in a bean pod.

*Trichome.* A hair or bristle growing from the epidermis.

*Umbel.* An inflorescence type with all flower pedicels originating at the same point.

*Verticillate.* Whorled with two or more leaves at a node, usually with several whorls in a row.

*Villous.* Provided with long, soft, shaggy hairs.

# Suggested References

Bailey, L. H. 1968. *Manual of Cultivated Plants.* New York: MacMillan Co. Mainly cultivated plants as well as those which have escaped from cultivation.

Correll, D. S., and M. C. Johnston. 1970. *Manual of Vascular Plants of Texas.* Renner, Tex.: Texas Research Foundation. A comprehensive and highly technical book on the flora of Texas.

Dormon, Caroline. 1934. *Wild Flowers of Louisiana.* New York: Doubleday, Doran & Co. The first publication on Louisiana wildflowers. Illustrated with 73 original paintings and many outline drawings. Nontechnical. Out of print.

———. 1958. *Flowers Native to the Deep South.* Baton Rouge: Claitor's Book Store. Illustrated with 67 original paintings and many line drawings. Nontechnical.

Gleason, H. A. 1952. *The New Britton and Brown Illustrated Flora of the Northeastern United States and Adjacent Canada,* 3 vols. New York Botanical Garden. An important technical work, with line drawings for most of the species described.

Justice, W. S., and C. R. Bell. 1968. *Wildflowers of North Carolina.* Chapel Hill: University of North Carolina Press. Contains 400 color reproductions, of which about 200 species occur in Louisiana. Nontechnical.

Radford, A. E., H. E. Ahles, and C. R. Bell. 1968. *Manual of the Vascular Flora of the Carolinas.* Chapel Hill: University of North Carolina Press. A technical manual, with line drawings and range maps. Superficially covers Louisiana.

Rickett, H. W. 1968. *Wildflowers of the United States,* Vol. II, *The Southeastern States;* Vol. III, *Texas.* New York: McGraw-Hill. Superbly illustrated with 1700 color plates in Vol. II and about as many in Vol. III. Nontechnical.

Small, J. K. 1933. *Manual of the Southeastern Flora.* New York: by author. Very technical.

Wharton, May E., and R. W. Barbour. 1971. *The Wildflowers and Ferns of Kentucky.* Lexington: University of Kentucky Press. 500 color illustrations. Nontechnical.

Wills, Mary M. (paintings), and H. S. Irwin (text). 1961. *Roadside Flowers of Texas.* Austin: University of Texas Press. Contains 257 painted illustrations. Semipopular.

# Index

*Acacia farnesiana*, 72
Acanthus family, 175
*Acer drummondii*, 106
*Acer rubrum*, 106
*Acer rubrum* var. *tridens*, 106
*Achillea millefolium*, 183
Adder's Mouth orchid, 40
*Aesculus pavia*, 107
African Daisy, 206
*Agalinis fasciculata*, 166
*Agalinis oligophylla*, 166
*Agalinis purpurea*, 166
Agave, 24
*Agave virginica*, 24
Ageratum, Wild, 199
*Aletris aurea*, 14
*Aletris farinosa*, 15
*Aletris lutea*, 15
*Allium arenicola*, 16
*Allium canadense*, 15
Aloe, American, 24
*Alophila drummondii*, 29
Alsike Clover, 90
Amaryllis family, 24–27
*Amelanchier arborea*, 66
American Aloe, 24
American Beauty Berry, 155
American Holly, 105
American lotus, 49
American Mistletoe, 45
*Amianthium muscaetoxicum*, 16

*Amorpha fruticosa*, 72
*Amsonia tabernaemontana*, 144
*Anemone caroliniana*, 50
*Antennaria plantaginifolia*, 185
*Antennaria solitaria*, 185
*Anthemis cotula*, 184
*Aphanostephus skirrobasis*, 185
*Apios americana*, 73
Apple, Southern Crab, 69
Apple, Wild Crab, 69
*Aralia spinosa*, 122
*Argemone albiflora*, 58
*Argemone mexicana*, 58
*Arisaema dracontium*, 8
*Arisaema triphyllum*, 8
*Aronia arbutifolia*, 69
Arrow-arum, 10
Arrowhead, 5
Arrow-wood, 179
Arrow-wood, Ash's, 179
Arum family, 8–10
*Asclepias humistrata*, 144
*Asclepias incarnata*, 142
*Asclepias lanceolata*, 143
*Asclepias rubra*, 143
*Asclepias tuberosa*, 144
*Asclepias variegata*, 144
*Asclepias viridiflora*, 145
*Asclepias viridis*, 145
*Asclepidora viridis*, 145
*Ascyrum stans*, 112

**235**

Ash family, 135
Ash's Arrow-wood, 179
*Asimina parviflora*, 57
*Asimina triloba*, 57
Asphodel, False, 70
Aster, 188
*Aster adnatus*, 187
*Aster, Chain-leaf*, 187
*Aster ericoides*, 186
Aster, Fall, 186
Aster, Frost, 186
*Aster lateriflorus*, 186
*Aster praealtus*, 188
*Aster* sp., 188
Aster, Stokes, 223
Aster, White, 186
*Astragalus distortus*, 73
*Astragalus soxmaniorum*, 73
Atamasco-lily, 27
*Aureolaria dispersa*, 166
*Avicennia germinans*, 154
*Avicennia nitida*, 154
Azalea, Orange-flowered, 131
Azalea, Summer, 132
Azalea, Swamp, 132
Azalea, Wild, 132

*Balduina uniflora*, 189
Banana-lily, 49
*Baptisia leucantha*, 74
*Baptisia leucophaea*, 74
*Baptisia nuttalliana*, 75
*Baptisia sphaerocarpa*, 75
*Bapitisia viridis*, 75
Barberry family, 53
Barb-d'Espanole, 12
Basket Flower, 195
Beach Morning-glory, 149
Bean, Coral, 79
Beard Flower, 41
Beard-tongue, 170, 171
Bear-grass, 23
Bear's-foot, 212
Beautyberry, American, 165
Beebalm, 158
Beebalm, Lemon, 157
Begger Ticks, 189
Bellwort, 21
Bergamont, 158
Berry, June, 66
Berry, Partridge, 176
Berry, Tea, 176
*Bidens aristosa*, 189
*Bidens cernua*, 190
*Bidens laevis*, 190
*Bidens pilosa*, 190
Big Blue Lobelia, 182
*Bigelowia nudata*, 191

*Bigelowia virata*, 101
Bigleaf Magnolia, 56
*Bignonia capreolata*, 171
Bignonia family, 169, 171–72
Bindweed, Hedge, 146
Birds-foot violet, 115
Birthwort family, 46
Bitter-bloom, 139
Bitterweed, 207
Black Cherry, 68
Black-eyed Susan, 114
Blackleaf Goldenrod, 221
Black Locust, 86
Black-mangrove, 154
Black-mangrove family, 154
Black-medic, 82
Black Titi, 104
Bladderwort family, 173–74
Bladderwort, Floating, 174
Blanket, Indian, 202
Blazing-star, 209–10
Bloodwort family, 28
Bluebell, 154
Bluebell family, 181–83
Bluebonnet, 80
Bluebonnet, Texas, 82
Blue-eyed-grass, 33
Blue-flag, Southern, 31
Blue Larkspur, 53
Blue Phlox, 151
Blue Sage, 161
Blue-star, 142
Blue Toadflax, 167
Bluets, 177
Blue Waterleaf, 152
Blue Water-lily, 49
Bog Batchelor Button, 99
*Boltonia asteroides*, 191
*Boltonia diffusa*, 191
Boneset, 200
Borage family, 153–54
*Borrichia frutescens*, 192
Bottle Gentian, 137
Bottomland Hardwoods and Cypress Region, xxxv
Bracted Cone-flower, 215
*Brasenia schreberi*, 50
Brush, Indian Paint, 167
Buckeye family, 107
Buckthorn family, 107
Buckwheat Tree, 104
Buffalo Clover, 91
Bull Nettle, 100
Bur Clover, 82
Bur-reed, 3
Bur-reed family, 3
Bush Lespedeza, 80
Buttercup, 121

Buttercup, Early, 52
Buttercup, Spiny, 52
Butterfly Pea, 77
Butterfly-weed, 144
Butterweed, 216
Butterwort, Dwarf, 173
Butterwort, Pale Blue, 173
Butterwort, Yellow, 174
Buttonbush, 175
Button Snake-root, 124
Buttonweed, 176

*Cacalia lanceolata*, 192
*Cacalia plantaginea*, 192
Cactus family, 117–18
California Bur-clover, 82
*Callicarpa americana*, 155
*Callirhoë papver*, 108
*Calopogon pallidus*, 35
*Calopogon puchellus*, 35
*Calycocarpon lyoni*, 54
*Calystegia sepium*, 146
Camass, 22
*Camassia scilloides*, 17
Camellia family, 111
Camellia, Silky, 111
Camellia, Wild, 111
Camomile, 184
Camphor-weed, 208
*Campsis radicans*, 172
Candy Root, 98, 99, 100
Canna family, 23
*Canna flaccida*, 23
*Canna glauca*, 24
Canna, Golden, 23
*Canna indica*, 24
*Canna X generalis*, 24
Caper family, 59
Cardinal Flower, 181
*Carduus spinosissimus*, 194
Carolina Lily, 18
Carolina Mallow, 111
Carolina Moonseed, 54
Carpetweed family, 47
*Carphephorous pseudo-liatris*, 194
Cashew family, 102–103
*Cassia fasciculata*, 76
*Castilleja indivisa*, 167
*Catalpa bignonioides*, 172
Catalpa, Hardy, 172
Catalpa, Northern, 172
Catalpa, Southern, 172
*Catalpa speciosa*, 172
Catchfly-gentian, 137
Catesby Lily, 17
Cat-tail, 3
Cat-tail family, 3
Cat-tail, narrow-leaved, 3

*Ceanothus americanus*, 107
Cedar, Salt, 114
Celestial-lily, 33
*Centaurea americana*, 195
*Centrosema virginianum*, 77
*Cephalanthus occidentalis*, 175
*Cercis canadensis*, 76
Chain-leaf Aster, 187
*Chaptalia tomentosa*, 195
Cherokee Rose, 70
Cherry, Black, 68
Cherry, Ground, 164
Cherry-laurel, 68
Chickasaw Plum, 67
Chickasaw Rose, 70
Chinese Wisteria, 95
Chinquapin, Water, 49
*Chionanthus virginica*, 135
Chokeberry, Red, 69
*Chondrophora nudata*, 191
*Chrysopsis graminifolia*, 196
*Cirsium horridulum*, 194
*Cirsium muticum*, 193
*Cirsium nutans*, 193
Clasping-leaf Cone-flower, 214
Classification, xiii
*Cleistes divaricata*, 35
Clematis, 51
*Clematis crispa*, 51
*Clematis dioscorelfolia*, 51
*Clematis virginiana*, 51
*Cleome houtteana*, 59
Clethra, 127
*Clethra alnifolia*, 127
*Cliftonia monophylla*, 104
Climbing Hempweed, 211
Climbing Hydrangea, 64
Clover, Alsike, 90
Clover, Buffalo, 91
Clover, Crimson, 90
Clover, Ladino, 92
Clover, Persian, 91
Clover, Rabbit Foot, 89
Clover, Red, 93
Clover, Sour, 83
Clover, Sweet, 83
Clover, White Dutch, 92
*Cnidoscolus stimulosus*, 100
*Cnidoscolus texanus*, 101
*Cocculus carolinus*, 54
Colic-root, 14, 15
*Colocasia antiquorum*, 8
*Commelina erecta*, 12
Common Goldenrod, 218
Common Morning-Glory, 147
Compass-plant, 217
Cone-flower, 198, 213, 214, 215
Cone-flower, Bracted, 215

Cone-flower, Clasping-leaf, 214
Cone-flower, Giant, 215
Cone-flower, Purple, 198
Congo-root, 87
*Conium maculatum*, 123
*Convolvulus sepium*, 146
*Cooperia drummondii*, 25
Copper-colored Iris, 30
Copper-lily, 24
Coral Bean, 79
Coral Honeysuckle, 178
Coral-root, Crested, 39
Coreopsis, 196, 197
*Coreopsis lanceolata*, 196
*Coreopsis major*, 197
*Coreopsis tinctoria*, 197
Cork-screw Orchid, 42
*Cornus florida*, 126
*Corydalis halei*, 58
*Corydalis micrantha*, 58
"Cowcumber," 56
Cow-itch, 172
Cow-lily, Yellow, 48
Cow-pea, Wild, 94
Crab Apple, 69
Crane-fly Orchid, 41
*Crataegus opaca*, 66
Creeping Spilanthes, 222
Creeping Spot Flower, 222
Cress, Water, 60
Crested-coral-root, 39
Crimson Clover, 90
*Crinum americanum*, 25
Crossvine, 171
Crowfoot family, 50–52
Crownbeard, Virginia, 225
Crownbeard, Wing-stem, 225
Crownbeard, Yellow, 224
Cucumber Leaf Sunflower, 204
Cucumber tree, 55
*Cucumis melo* var. *dudain*, 181
Cupseed, 54
*Cuscuta gronovii*, 146
Custard-apple family, 57
Cypress Vine, 148
Cypress-weed, 202
*Cypripedium calceolus*, 36
Cyrilla, 104
*Cyrilla racemiflora*, 104

Daisy, African, 206
Daisy Fleabane, 198
Daisy, Lazy, 185
Dandelion, 223
Dandelion, Dwarf, 209
Dandelion, False, 212
Dandelion, Potato, 209
Dangleberry, 127

*Datura stramonium*, 163
*Daubentonia punicea*, 77
*Daubentonia texana*, 78
Day-flower, 12
Day-flower family, 12
Dead-nettle, 157
Deciduous Holly, 105
*Decumaria barbara*, 64
Deerberry, 130
Deer Pea, 94
Deer's-tongue, 224
*Delphinium carolinianum*, 53
*Desmanthus illinoensis*, 78
Devil's-walking-stick, 122
Dewberry, Southern, 71
*Dichromena colorata*, 6
Dicotyledons, Part II., 43
*Diodia teres*, 176
*Diodia virginiana*, 176
Dodder, 146
Dogbane family, 142
Dog Fennel, 184
Dogwood family, 126
Dogwood, Flowering, 126
Dollar-grass, 125
Downy Phlox, 152
*Drosera brevifolia*, 62
*Drosera filiformis*, 63
*Drosera intermedia*, 63
Drummond Rain-lily, 25
Drummond Red Maple, 106
Drummond's Evening Primrose, 120
*Duchesnea indica*, 67
**Dudaim Melon, 181**
Dwarf Butterwort, 173
Dwarf Dandelion, 209

Early Buttercup, 52
*Echinacea pallida*, 198
*Echinacea purpurea*, 198
*Eichhornia crassipes*, 13
Elderberry, 180
Elephant's-ear, 8
Elm-leaf Goldenrod, 219
Empress Tree, 169
*Endorima uniflora*, 189
**Epidendrum conopseum, 36**
*Erigeron philadelphicus*, 198
*Eriocaulon decangulare*, 11
*Eryngium integrifolium*, 123
*Eryngium yuccifolium*, 124
Eryngo, 123
*Erythrina herbacea*, 79
*Eupatorium album*, 199
*Eupatorium capillifolium*, 202
*Eupatorium coelestinum*, 199
*Eupatorium fistulosum*, 200
*Eupatorium perfoliatum*, 200

*Eupatorium purpureum*, 200
*Eupatorium rotundifolium*, 201
Eupatorium, Roundleaf, 201
*Eupatorium rugosum*, 201
*Euphorbia bicolor*, 101
*Euphorbia dentata*, 102
*Euphorbia heterophylla*, 102
*Euphorbia marginata*, 101
*Eustoma exaltatum*, 137
*Eustylis purpurea*, 29
Evening Primrose, 120
Evening Primrose family, 120–21
Evergreen Magnolia, 56

Fall Aster, 186
False Asphodel, 20
False Dandelion, 212
False Foxglove, 166
False Garlic, 18
False-hoarhound, 201
False Liatris, 194
Featherbells, 16
Feather, Gay, 209
Fennel, Dog, 184
Fetterbush, 128
Figwort family, 166–71
Fire Pink, 47
Flags, 31
Flag, Southern blue, 32
Flag, Yellow, 32
Flame Flower, 168
Flat-topped Goldenrod, 221
Fleabane, Daisy, 198
Floating Bladderwort, 174
Floating Heart, 141
Flower, Flame, 168
Flowering Dogwood, 126
Fly Catcher, 61
Fly Poison, 16
*Forestiera acuminata*, 135
Foxglove, False, 166
Foxglove, Pink, 166
*Fragaria virginiana*, 67
Fragile Cactus, 118
Fragrant Ladies' Tresses, 42
French Mulberry, 155
French Tamarisk, 114
Fringetree, 135
Frog Belly, 61
Frog's-bit family, 5
Frost Aster, 186
Fumitory family, 58

*Gaillardia aestivalis*, 202
*Gaillardia pulchella*, 202
Garlic, False, 18
*Gaura lindheimeri*, 121
Gay Feather, 209

*Gaylussacia frondosa*, 127
*Gelsemium sempervirens*, 136
General Ecology, xxv
Gensing family, 122
Gentian family, 137–40
*Gentiana saponaria*, 137
*Gentiana villosa*, 138
*Gentiana virginica*, 138
*Geranium carolinianum*, 97
*Geranium dissectum*, 97
Geranium family, 97
German Iris, 31
Giant-blue Iris, 31
Giant Cone-flower, 215
*Gilia rubra*, 151
Ginger, Wild, 46
Glossary, 227
Goat-foot Morning-glory, 148
Goat's Rue, 89
Gold-crest, 28
Golden Alexanders, 126
Golden Aster, 196
Golden Canna, 23
Golden-club, 9
Golden-corydalis, 58
Goldenrod, 220–21
Goldenrod, Blackleaf, 221
Goldenrod, Common, 218
Goldenrod, Elm-leaf, 219
Goldenrod, Flat-topped, 221
Goldenrod, Seaside, 220
Goldenrod, Sweet, 218
Golden-torch, 9
*Gordonia lasianthus*, 112
Gourd family, 181
Grancy-greybeard, 135
Grape family, 108
Grass-pink Orchid, 35
*Gratiola brevifolia*, 168
Green Adders-mouth Orchid, 40
Greenbriar, 19, 20
Green Dragon, 8
Green-flowered Milkweed, 145
Green-fly Orchid, 36
Gromwell, Narrowleaf, 153
Ground Cherry, 164

*Habenaria blephariglottis*, 37
*Habenaria ciliaris*, 37
*Habenaria cristata*, 38
*Habenaria leucophea*, 37
*Habenaria nivea*, 38
*Habenaria repens*, 39
*Habranthus texanus*, 24
Hairy Lupine, 81
Hairy Pepperbush, 127
Halberd-leaved Rose-mallow, 110
*Halesia diptera*, 134

**239**

*Hamamelis virginiana*, 65
Hard-heads, 11
Hardy Catalpa, 172
Hat, Mexican, 213
Haw, Possum, 180
Hawthorn, Riverflat, 66
Hazel, Witch, 65
Heath family, 127–33
Hedge Bindweed, 146
Hedge-hyssop, 168
Hedge-nettle, Tuberous, 162
*Helenium amarum*, 207
*Helenium autumnale*, 207
*Helenium tenuifolium*, 207
*Helianthus augustifolius*, 203
*Helianthus annuus*, 203
*Helianthus cucumerifolius*, 204
*Helianthus divaricatus*, 205
*Helianthus heterophyllus*, 205
*Helianthus mollis*, 204
*Helianthus simulans*, 206
*Helianthus strumosus*, 206
Hempweed, Climbing, 211
Henbit, 157
Herbertia, 29
*Herbertia caerulea*, 29
Hercules-club, 122
*Heterotheca graminifolia*, 196
*Heterotheca subaxillaris*, 208
*Hexalectris spicata*, 39
*Hexastylis arifolia*, 46
*Hibiscus aculeatus*, 109
*Hibiscus lasiocarpos*, 109
*Hibiscus militaris*, 110
Hog Peanut, 73
Holly, 105
Holly, American, 105
Holly, Deciduous, 105
Holly family, 105–106
Honey-mangrove, 154
"Honeysuckle," 132
Honeysuckle, Coral, 178
Honeysuckle family, 178–80
Honeysuckle, Japanese, 178
Honeysuckle, Trumpet, 178
Horsebean, 84
Horsemint, 158
Horse-nettle, 165
Horse Sugar, 133
*Houstonia caerulea*, 177
*Houstonia patens*, 177
*Houstonia purpurea*, 177
Huckleberry, Tree, 133
Huckleberry, Winter, 133
Huisache, 72
Hyacinth, Water, 13
Hyacinth, Wild, 17
*Hydrangea arborescens*, 64

Hydrangea, Climbing, 64
Hydrangea, Oak-leaved, 64
*Hydrangea quercifolia*, 64
*Hydrocotyle bonariensis*, 124
*Hydrocotyle umbellata*, 125
*Hydrocotyle verticillata*, 125
*Hydrolea ovata*, 152
*Hymenocallis eulae*, 26
*Hymenocallis occidentalis*, 26
*Hymenopappus scabiosaeus*, 208
*Hypericum cistifolium*, 113
*Hypericum densiflorum*, 113
*Hypoxis hirsuta*, 26

*Ilex decidua*, 105
*Ilex longipes*, 105
*Ilex opaca*, 105
*Ilex vomitoria*, 106
*Illicium floridanum*, 55
Indian Blanket, 202
Indian Paint Brush, 167
Indian Pink, 136
Indian Pipe, 129
Indian Plantain, 192
Indian-turnip, 8
Indigo, 79
*Indigofera suffruticosa*, 79
Introduction, ix
*Ipomoea coccinea*, 148
*Ipomoea hederacea*, 150
*Ipomoea lacunosa*, 147
*Ipomoea pandurata*, 147
*Ipomoea pes-capre*, 148
*Ipomoea quamoclit*, 148
*Ipomoea sagittata*, 149
*Ipomoea stolonifera*, 149
*Ipomopsis rubra*, 151
*Iris brevicaulis*, 30
Iris, Copper-colored, 30
Iris family, 29–34
*Iris foliosa*, 30
*Iris fulva*, 30
*Iris germanica*, 31
Iris, Giant-blue, 31
*Iris giganticaerulea*, 31
*Iris pseudoacorus*, 32
Iris, Red, 30
*Iris virginica*, 32
Iris, Zig-zag-stem, 30
Ironweed, 226
*Itea virginica*, 65

Jack-in-the-pulpit, 8
*Jacquemontia tamnifolia*, 150
Japanese Honeysuckle, 178
Japanese Virgins-bower, 51
Japanese Wisteria, 95
Jerusalem-cherry, 165

Jerusalem thorn, 84
Jimson-weed, 163
Joe-pye Weed, 200
Jug-plant, 46
June-berry, 66

*Kalmia latifolia*, 128
Knotweed family, 46
*Kosteletzkya virginica*, 110
*Krigia dandelion*, 209
Kudzu, 85

*Lachnanthes caroliana*, 28
Ladies' Tresses, Fragrant, 42
Ladino Clover, 92
Lady Lupine, 81
Lady's-slipper, Yellow, 36
*Lamium amplexicaule*, 157
Lance-leaved Indian Plantain, 192
Langlois Violet, 114
Larkspur, Blue, 53
Laurel-cherry, 68
Lazy Daisy, 185
Lead Plant, 72
Leafy Three Square, 6
Leather flower, 51
Legume family, 72–95
Lemon Beebalm, 157
Leopard Lily, 17
*Lespedeza capitata*, 80
*Leucothe racemosa*, 128
*Liatris elegans*, 209
Liatris, False, 194
*Liatris pycnostachya*, 211
*Liatris squarrosa*, 210
*Liatris squarrulosa*, 210
"Lilie," 13
*Lilium catesbaei*, 17
*Lilium michauxii*, 18
Lily, Atamasco, 27
Lily, Celestial, 33
Lily, Copper, 24
Lily family, 14–23
Lily, Pinewoods, 29
Lily, Spider, 26
*Linaria canadensis*, 167
Lindheimer Cactus, 118
*Liriodendron tulipifera*, 54
*Listera australis*, 40
*Lithospermum caroliniense*, 153
*Lithospermum incisum*, 153
Lizard's-tail, 45
Lizard's-tail family, 45
*Lobellia appendiculata*, 182
Lobelia, Big Blue, 182
*Lobelia cardinalis*, 181
Lobelia, Pale, 182
*Lobelia siphilitica*, 182

Loblolly Bay, 112
Locust, Black, 86
Logania family, 136
Longleaf Pine Region, xxxiv
*Lonicera japonica*, 178
*Lonicera sempervirens*, 178
*Lophiola americana*, 28
Lousewort, 169
Love-vine, 146
*Lupinus subcarnosus*, 82
*Lupinus texensis*, 80
*Lupinus villosa*, 81
*Lycium carolinianum*, 164
*Lyonia lucida*, 128

Macartney Rose, 70
*Macranthera flammea*, 168
Madder family, 175–77
*Magnolia acuminata*, 55
Magnolia, Bigleaf, 56
Magnolia, Evergreen, 56
Magnolia family, 55–57
*Magnolia grandiflora*, 56
*Magnolia macrophylla*, 56
Magnolia, Southern, 56
*Magnolia virginiana*, 57
*Malaxis uniflora*, 40
Mallow family, 108–11
*Malus angustifolia*, 69
Mamou, 79
Mandrake, 53
Mangrove, Black, 154
Man-of-Earth, 147
Maple family, 106
Maple, Red, 106
Maple, Swamp Red, 106
Marsh Region, xxx
*Martynia louisianica*, 173
May-apple, 53
Mayhaw, 66
Maypop, 116
Mayweed, 184
Meadow Beauty, 119
*Medicago arabica*, 82
*Medicago hispida*, 82
*Medicago lupulina*, 82
Melastoma family, 119
*Melilotus alba*, 83
*Melilotus indica*, 83
Melon, Dudaim, 181
Melon, Smell, 181
*Mertensia virginica*, 154
Mexican Hat, 213
Mexican Poppy, 58
Mexican Primrose, 121
*Mikania scandens*, 211
Milk-weed, 102
Milkweed family, 142–45

Milkweed, Green-flowered, 145
Milkweed, Orange, 144
Milkweed, Red, 143
Milkweed, Spider, 145
Milkweed, Swamp, 142
Milkweed, White-flowered, 144
Milkwort family, 98–100
Mimosa, 83
*Mimosa strigillosa*, 83
Mint family, 157–63
Mist-flower, 199
Mistletoe, American, 45
*Mitchella repens*, 176
Mock Bishop's-weed, 125
Mock-orange, 68
*Modiola caroliniana*, 111
*Monarda citriodora*, 157
*Monarda fistulosa*, 158
*Monarda punctata*, 158
Monocotyledons, Part I, 1
*Monotropa hypopithys*, 129
*Monotropa uniflora*, 129
Moonseed, Carolina, 54
Morning-glory, 149–50
Morning-glory, Common, 147
Morning-glory family, 146–50
Moss Verbena, 156
Mountain Laurel, 128
Mountain-mint, 162
Mulberry, French, 155
Musk Thistle, 193
Mustard family, 59

Narrowleaf Gromwell, 153
Narrow-leaved Cat-tail, 3
Narrow-leaved Sundew, 63
Narrow-leaved Sunflower, 203
Narrow-leaved Vetch, 93
*Nasturtium officinale*, 60
*Nelumbo lutea*, 49
*Nemastylis geminiflora*, 33
*Nemastylis purpurea*, 29
*Neptunia lutea*, 84
New Jersey Tea, 107
Nightshade family, 163–65
Nodding Indigo, 74
Nodding Sticktight, 190
Nodding Thistle, 193
Nomenclature, xii
Northern Catalpa, 172
*Nothoscordum bivalve*, 18
*Nothoscordum fragrans*, 18
*Nuphar advena*, 48
Nuttall Indigo, 75
*Nymphaea elegans*, 49
*Nymphaea mexicana*, 49
*Nymphaea odorata*, 48
*Nymphoides aquatica*, 141

*Nymphoides peltata*, 141

Oak-leaved Hydrangea, 64
Oak, Poison, 102
Obedient Plant, 159
*Obolaria virginica*, 138
*Oenothera biennis*, 120
*Oenothera drummondii*, 120
*Oenothera speciosa*, 121
Onion, Wild, 15, 16
Opopanax, 72
*Opuntia compressa*, 117
*Opuntia drummondii*, 118
*Opuntia lindheimeri*, 118
Orange Candy Root, 99
Orange Flowered Azalea, 131
Orange Milkweed, 144
Orchid, Crane-fly, 41
Orchid, Cork-screw, 42
Orchid family, 35–42
Orchid, Grass-pink, 35
Orchid, Green Adders-mouth, 40
Orchid, Green-fly, 36
Orchid, Snowy, 38
Orchid, Water-spider, 39
Orchid, White fringed, 37
Orchid, Yellow Crested, 38
Orchid, Yellow Fringed, 37
*Orontium aquaticum*, 9
Ottelia, 5
*Ottelia alismoides*, 5
*Oxalis rubra*, 96
*Oxalis stricta*, 97
*Oxalis violacea*, 96
Ox-eye, Sea, 192
*Oxydendrum arboreum*, 130

Paint Brush, Indian, 167
Pale Blue Butterwort, 173
Pale Lobelia, 182
Palmetto, 7
Palmetto, Saw, 7
Palm family, 7
*Parkinsonia aculeata*, 84
Parrots Pitcher-plant, 62
Parsley family, 123–26
*Parthenocissus quinquefolia*, 108
Partridge Berry, 176
Partridge Pea, 76
*Passiflora incarnata*, 116
*Passiflora lutea*, 117
Passion Flower, 116
Passion Flower family, 116–117
Passion Flower, Yellow, 117
*Paulownia tomentosa*, 169
Pawpaw, 57
Pawpaw, Dwarf, 57
*Pedicularis canadensis*, 169

*Peltandra sagittaefolia*, 9
*Peltandra virginica*, 10
Pencil Flower, 88
Pennywort, 138
Pennyworts, 125
*Penstemon digitalis*, 170
*Penstemon laxiflorus*, 170
*Penstemon murrayanus*, 170
*Penstemon tubaeflorus*, 171
Penstemon, Red, 170
Peppernush, Hairy, 127
Persian Clover, 91
*Petalostemon candidum*, 85
*Petalostemon purpureum*, 85
Petunia, Wild, 175
Phlox, Blue, 151
*Phlox divaricata*, 151
Phlox, Downy, 152
Phlox family, 151–52
*Phlox pilosa*, 152
Phlox, Prairie, 152
*Phoradendron flavecens*, 45
*Phoradendron tomentosum*, 45
*Physalis angulata*, 164
*Physostegia, digitalis*, 159
*Physostegia virginiana*, 159
Pickerel-weed, 14
Pickerel-weed family, 13–14
Pineapple family, 12
Pineland Hibiscus, 109
Pine Lily, 17
Pinesap, 129
Pinewoods-lily, 29
*Pinguicula caerulea*, 173
*Pinguicula lutea*, 174
*Pinguicula pumila*, 173
Pink family, 47
Pink, Fire, 47
Pink Foxglove, 166
Pink, Indian, 136
Pink Sensitive Briar, 88
Pipewort, 11
Pipewort family, 11
*Pistia stratiotes*, 10
Pitcher-plant, 61
Pitcher-plant family, 61–62
Pitcher-plant, Parrots, 62
Pitcher-plant, Purple Trumpet, 61
Plantain, Indian, 192
Plantain, Lance-leaved Indian, 192
Plum Chickasaw, 67
*Podophyllum peltatum*, 53
*Pogonia ophioglossoides*, 41
Pogonia, Spreading, 35
Poison Hemlock, 123
Poison Ivy, 103
Poison Oak, 102
Poison Sumac, 103

*Polycodium stamineum*, 130
*Polygala cruciata*, 98
*Polygala cymosa*, 98
*Polygala incarnata*, 99
*Polygala nana*, 100
*Polygala ramosa*, 98
*Polygonum hydropiperoides*, 46
*Polygonum orientale*, 46
*Polygonum punctatum*, 46
*Polymnia uvedalia*, 212
*Pontederia cordata*, 14
Poor Joe, 176
Poppy family, 58
Poppy-mallow, 108
Poppy, White Prickly, 58
Possom Haw, 180
Possom-haw, 105
Potato Dandelion, 209
Prairie Phlox, 152
Prairie Region, xxxiii
Prickly Pear Cactus, 117
Primrose-leaved Violet, 115
Prince's Feather, 46
Princess Tree, 169
*Proboscidea louisianica*, 173
Prunella, 160
*Prunella vulgaris*, 160
*Prunus angustifolia*, 67
*Prunus caroliniana*, 68
*Prunus serotina*, 68
*Psoralea psoralioides*, 87
*Ptilmium capillaceum*, 125
*Ptilmium costatum*, 125
Puccoon, 153
*Pueraria lobata*, 85
Purple Cone-flower, 198
Purple Prairie-clover, 85
Purple Trumpet Pitcher-plant, 61
Purple Vetch, 94
Pussy's Toes, 185
*Pycanthemum tenuifolium*, 162
*Pyrrhopappus carolinianus*, 212
*Pyrus angustifolia*, 69
*Pyrus arbutifolia*, 69

Quamasia. *See* Camassia, 19

Rabbit Foot Clover, 89
Railroad Vine, 148
Rain-lily, Drummond, 25
Rain-lily, White, 27
*Ranunculus fascicularis*, 52
*Ranunculus muricatus*, 52
*Ratbida columnaris*, 213
*Ratbida pinnata*, 213
Rattlebox, 78
Rattlesnake-master, 124

Rayless Goldenrod, 191
Red Buckeye, 107
Redbud, 76
Red Chokeberry, 69
Red Clover, 93
Red Iris, 30
Red Maple, 106
Red Milkweed, 143
Red Penstemon, 170
Red Rattlebox, 77
Redroot, 28
Red Trillium, 21
Relationship to other floras, xxix
Retama, 84
*Rhexia alifanus*, 119
*Rhexia lutea*, 119
*Rhexia mariana*, 119
*Rhexia petiolata*, 119
*Rhododendron austrinum*, 131
*Rhododendron canescens*, 132
*Rhododendron serrulatum*, 132
*Rhus aromatica*, 102
*Rhus copallina*, 102
*Rhus glabra*, 102
*Rhus quercifolia*, 102
*Rhus radicans*, 103
*Rhus toxicodendron*, 102
*Rhus vernix*, 103
*Rhynchosia latifolia*, 86
*Rhynchosia minima*, 87
*Rhynchosia reniformis*, 87
Riverflat Hawthorn, 66
*Robinia pseudoacacia*, 86
*Rosa bracteata*, 70
*Rosa carolina*, 70
*Rosa laevigata*, 70
*Rosa setigera*, 70
Rose, Cherokee, 70
Rose, Chickasaw, 70
Rose family, 66–71
Rose-gentian, 139
Rose, Macartney, 70
Rose-pink, 139
Rose Pogonia, 41
Rose Vervain, 155
Rosin Weed, 216–17
Rough Skullcap, 160
Roundleaf Eupatorium, 201
*Rubus clair-brownii*, 71
*Rubus sons*, 71
*Rubus trivialis*, 71
*Rudbeckia amplexicaulis*, 214
*Rudbeckia fulgida*, 215
*Rudbeckia hirta*, 214
*Rudbeckia maxima*, 215
Ruellia, 175
*Ruellia caroliniensis*, 175

*Sabal minor*, 7
*Sabatia angularis*, 139
*Sabatia brachiata*, 139
*Sabatia dodecandra*, 140
*Sabatia gentianoides*, 140
*Sabatia macrophylla*, 140
Sage, Blue, 161
Sage, Wood, 163
*Sagittaria graminea*, 4
*Sagittaria lancifolia*, 4
*Sagittaria latifolia*, 5
St. John's-wort, 113
St. John's-wort family, 112–113
St. Peter's-wort, 112
Salt Cedar, 114
Salt Marsh-mallow, 110
Salt Matrimony Vine, 164
Salt Pennywort, 124
*Salvia azurea*, 161
*Sambucus canadensis*, 180
Sampson Snake Root, 87
Sampson's Snakeroot, 138
*Sarracenia alata*, 61
*Sarracenia drummondii*, 61
*Sarracenia leucophylla*, 61
*Sarracenia psittacina*, 62
*Sarracenia purpurea*, 61
*Sarracenia sledgei*, 61
*Saururus cernuus*, 45
Sawbriar, 19
Saw Palmetto, 7
Saxifrage family, 64–65
*Schrankia hystricina*, 88
*Schrankia microphylla*, 88
*Schrankia uncinata*, 88
*Scirpus olneyi*, 6
*Scirpus robustus*, 6
Scope, x
*Scutellaria integrifolia*, 160
Sea Ox-eye, 192
Sea-purslane, 47
Seaside Cedar, 114
Seaside Goldenrod, 220
Sedge family, 6
Suggested References, 233
Self-heal, 160
*Senecio aureus*, 216
*Senecio glabellus*, 216
Sensitive-plant, 83
*Serenoa repens*, 7
Service-berry, 66
*Sesuvium portulacastrum*, 47
*Sesuvium maritimum*, 47
Shad-bush, 66
Shame-plant, 83
Shepherd's Needle, 190
Shortleaf Pine-Oak-Hickory Region, xxxiv

Silk-grass, 196
Silky Camellia, 111
*Silphium asperrimum*, 216
*Silphium gracile*, 217
*Silphium laciniatum*, 217
Silver Bell, 134
*Sisyrinchium atlanticum*, 34
*Sisyrinchium capillare*, 33
*Sisyrinchium exile*, 34
Skullcap, Rough, 160
Smartweed, 46
Smell Melon, 181
*Smilax bona-nox*, 19
*Smilax laurifolia*, 19
*Smilax walteri*, 20
Snake Root, Sampson, 87
Snakeroot, Sampson's, 138
Snakeroot, White, 201
Sneezeweed, 207
Snout Bean, 87
Snowbell, 134
Snow-on-the-mountain, 101
Snowy Orchid, 38
Soapwort Gentian, 137
*Solanum carolinense*, 165
*Solanum elaeagnifolium*, 165
*Solanum pseudocapsicum*, 165
*Solanum rostratum*, 165
*Solidago altissima*, 218
*Solidago microcephala*, 221
*Solidago nitida*, 221
*Solidago odora*, 218
*Solidago rugosa*, 219
*Solidago sempervirens*, 220
*Solidago tenuifolia*, 221
*Sonchus asper*, 222
*Sonchus oleraceus*, 222
Sourwood, 130
Southern-blue Flag, 32
Southern Crab Apple, 69
Southern Dewberry, 71
Southern Magnolia, 56
Southern Sweet Bay, 57
Southern Twayblade, 40
Sow-thistle, 222
Spanish-moss, 12
*Sparganium americanum*, 3
Spatterdock, 48
*Specularia perfoliata*, 183
Spiderflower, 59
Spider-lily, 26
Spider milkweed, 145
Spiderwort, 13
*Spigelia marilandica*, 136
*Spilanthes americana*, 222
Spilanthes, Creeping, 222
Spiny Buttercup, 52
Spiny Thistle, 194

*Spiranthes gracilis*, 42
*Spiranthes grayi*, 42
*Spiranthes longilabris*, 42
*Spiranthes odorata*, 42
*Spiranthes praecox*, 42
*Spiranthes vernalis*, 42
Spotted Bur-clover, 82
Spotted-medic, 82
Spreading Pogonia, 35
Spurge family, 100–102
Squaw Huckleberry, 130
*Stachys floridana*, 162
Standing-cypress, 151
Star-anise, 55
Star, Blazing-, 209
Star-bush, 55
Star-grass, Yellow, 26
Star-thistle, 195
*Stenanthium gramineum*, 16
*Stewartia malacodendron*, 111
Sticktight, 189
Sticktight, Nodding, 190
Stokes Aster, 223
*Stokesia laevis*, 223
Storax family, 134
Strawberry, Wild, 67
*Streptanthus hyacinthoides*, 59
*Styrax americana*, 134
*Stylosanthes biflora*, 88
Sumac, Poison, 103
Summer Azalea, 132
Sunbonnet, 195
Sundew, 62
Sundew family, 62–63
Sundew, Narrow-leaved, 63
Sundew, Thread-leaf, 63
Sunflower, 203–206
Sunflower family, 182–226
Susan, Black-eye, 214
Swamp Azalea, 132
Swamp Bay, 57
Swamp Fetterbush, 128
Swamp-lily, 25
Swamp Milkweed, 142
Swamp-privet, 135
Swamp Red Maple, 106
Swamp Thistle, 193
Sweet-acacia, 72
Sweet Bay, 57
Sweet Goldenrod, 218
Sweetleaf, 133
Sweetleaf family, 133
*Symplocos tinctoria*, 133

Tamarisk family, 114
*Tamarix gallica*, 114
Tangleberry, 127
*Taraxacum officinale*, 223

Tea Berry, 176
Tea family, 111–112
*Teucrium canadense*, 163
*Tephrosia virginiana*, 89
Texas Bluebonnet, 80
Texas Bull Nettle, 101
Thistle, Musk, 193
Thistle, Nodding, 193
Thistle, Spiny, 194
Thistle, Swamp, 193
Thistle, Sow, 222
Thoroughwort, 200
Thoroughwort, White, 199
Thread-leaf Sundew, 63
Three-square Sedge, 6
Ticks, Beggar, 189
Tickseed, 196
Tie Vine, 150
*Tillandsia usneoides*, 12
*Tipularia discolor*, 41
Titi, 104
Titi family, 104
Toadflax, Blue, 167
*Tofieldia racemosa*, 20
*Tradescantia hirsutiflora*, 13
*Tradescantia ohioensis*, 13
*Tradescantia virginiana*, 13
Tree Huckleberry, 133
Tree Orchid, 36
Trident Red Maple, 106
*Trifolium arvense*, 89
*Trifolium hybridum*, 90
*Trifolium incarnatum*, 90
*Trifolium pratense*, 91
*Trifolium reflexum*, 91
*Trifolium repens*, 92
*Trifolium resupinatum*, 91
*Trilisa odoratissima*, 224
*Trillium ludovicianum*, 21
*Trillium recurvatum*, 21
Trillium, Red, 21
*Trillium sessile*, 21
*Triodanis biflora*, 183
*Triodanis perfoliata*, 183
Trumpet-creeper, 172
Trumpet Honeysuckle, 178
Tuberous Hedge-nettle, 162
Tuber Vervain, 156
Tulip-tree, 54
Twayblade, Southern, 40
*Typha domingensis*, 3
*Typha latifolia*, 3

Unicorn-plant family, 173
Upland Hardwood Region, xxxvi
*Utricularia inflata*, 174
*Uvularia perfoliata*, 21
*Uvularia sessilifolia*, 21

*Vaccinium arboreum*, 133
Vanilla-plant, 224
Vanishing Wildflowers, xxi
Vegetation Regions, xxx
Venus' Looking-glass, 183
Verbena, 155
*Verbena canadensis*, 155
Verbena, Moss, 156
*Verbena rigida*, 156
*Verbena tenuisecta*, 156
*Verbesina helianthoides*, 224
*Verbesina virginica*, 225
*Verbesina walteri*, 225
*Vernonia altissima*, 226
*Vernonia missurica*, 226
Vervain family, 155–56
Vervain, Rose, 155
Vervain, Tuber, 156
Vetch, Narrow-leaved, 93
Vetch, Purple, 94
*Virburnum ashei*, 179
*Viburnum dentatum*, 179
*Viburnum nudum*, 180
*Vicia angustifolia*, 93
*Vicia dasycarpa*, 94
*Vigna luteola*, 94
Vine, Cypress, 149
Vine, Salt Matrimony, 164
*Viola affinis*, 114
*Viola langloisii*, 114
*Viola pedata*, 115
*Viola primulifolia*, 115
*Viola rosacea*, 116
Violet, Birds-foot, 115
Violet family, 114–16
Violet, Langlois, 114
Violet, Primrose-leaved, 115
Violet Wood Sorrel, 96
Virginia Creeper, 108
Virginia Crownbeard, 225
Virginia-willow, 65
Virgin's-bower, 51

Wake Robin, 21
Water-chinquapin, 49
Water Cress, 60
Water-hyacinth, 13
Waterleaf Blue, 152
Waterleaf family, 152
Water-lettuce, 10
Water-lily, Blue, 49
Water-lily family, 48–50
Water-lily, White, 48
Water-lily, Yellow, 49
Water-plantain family, 4
Water-shield, 50
Water-spider Orchid, 39
White-alder family, 127

White-arum, 9
White Aster, 186
White Astragalus, 73
White Colic-root, 15
White Dutch Clover, 92
White-flowered Milkweed, 144
White Fringed Orchid, 37
White Indigo, 74
White Prairie Clover, 85
White Prickly-poppy, 58
White Rain-lily, 27
White Snakeroot, 201
White Sweet Clover, 83
White Thoroughwort, 199
White-topped Sedge, 6
White Water-lily, 48
Whitewood, 135
Why Study Plants, x
Wild Ageratun, 199
Wild Azalea, 132
Wild Camellia, 111
Wild Cowpea, 94
Wild Crab Apple, 69
Wild Geranium, 97
Wild-ginger, 46
Wild hyacinth, 17
Wild Onion, 15, 16
Wild Petunia, 175
Wild Poinsettia, 102
Wild Potato, 147
Wild Strawberry, 67
Wild Wisteria, 95
Willow, Virginia, 65
Wind-flower, 50
Wing-stem Crownbeard, 225
Winter Huckleberry, 133
Wisteria, Chinese, 95
*Wisteria floribunda*, 95
*Wisteria frutescens*, 95
Wisteria, Japanese, 95
*Wisteria macrostachya*, 95
*Wisteria sinensis*, 95
Wisteria, Wild, 95
Witch-hazel, 65
Witch-hazel family, 65
Woodbine, 108
Wood Sage, 163

Wood Sorrel family, 96–97
Wood-vamp, 64
Woolly Rose-mallow, 109

*Xyris iridifolia*, 11

Yankee-weed, 202
Yarrow, 183
Yaupon, 106
Yellow Butterwort, 174
Yellow Cow-lily, 48
Yellow Crested Orchid, 38
Yellow Crownbeard, 224
Yellow-eyed Grass, 11
Yellow-eyed Grass family, 11
Yellow Flag, 32
Yellow Floating Heart, 141
Yellow-flowered Strawberry, 67
Yellow Fringed Orchid, 37
Yellow Jessamine, 136
Yellow Lady's-slipper, 36
Yellow Passion Flower, 117
Yellow Pitcher-plant, 61
Yellow Polygala, 98
Yellow-poplar, 54
Yellow Rhexia, 119
Yellow Sensitive-plant, 84
Yellow Sour Clover, 83
Yellow Star-grass, 26
Yellow Top, 216
Yellow Water-lily, 49
Yellow Wood Sorrel, 97
Yucca, 23
*Yucca aloifolia*, 23
*Yucca filamentosa*, 23
*Yucca louisianensis*, 23
*Yucca smallii*, 23
*Yucca treculeana*, 23

*Zephyranthes atamasco*, 27
*Zephyranthes candida*, 27
*Zephyranthes grandiflora*, 27
*Zigadenus glaberrimus*, 22
*Zigadenus leimanthoides*, 22
Zig-zag-stemmed Iris, 30
*Zizia aurea*, 126